DAWN OF CHAOS

DAWN OF CHAOS

THE CAITLIN CHRONICLES BOOK ONE

DANIEL WILLCOCKS

MICHAEL ANDERLE

DISRUPTIVE IMAGINATION

DAWN OF CHAOS TEAM

Thanks to the JIT Readers

Mary Morris
Peter Manis
Larry Omans
Paul Westman
Micky Cocker

If we've missed anyone, please let us know!

Editor
Lynne Stiegler

For Bailey. Your daddy did this.
—Dan

To Family, Friends and
Those Who Love
To Read.
May We All Enjoy Grace
To Live The Life We Are
Called.

—Michael

PROLOGUE

It's incredible, looking back now, how quickly the world fell into madness.

The Madness...

That's what the people called it, and I suppose it's apt.

Where the disease came from, I still cannot tell. At first, I thought it would perhaps be one of those epidemics, much like the Black Death that swept England and lasted for three years or so.

Yeah, right.

How much more wrong could I have been?

It's now been seventy years since I first sighted the Mad in my Canadian homeland, and it doesn't appear as though their numbers are decreasing. Lord, I wish I could say otherwise. I wish I had better news. Years of experimentation and examination have led to nothing more than a few near-misses with the infected—and a load of extra confusion.

I simply don't have the equipment.

Or the staff.

My observations tell me that the world is dying. I used to travel. I used to see people and speak to people, but now, that way

1

of life is fading. Men and women have holed themselves up in tight-knit colonies, towns have become so withdrawn that there are some who believe there are no humans left out there in the wider world, and there are some survivors who simply batten down the hatches and try to hide away from it all—but even that isn't a foolproof method to keep the Madness from finding its way through.

If I can do one thing before I die—and I know that death isn't far off for me—it will be to find the cure. Or at least to loosen the lid of the pickle jar that contains it.

For the sake of humanity, there has to be a cure.

There must.

Helena Millican, MD—circa seventy years post spread of Madness

CHAPTER ONE

Carter Manor, Silver Creek Forest, Ontario, Canada

It was far too late to save her.

"Kiera!" Caitlin screamed from the top of the stairs. A cold draft blew in through the open door where the Mad had broken in.

Kiera stared up at her through the horde of Mad attacking her—scratching, tearing, and biting, their eyes glowing fiercely red. She tried to speak, but no words would come.

This hadn't been the plan at all.

Earlier that day, Caitlin had been delighted when she had been told she was to join Silver Creek's ranger troop —a hardened band of men who patrolled the perimeter outside their town's wooden walls. For as long as she could remember, she had wanted to see the outside world beyond the gates. To see the overgrown forests and smell the fresh air.

There was just one problem with that...

For the last seven decades, the forest had crawled with

Mad-infected zombies— humans who had contracted the Madness and stalked the forests as though they were the walking dead.

They were very much alive, unfortunately. Death would have been a kinder end.

Governor Trisk's law stated that only specified civilians would *ever* leave the confines of the walls, under the penalty of death. Rangers were among the few who could, which was annoying for Caitlin because her brother was the Captain of the Rangers troop.

Caitlin had to watch her own flesh and blood leave every night to travel the woods. The rangers eradicated any Mad who might have wandered within Silver Creek's borders that day. *She* stayed at home to clean, cook, and scratch at the walls in frustration while Jaxon, her pet German Shepherd, cocked his head and watched her with interest.

Where was the justice in that?

Caitlin couldn't count the nights she'd spent imagining what the overgrown world out there was like.

Her excitement had exceeded all her imaginings when Dylan came home earlier that day. He'd worn a confused expression on his face and delivered the news that Caitlin, Kiera, and a handful of other women were to join the rangers that evening to patrol for the first time.

"Why? Why now?" Caitlin had asked.

Dylan explained that Trisk was looking to increase his security. The plan was to train more rangers to travel further afield and to push the perimeters of their territory outward. They had also come across something in the woods that needed exploration. Though he didn't say much more, Dylan had gotten the impression that the governor was looking for something beyond their borders.

Not that Caitlin had minded at all, as she had prepared for this for years. Every available moment had been used to train in secret with her brother's bo staff while he was away in the hopes that one day, she'd have the chance to join his ranks. It was the only way to leave the musty oppression of day to day life in the Creek.

Now, though…

Now, she wished she'd stayed home.

Caitlin and Kiera had become separated from their group in the forest when the horde had first attacked. It was full dark, with thick clouds covering the moon. The first bunch came out of nowhere—at least fifty of them, with laser-red eyes.

Caitlin had drawn her bo staff and swung at one of them, connecting with a satisfying *thunk*. The one she struck fell to the floor.

"Damn! Did you see that?" she'd shouted. She wanted to impress Kiera with her skills…but Kiera was running in the opposite direction.

Caitlin spared one glance at Dylan and his men—who were hacking at any Mad within their reach, ganging up on each in turn as their poor excuse for blades struggled to break the skin—before racing after Kiera.

She leapt over brambles and did her best to avoid tripping over roots as she followed her friend. She could hear Mad following them, although they were nowhere near as coordinated and calculated as humans. They stumbled and fell but never quite lost sight of their targets.

At the time, it had seemed like a blessing when the

manor came into view—a decrepit old building with fallen roof tiles and rotten beams, at least three stories tall. The place the governor had instructed them to find and explore.

Now, Caitlin clung to the railing and watched in horror while the Mad did what they did best...

They ripped Kiera apart and ate her.

Caitlin fell to her knees, unable to turn away from the horror downstairs. Her bo staff had fallen to the floor beside her. Her eyes filled with tears, and an anger she couldn't quite understand burned deep in her gut.

Kiera was *supposed* to have followed her.

Kiera was *supposed* to have run up the stairs with her to find a safe place.

None of this was *supposed* to have happened.

As Caitlin wrestled with the injustice of it all, she failed to hear a door creak open behind her and the labored footsteps of a stray zombie approaching.

It was the smell that brought Mary-Anne to her senses—that metallic, earthy smell of decay and blood.

Never mind the dust raining from the floorboards above and the thundering footsteps of what had to be Mad.

They were a noisy bunch. Definitely wouldn't win a game of hide and seek.

She blinked and stretched, her eyelids feeling heavier than they had in decades.

What happened to the days of being awakened by a rooster?, it's all "bloodlust this" and "bloodlust that."

With her vampiric eyesight, Mary-Anne could see almost perfectly in the dark, though her body ached and she wished only that her sleep had not been disturbed yet again. This was the third time in a week she'd been wakened by intruders and had to drive them away. She was annoyed.

Mary-Anne groaned. She had been comfortable—and tired.

More tired with every passing day.

In the days since the Madness had taken over, the world had changed beyond description. Humans had withdrawn into medieval-style colonies, Weres had all been killed or gone into hiding, and there weren't many vamps around anymore either.

Mary-Anne had experienced her fair share of encounters with the Mad—hell, there were few who hadn't—and had learned very quickly from watching her kin die off one by one that the only way to survive was through avoiding human contact at all costs. Drinking from a human who didn't know they were infected yet…well, that risk was not worth taking.

Still, there was little to be gained from sucking a rabbit or a deer dry. It was enough to sustain but not to flourish.

Mary-Anne's stomach rumbled, and her eyes narrowed as she looked at the floor above her, able to smell the humans but unable to eat.

She sighed, trying to remember the days before the Madness. It had begun long after the fall. There had been a sweet period after the world had nearly ended and before the Madness began, when giant ships flew, and cities were full and thriving. Before the world turned to feral bloodlust and her brothers and sisters had begun to degenerate and die.

Someone screamed above.

Mary-Anne stood up and cracked her neck, then ran at vampire speed through the basement and up two flights of stairs. She navigated through the back corridors as only she would know how to do. Her family manor was a labyrinth, a maze of rooms and hallways and staircases. Portraits thick with spiderwebs rocked gently on their hooks as she sped past. Her eyes glowed as red as those of the Mad.

When she reached the shadows of the second floor, she crept along in silence toward an opening from a side corridor. It gave her a perfect view of what was happening below.

A girl, no more than shreds of meat and blood, and a horde of Mad screeching and chittering in delight.

No fair, she thought. *How come they get to eat and I don't?*

And then she heard the sobs.

Another girl had collapsed to her knees not twenty feet away from where she stood. She was young, at least by Mary-Anne's standards—probably in her mid-twenties. Her long brown hair fell over her shoulders and face, and her frame was covered by a dark green cloak.

Mary-Anne cocked her head. This was certainly a strange new development.

The last few intruders to her home had been men armed with rusted swords and bows. They had done a much better job sneaking up on Mary-Anne, almost managing to cause her harm before Mary-Anne went all vamp and handed them their asses.

But this girl seemed...different. She certainly wasn't there for Mary-Anne. Maybe the girls had made their way here by accident? Mary-Anne couldn't remember the last time she'd seen genuine compassion from a human.

In the days when the Madness had spread far and wide, Mary-Anne had seen humans switching into survival mode —grouping into their colonies and purging anything or anyone that might have been a threat in some way. Cama-raderie, bravery, and honor had crumbled as quickly as civilization did.

Now, there was a girl frozen to the spot with emotion as her companion was killed—

Well, that stirred something in Mary-Anne she couldn't quite explain.

So when the stray zombie crept out of the room that had once been her sister's playroom, Mary-Anne took action.

Awareness of the zombie behind her finally penetrated Caitlin's consciousness when it was only a foot or so away.

She could smell it—that putrid stench of rotten eggs pouring from a mouth that might once have had a full set of teeth but which now held only a few.

"*Fuuu—*" Her instinctive curse was cut off as a person hurtled from nowhere and smacked into the zombie.

What the shitbags? Caitlin watched, fascinated, as they wrestled on the floor.

Well...*kind* of wrestled. The zombie had no hope. A woman with dark skin, fangs, and glowing red eyes had grabbed a handful of the zombie's thin, greasy hair and now used her other hand to separate his head from his body. She straddled him and held up the head as if in triumph.

Caitlin's stomach curdled as the zombie's head continued to chomp and gnash its teeth for a few seconds after the separation.

The vampire climbed off the zombie, panting heavily and looking as though she'd just run a mile.

"Are you okay?" she asked Caitlin, her eyes now pulsing a dull red.

Caitlin couldn't believe it. A *vampire* was asking if she was okay.

When Caitlin was a child, her parents had told her about vampires and Weres. She remembered a night around the fire when she had probed and prodded with question after question. Were they really real? If they had been so powerful, where were they now? How would they respond if they contracted the Madness?

Her mother and father had deflected her questions and rolled their eyes at her childish curiosity. Their response confirmed her belief that they were nothing more than fiction, stories to keep the fenced-in children of Silver Creek amused as time went by.

And after Father had contracted the Madness and her mother died from food poisoning after eating a tainted fox, there had been no one left whom Caitlin felt she could question without people thinking she was crazy.

She looked at the woman with fangs and black hair that fell to her shoulders and knew without a doubt that vampires were real.

Caitlin wiped away a tear, her voice catching as she said, "Thanks?"

"Don't mention it." The vamp stretched her back. She looked tired. "But don't rely on it, either."

She nodded to the floor below. Some of the Mad who had killed Kiera now turned their attention upstairs in the wake of the commotion. A few eager forerunners were already on the bottom steps.

"Your friend may be dead, but you have a chance to live. Tears can wait until you're safe. Here, take this. It should help you," the vamp said, reached inside the folds of her cloak and unfastened something Caitlin couldn't see.

She withdrew a sheath and pulled out a sword unlike anything Caitlin had ever seen. Its blade gleamed silver and its edge was flawless.

The blacksmiths of Silver Creek could forge nothing like this. The only blades Caitlin had ever seen leave that place were bent and notched pieces of crap recovered from the old world. The only people to bear the blades were the governor's guards and rangers.

Except for Kiera and Caitlin. According to the head of the guards, Hank Newman, they were too new to the squad to warrant proper blades.

Maybe if they'd had something better than glorified sticks, they wouldn't be in this mess.

Mary-Anne handed the sword to her. It was light, and the hilt fit Caitlin's hand perfectly. In fact, nothing had ever felt more natural in her life.

"It is silver-tipped," the vampire said. "A perfect bringer of death to those of the UnknownWorld. Stab this through a Mad's heart, and it shall be no more."

"Oh, great advice. Stab the Mad in the heart and it dies?" Caitlin smiled at the vampire. "Thanks again."

Most of the Mad on the stairs had fallen over as they tried to lift their feet to the next step.

Despite herself, Caitlin laughed at their ridiculousness.

The vampire joined in the laughter, an oddly humorless sound, then turned back to Caitlin. "Take care of yourself, flesh sack. No one else will. The world has turned Mad, and there are very few people alive who have honor, love, or compassion. Don't let them take it."

And with that, she was gone.

More groaning and frustrated cries came from the stairs. Caitlin weighed the sword in her hand and took the defensive stance she had practiced in her bedroom over so many years with little hope she'd ever get a chance to test it. She waited for them to attack.

Well, dickweeds, you wanted it. Come and get it!

They hesitated, the stairs hindering their progress, and Caitlin's instincts pushed her forward. She worked her way down the stairs and stopped just beyond the grasp of a middle-aged man. His skin was blistered and dotted with weeping sores, and his hair was falling out in clumps. Scratches and gashes laced his arms, and the tattered remnants of clothing were covered in dirt and dried blood.

Caitlin spared a half second to wonder what his name might once have been.

"Phil?" she mused as she swung with all her strength.

The sword broke through his skin with ease, though it stopped at the bone. Caitlin yanked the blade clear and made another swing, then another. She struck again and again, hacking until she heard bone crack beneath the metal. Thankfully, it took only a single final swing before the Mad toppled and began bouncing down the stairs.

"I guess we'll never know," she said, breathless.

She pressed forward to the next—a twenty-something woman with a large frame and bingo wings—and drew her sword back to hack at the head again.

Until she remembered the effort it took to take down Phil.

Caitlin pulled back, stabbed the sword forward in the place where she figured the heart would be, and watched as the light died in the woman's eyes.

This one she called "Sarah," though she wasn't sure why. She simply looked like a Sarah.

Before long, bodies littered the stairs. The rest of the horde shrieked their protest, obviously infuriated by the mere sight of Caitlin. Though some were too far deteriorated to really pose much of a threat—they could barely climb the steps—a handful of fresher Mad took the stairs with ease.

It was these which nearly caught Caitlin off-guard, but at the last moment, she twisted to avoid their grasp and within minutes, had covered her sword with their blood.

When they were down, Caitlin took a few steps back up the stairs and out of reach of the crawlers. She panted heavily, wondering why the vampire hadn't stuck around to help her out. Sure, the sword was useful, but she could really do with some extra bodies.

As if answering her plea, Caitlin heard Dylan's voice calling outside the front of the manor. "Get 'em, boys!"

A rallying cry.

The remaining Mad turned as the door was kicked fully

wide. Within seconds, several of the rangers had loosed arrows and followed immediately with a charge. The Mad went from zombies to pincushions in seconds, collapsing to the floor.

Caitlin quickly wiped her blade clean across her thigh and replaced it in its sheath. She wrapped her cloak tightly around herself. She wasn't sure why she wanted to hide the blade, but something told her that it was in her best interest.

"Cat!" Dylan exclaimed, running to meet his sister once they were sure the Mad were dead.

They hugged each other tightly. "I thought we'd lost you." He pulled back and made his "man of the family" face. "Don't you ever run off like that again, okay? I was worried sick."

Caitlin pushed Dylan away playfully and smiled. "Shut up! I'm fine, I'm fine."

Dylan grinned back, then looked around the foyer. "Where's Kiera?"

Caitlin's expression changed. In all the chaos and the excitement of meeting the vampire and the adrenaline unleashed in taking on the Mad, she had almost forgotten her friend.

She scanned the floor, hunting for Kiera beneath the bodies now piled around the place. She found what was left of Kiera's body and pointed. Her eyes welled up, and her lip wobbled, though she was careful not to break down and cry in front of the other men.

Dylan's eyes widened. He sighed and pulled Caitlin close to his chest, covering her eyes and stroking her hair.

"Cat... I'm so sorry." Behind him, several of the rangers shuffled awkwardly.

Dylan pulled away and held Caitlin at arm's length, his expression one of concern and affection. She admired how tough he was and wondered how many men of his own he had lost through the years.

"C'mon," he said as he wrapped an arm around Caitlin and led her out the door. "Let's get you out of here."

Caitlin spared one last glance up the stairs, almost certain she could see two red eyes staring after her from the shadows.

CHAPTER TWO

Silver Creek

Morning was crowing by the time the gates of Silver Creek came into view. A violent splash of red appeared over the tops of the skeletons of trees like fire.

"Oh, we're gonna have some explaining to do," Dylan whispered to Caitlin as they walked side-by-side. She shot him a look, and he zipped his lips. She smirked, acknowledging the power only she had over her brother.

"Halt. In the name of Governor Trisk, who goes there?" came the call from one of several guards atop the walkway above the gate. Their uniform was made of dark leather and each guard was equipped with a bow.

"Oh, give it a rest, Clint. You know who we are. Now, open up before I lose my patience," Dylan said, earning a few sniggers from his comrades behind him.

"Very well." Clint snapped instructions to someone hidden from view, and a moment later, the gates creaked open.

Despite its appearance to the contrary from the outside,

Silver Creek was a fair size on the inside. Caitlin was old enough to have heard tales of when Silver Creek was nothing more than a shy outpost of Toronto. It had been founded as a last-ditch effort to try to re-expand the colonies and spread humanity back across the country in a world that had shriveled the population like a flame to cotton wool.

As she understood it from the stories her mother had told her, the world had once been densely populated by men and women alike. Cars and trains and vehicles which flew the skies allowed people to cross the seas. Guns and weapons of great power were made available over the counter and weren't restricted solely to dictators. Electricity had been available to nearly everyone and anyone who wished to could use it on a regular basis. And the Mad, alongside the rest of the UnknownWorld—vampires, Weres, and the like— had been little more than material for myths and legends.

There were streets where people could roam safely from town to town, roads to enable fast travel, medicines in abundance—the whole shebang.

It all sounded like a perfect vision of a life far removed. That old reality was a far cry from the life that Caitlin and the people of Silver Creek were used to.

Though despite its miseries, life somehow went on.

Already, the town bustled with life. Few eyes turned as the ranger troop walked through the gates and across the mud-packed streets. Most inhabitants were used to the early-morning arrival of the rangers and had grown indifferent to their appearance. Others merely looked away out of respect for the brave souls who put their lives on the line on a nightly basis to clear the forested area and ensure that the Mad stayed as far away from their perimeter as possible.

The troop moved in formation through the center of the streets, navigating around market stalls where stall-holders had already laid out their wares and were looking for their first sales. The off-color fruit and vegetables were grown locally in gardens so small that it was a wonder anything grew at all. Some stalls sold malnourished live-stock which looked to be so skinny and ill that Caitlin thought it would be much kinder to kill the fuckers and put them out of their misery.

Some tables displayed jewelry crafted of rocks and wood. Other vendors offered clothing woven from wool and various fibers, no doubt salvaged from desolate and abandoned houses that had been tracked and pillaged from brave husbands who had fallen to the Mad through the years gone by.

Dylan caught Caitlin's eye as they passed a stall selling leather sheaths and wooden swords. She had hidden her own sword within her jacket where it nestled safely and out of sight of the other troops.

She began to doubt whether she had been sneaky enough to hide the sword from Dylan.

He stopped suddenly. The troop came to a halt obedi-ently behind him. "I can take her from here. All are dismissed."

His men nodded as one, turned on their heels, and began to disperse into the thickening crowd.

"Except you, Sullivan."

A thick-set ranger with muddied skin and a grizzled beard answered, "Me, sir?"

Dylan waited a moment to double-check that the other rangers were out of hearing. "Cut the crap, Sullivan. You don't need to 'sir' me when the others aren't around."

"Of course, sir...er...I mean... Yes, Dylan." Sullivan shuffled his feet, displaying open discomfort at the directive.

Dylan turned to Caitlin. "He's cute when he's nervous, don't you think, sis?"

"I suppose—I mean, maybe if he cleaned himself up a bit." She folded her arms. "What are we doing? Can we go home?"

Somewhere nearby, they heard the deep, booming voice of a stallholder announcing the discounted price of his rugs and blankets.

"Sullivan, I need you to do something for me."

"Anything, sir," Sullivan said eagerly.

Dylan gritted his teeth as if he was about to lash Sullivan again for not using his name, but evidently decided to let it go.

"Caitlin, here, has something valuable that I need you to take back to our home."

"Wait, what?" Caitlin said, her eyes wide as she took a defensive step back and clutched the package beneath her clothes. "If fudge nuggets so much as touches this, I'll bite his hand off."

Dylan grinned, grabbed Caitlin's elbow, and pulled her closer.

"You'll do no such thing. Look, here's the deal. I need to report to the governor to update him on the night's events.

I'm taking you with me to give a first-hand account of whatever the fuck went down at that manor and to explain why we're returning with two fewer rangers than we left with."

"Two?" Caitlin said, confused.

"While you were off playing with zombs, Francis was mauled by a bear."

"Ouch," Caitlin said and took in a hiss of breath.

"Right. And what do you think Governor Trisk will think of your shiny new addition if he sees you clutching it to your breasts like Sullivan clutches his ale at Mother Wendy's tavern?"

Realization suddenly dawned. Caitlin wasn't sure what it was that made her so protective over her sword, but did know it would be much better to part with it for an hour than for the governor to confiscate her weapon permanently.

She knew the official's temper could be volatile at the best of times. Only last week, she'd heard that he had sentenced a former guard to two days out in the woods with nothing more than the clothes on his back as punishment for turning up five minutes late to a shift.

The man had died some twelve hours later, attacked and mauled by Mad within view of the town walls. The guards on the wall had been instructed, under pain of their own death, not to help him out.

Sullivan shuffled his feet. Small beads of sweat peppered his brow.

"It's okay, Sullivan. Just get back nice and quick and hide it beneath *my* bed," Caitlin said. "You'll know which one it is. It's the one that doesn't smell of BO and shit."

Dylan tutted.

"But if I find you hiding beneath my sheets when I get back, I'll be sure to cut your cock off."

Caitlin opened her cloak cautiously, shielding the sword from view. Someone watching from afar could be mistaken for thinking that she had given the ranger a hug. When she moved away, she felt a sudden overwhelming emptiness in knowing she was defenseless. Despite her brother's trust in this ranger, Caitlin couldn't help her reservations.

"Do *not* lose it," Caitlin said through gritted teeth.

Sullivan nodded and disappeared into the crowd.

When Sullivan was out of sight, Dylan said, "Now, are you ready to give your first morning report?"

Despite his reassuring tone, she couldn't help but feel a little nervous. She had been given this one chance to help out on ranger patrol, and already, she had found herself mixed up with the Mad, played with a vamp, and had lost a friend.

What kind of governor would want such a liability out there on patrol?

"Sure. Though I guess it'll likely be my last," Caitlin said as they headed through the streets.

Governor's Quarters, Silver Creek

Caitlin didn't know what to expect when they arrived at Trisk's quarters. Life as she knew it in Silver Creek was certainly a far stretch from anything she had ever considered 'lavish.'

Sure, she had heard tales of comfort and convenience of

times long gone, but day-to-day life was about as basic as you could get.

Her own home—along with so many others—was little more than a boarded wooden shack. A series of cubes attached to one another that ran in rows like shanty towns of old. Floors were nothing more than dirt. Beds were nothing more than basic, and on stormy nights when the rain poured down and the wind roared loud enough to cover the far-off screams of the Mad, the only defense to keep out the cold was the curtains covering the holes where, generations before, windows would have been.

But this…

Ho-lee-shit.

As the guards opened the doors and Caitlin stepped into the governor's quarters, a whole range of emotions punched her in the face. At first, she reveled in the warmth that greeted her instantly from a large fire in the hearth along the far wall. Then she stared in awe at the ornate decoration, felt the softness of carpet beneath her feet for the first time, and looked at the paintings that lined the walls in frames that looked to be cast in gold. In a way, it reminded her a little of what the vampire's manor could have looked like—after a good clean.

And then a little bubble of anger popped inside her, frustration at how one man could live so royally in a town where Caitlin had seen people sleeping in muddied puddles on the street. Where it was more common to have dirt smeared across your face than it was to be clean.

"Aha!" Governor Trisk bellowed. "There he is, my favorite of *all* the ranger party."

Caitlin couldn't hide her surprise.

The man was a slob. The man before her presented a far sight from what Caitlin had seen when he made public appearances wearing outfits that were pristine and invariably regal.

Usually, the only sightings of Trisk would have been on Friday afternoons when the bell sounded and the town gathered in the market square for what some had begun to call the Governor's Gabble.

For several hours, he would preach and speak in his droning tone, inviting guests up to provide updates and orders to the residents of the town.

Well, perhaps not exactly 'inviting' people...

Guided by Trisk's number one guard, Hank Newman, most residents were *forced* to go up on the platform. Those who refused would be used quickly as an example of what not to do when given a direct order from Governor Trisk.

Caitlin had seen it several times, now. On one occasion, she could remember a timid old woman with graying hair and arthritic legs unable to take to the platform to speak. Her son had gone toe-to-toe with Hank after he had pulled out his rusted sword and said, loud enough for all to hear, "The governor would like *you* to speak, ma'am. Whether you can walk up the stairs or not is not my concern. Talk, or say goodbye to the kiddo here, because I haven't got all fucking day."

The journey up the stairs was painful. The woman had given her report through wracked sobs and tears. Her son was dragged away and out of sight. It took a long while after that before anyone refused again.

"Good morning, Governor," Dylan replied, dropping to

one knee and bowing. When Caitlin didn't follow suit, he tugged on her cloak.

"What?" Caitlin asked absently, still stunned by this version of the governor.

The man waddled forward to greet Dylan, his stomach leading the way. His tits wobbled back and forth. The only items Caitlin could identify were a graying pair of briefs and a golden chain which hung around Trisk's neck.

Dylan tugged again, more fiercely this time.

"Oh, right," Caitlin said, falling to her own knee.

Somewhere back in the room he had emerged from, Caitlin heard the mumbles and giggles of several women.

"Oh, and look, you've even brought me a present," Trisk said, seemingly noticing Caitlin for the first time.

At first, she wasn't sure if he was joking. But when she saw the way his eyes scanned her from bottom to top, pausing for far too long as he reached her chest, she opened her mouth to speak.

"Excuse me? I'm *not* a—"

"Governor, this is my sister, Caitlin," Dylan interjected. "One of the first women to join the rangers under your orders."

Caitlin's mouth snapped shut.

"Ah, yes," he said delightedly, clapping his hands together. He walked to the far side of the room. Several goblets were lined atop a dressing unit beside a jug from which he poured a thick purple liquid. "I assume all went well?" He drained his cup in one, held up an empty cup to Caitlin and Dylan, who both shook their heads, then poured himself another.

As Dylan spoke, the governor drank, wine dribbling out

of either side of his mouth to trickle down the peaks and troughs of his body.

"Unfortunately, there were some complications. As we approached the borders near Mossy Hollow, we ran into a horde of Mad. More than we've seen in years, now. While we did our best to take them down, we lost two rangers along the way."

Trisk's eyebrow raised. His voice was level and calm, almost too steady for Caitlin's liking. "Oh? Who?"

"Drek Francis, sir. One of our finest. Amidst the onslaught, the disturbance attracted a nearby bear who caught him by surprise. There was little we could do to save him."

"That's a damn shame. Did you kill it?" the Governor asked, taking a seat at the side of the room with another goblet of wine full to the brim.

"No. We were preoccupied with the Mad. By the time we'd seen to them, the bear had gone."

"Nasty fuckers."

"Indeed."

The governor seemed lost in thought a moment. "And the other ranger?"

Dylan took a deep breath, but it was Caitlin who spoke. "Kiera Crane, a good friend of mine, and a damned brave woman. She fought against the Mad, finding her way into a manor out there in the woods. She fought tooth and nail until the end when the Mad overpowered her. There was nothing she could do."

She felt Dylan's elbow in her side as his eyes flicked from her to Trisk.

Caitlin rolled her eyes. "*Sir.*"

"Right…" For a moment, their leader sat in silence. Caitlin wasn't even sure he'd heard what she had said. Again, the giggles and moans of women were heard through the door to the bedroom. From where they stood, they could barely make out a sliver of the room itself, and Caitlin could count at least three women rolling around naked on the bed. Their bodies looked oiled and slick from what she hoped was their own sweat and not the governor's fluids.

He took a deep breath. "And the vampire?"

Ice ran through Caitlin's body.

"I'm sorry?" Caitlin asked.

"What about the vampire? You saw her, no?"

"Excuse me, sir?" Dylan asked. "Did I just hear you right?"

The man stood, his calm, mirthful demeanor fading to be replaced with steel-like cold. "You heard me perfectly well. Caitlin, what about the vampire?"

Realization dawned.

She had been worried, at first, that no one would believe her. In fact, she hadn't even mentioned the vampire to Dylan through fear that he would call her crazy and think she couldn't handle being out on ranger duty. After all, who in their right mind would believe someone when they said they'd seen a real-life vampire?

No one. That's who.

Or at least Caitlin had thought so.

"You knew there was a vampire there?" she said. "You knew about the manor?"

"Of course I knew," Trisk said, slurping his wine. "You think I'd blindly send my men to explore an area without reason? You think I haven't *already* sent people out there the moment I caught wind of that place? I've already lost three of my best men to that fucking blood drainer."

Dylan stepped forward. "Sir, you told us to go and explore Mossy Hollow. You didn't say anything about this" —he paused, almost as if he couldn't believe what he was about to say—" this...vampire."

"Of course I didn't. If I'd told you to go out and track a Werebear, a hell-hound—hell, even a deer armed with super speed and brute strength—do you think you'd have gone willingly? It took enough convincing to get Murphy to go last week, and even then, the bastard never came back."

He shook his head in disappointment.

Caitlin couldn't believe what she'd heard. What she had thought had been a gesture of good will from the governor —allowing women to become rangers—had been nothing more than...what? A trap? A trick?

Clearly, Dylan was struggling with this information too.

"You sent us in there to die?" he asked, his lips barely moving around the words.

Trisk's face turned from disappointment to one of concern. He topped up his wine. "Oh, no, my dear boy. Not at all. The last thing I'd want is for any of my people to die."

His voice turned sickly sweet, and Caitlin knew he was lying.

"Then why send Dylan?" Caitlin asked, finding it harder to keep her anger hidden. "Why send me? Why send Kiera? Couldn't you simply mass an army of your people to march in there and get her?" Caitlin fought at the tears in her eyes and reached instinctively to her hip for a sword that wasn't there, noting that her brother noticed it too. "What kind of coward sends two innocent girls to a suspected slaughterhouse?"

And it was there that the governor smiled, a despicable grin which crept up his face. "Because, my dear, war is all about the long game. About poking at the weak points of your opponent's defense until you find the sweet spot to attack. Clearly, my men weren't getting anywhere with this bitch, so I thought, if we sent a couple of women in there, maybe the outcome would be different. Maybe you'd end up chatting and forming a sisterhood, able to later convince her to come back and join us here in Silver Creek. It was merely one variation of a carefully laid-out plan."

He swept his hand to a dresser at the side of his room where yellowing leaves of parchment were stacked precariously high.

"And, in truth, though I'd rather you'd not die, I think I'd rather lose the expendables than waste the blood of any more good, strong men. Wouldn't you?"

"You can't be serious—" Dylan began.

Caitlin shouted in frustration, ran forward, and punched the governor in the face. Her fist met with his doughy skin and dug deep until she felt the hardness of his cheekbone.

He stumbled backwards in shock. Then, as Caitlin raised her other hand for another beating, he grabbed her wrist with a speed that was frightening and shoved her away.

Whether it was his weight or his strength, Caitlin was thrown back into the arms of her brother.

Trisk brought his hand to his face, wiping away a small trail of blood from where his cheek had split. His face was red with rage, and as he spoke, spittle flew from between his lips.

"You dumb whore," he said, advancing on them both now.

A door creaked loudly behind them. He turned and saw one of his ladies waiting in the doorway, her naked body glistening in the morning light. "We heard noises," she said, her voice sickly sweet. "Is everything okay?"

"Yeah, come back. We're *looonely*," another voice added.

The man's anger dampened at that. "Just one moment and I'll be with you."

The girl winked, giggled, then returned to the bedroom.

"Here's what's going to happen," the governor said, his voice flooded with command. "Tonight, at sundown, you two will go back to that manor and get me that vampire."

Caitlin opened her mouth to speak. Dylan trod on her foot.

"And if you don't return with her by morning—*alive*—I'll kill you both myself. Have you got that?"

Dylan nodded. Caitlin simply stared at the man, the urge to sock another mean one to his cheek almost too great to rein back.

"Good."

Trisk called for his guards to escort them out into the bustling street.

CHAPTER THREE

Silver Creek

Jaxon, a young German Shepherd with dark patches round each eye, began barking the minute Caitlin entered the front door with Dylan a few steps behind.

"And good morning to you, too," Caitlin said, falling to her knees and scratching Jaxon behind the ears.

Compared to the luxury of the governor's home, her own space was little more than a stable out in the Wolds—a barn for the animals to be kept in. She thought back to Trisk's house and the luxuries it held and found herself angry again. Every house she had ever entered in Silver Creek had been bare, little more than plain walls with only the necessities which people needed to survive. What gave the man the right to hoard it all for his own comfort?

Dylan removed his traveling cloak, laid his sword down at the door, and took a seat. He rubbed his forehead with his fingers.

"Are you okay?" Caitlin asked, unable to remember the last time her brother had ever looked so tired.

Dylan nodded. "You've got a mean hook, you know? Where did you learn to punch like that?"

Caitlin blushed. "Oh, you know. Whenever you're off doing your rangerly duties, I run off to Mother Wendy's, buy the biggest dude there a drink, and then throw it in his face to start a fight."

Dylan chuckled, obviously imagining it in his head. Mother Wendy's was the town's only tavern. Simple and homely, it provided a quaint place where any man or woman could pop in and find someone to talk to, a quiet corner to hide in, or a cup of wine or mead to fall to the bottom of.

"If that was true, I'm sure I would have heard something by now," Dylan said. He cleared his throat and held his hand to his chest. "You think the governor's the only person with spies out there?"

They laughed. Dylan's impression of their leader was actually pretty spot on, aside from the fact that he lacked the colossal gut and overpowering man odor.

When the laughter subsided and Jaxon settled down on Dylan's lap, he said. "I'm sorry that you and Kiera were... well...y'know. She deserved more than that. You both did."

"It's not your fault." Caitlin sat herself down and whistled for Jaxon to come on to her lap. The dog hopped down obediently, crossed the room, and jumped up. His fur was soft between Caitlin's fingers as she kneaded and petted him.

They sat for a while and discussed their visit with Trisk, making jokes about his size and what horrors the whores he kept in the bedroom had been exposed to.

It seemed like an easier thing to do than to dwell on the memories of Kiera as she was chewed and spat on by Mad. Or the fact that they were almost certainly being sent off to their deaths tonight.

At least, she assumed that was what Dylan was thinking. Caitlin's encounter with the vampire had been considerably different to that of the governor's men. She hadn't seen any harm in the creature's eyes.

"What do you think he meant about getting the vampire to join Silver Creek?" Caitlin said, pretending to rub tiredness from her eyes as she thought of Kiera and another fresh wave of sadness passed. "Why would the governor of a small town *want* a vampire here? It's not like he's not living in luxury, is it?"

"I don't know." Dylan stroked his chin. "I still can't believe we're talking about a *real* vampire here. Y'know, fangs and bat wings." He flapped his arms, looking ridiculous. "Is that really what you saw in there?"

Caitlin nodded. Jaxon shifted and nestled into her lap, his tongue hanging out the side of his mouth.

She told him all about her encounter with the vampire. About how she had almost been caught off-guard by the Mad until the vamp had wrestled it to the ground and ripped its head off. About how the vampire had given her the sword to combat the remainder of the group and fight her way out.

"*She* gave you the sword?" Caitlin almost laughed at the expression on her brother's face. "Am I in a weird dream or something? Did I wake up in looney world? Not only are vampires actually real, but this one decided to save your life and give you a sword?" Dylan cast a look down at his poor excuse for a blade by the door. "No fair…"

"No fair? I almost died. Kiera *did* die! And now that man is sending us back there to…what, hunt and trap a vampire? Take her hostage and bring her back?" Caitlin stood, forcing Jaxon to leap off in surprise and bark loudly. "We can't do it, Dylan. I won't do it. She saved my life. How can I possibly go back there and thank her by capturing her and dragging her back to Silver Creek?"

"We have to, Cat." Dylan stood and took Caitlin by the shoulders. "If we don't, we're as good as dead. You know Trisk. He's true to his promises. He won't think twice about it."

Caitlin's eyes suddenly lit up. "Unless…"

"Unless what?"

"We run away?"

"Cat…"

"No, Dylan. Think about it. We leave here now. Grab our things and head out from Silver Creek. What is there here that's really holding us back, anyway? Life here is obeying orders and living the same day on repeat. Nothing changes. People are too scared of being out there in the wild, but if we were to go *together*, maybe we could find somewhere…better."

"And then what?" Dylan replied, a pitiful look on his face. "Cat, the world outside has changed. It's not safe anymore."

"But how do we *know*? When was the last time anyone went beyond our borders? It can't only be us left, surely. We're not the only humans left in the world."

"What if we are?" Dylan asked.

At first, Caitlin thought Dylan must be joking until she saw the expression on his face.

The truth was that no one they knew of had been beyond the patrol borders in decades. There was no need. Life was self-sustaining in Silver Creek, and those who were born there would go on to die there. All they knew of the forest was the Mad, and was it really worth braving hordes of zombies for the sake of discovering new life?

For Dylan, that was a definite no.

For Caitlin, she was starting to think that maybe it was a yes. If a vampire's manor had been discovered out there, what else was there to find? Villages? Towns? Cities?

"And what if the governor catches us? How are we supposed to *sneak* out of the walls without being seen before tonight's mission? Remember what happened to Monica?"

Caitlin suddenly deflated. The story of Monica Chapman was almost legendary amongst Silver Creek residents.

It had happened years ago. On a drizzly morning when the skies were gray and spirits were already low, Trisk had taken to the podium for the weekly Gabble accompanied by the thick mass of muscle that was Hank Newman.

And it was on that rainy morning that their leader had decided a public display of civilian negligence was in order.

After a booming speech met by a forced round of applause, Hank had dragged a bedraggled-looking woman with hair which hung in dirty strands and clothes which were tattered and torn to the front of the raised platform. She screamed behind her gag, and the residents of the

DANIEL WILLCOCKS & MICHAEL ANDERLE

town did their best to tune out her cries, tears burning hot in the corners of the eyes of many.

The woman, Monica Chapman, had been well-loved by the town. Over the years, she had made a name for herself as something of an inventor. By day, she paid her due diligence, joining the other women in their daily duties, but by night, she tinkered.

At first, it had been simple stuff. Wooden constructions with hidden compartments made of nothing more than discarded boards and homemade glue. Over time, she had become friendly with the local smithy, requesting small pieces of metal she could use for sturdier frames, hinges, and the like.

Her creations were distinctly unique, her mind working similarly to the minds of those who lived some two hundred years before, when the world was vibrant and humanity thrived. People paid her handsomely—or as handsomely as they could afford—for her creations, and soon, her name rang through the town with the same sort of timbre that had once been assigned to heroes and legends.

Yet, like Icarus, Monica flew too close to the sun. Her husband, a ranger by the name of Zach Chapman, stumbled across a relic from the old world on one of his midnight patrols. An old revolver, rusting and filthy, lay half-buried in the dirt.

Zach had picked the gun up instinctively, hiding it inside his jacket, and continued on his way. He had gifted it to Monica who reveled in the challenge of repairing something so ornate and well-crafted. There were still three bullets in the chamber, and the writing on the side had

faded. It read S_it_ & ___son. She referred to it affection-
ately as her 'Sitson.'

Many nights were spent cleaning the barrels and exper-
imenting with different powders and parts in order to
make it work again. She understood the dangers of toying
with explosives and that she would have to lose a bullet or
two during the repairs and tests.

But one night, the gun fired, creating a large hole in her
floor, and the shot was like a thunderclap across the town.

A thunderclap which reached the ears of Governor
Halrod Trisk.

In a turn of cruel irony, on that miserable Friday morning, the governor had instructed a young Hank Newman to
point Monica's gun at her own husband's head. Without
hesitation, Hank placed his hands over hers and pulled the
trigger, sending a spray of blood across the platform.

No one had seen a gun fired in years. Even the eldest of
the town had only heard the sound of bullets, never seen
the effects. Hands clapped to ears and many fell to their
knees.

Monica was left to live, though she was never the same
again. And that final bullet in the Sitson? Well, that still
nestled in the chamber, locked up tight in Hank's quarters
in the bedside table he had purchased a year earlier from
none other than Monica herself.

"Well?" Dylan asked, his face set. He sat back down and
placed his head in his hand. "I rest my case."

Jaxon whined, clearly disgruntled at having to stand
and wait for his masters to sit down again.

Caitlin's nostrils flared. She paused a moment, toying
between a reply and a reaction. She scanned the room, her

eyes falling on Dylan's sword by the door. An idea struck her.

She turned and disappeared into her bedroom.

Caitlin's heart thumped as she sprinted through the door and flipped the mattress.

Please say Sullivan did as he was told. Please say that he can follow simple instructions—Ha!

She let out a sigh of relief as she saw the silver of the sword gleaming in a ray of sunlight that had entered through her window. In the dark, the sword had been beautiful, but now, in the golden beams of the sun, it was absolutely stunning.

There were markings on the blade in a language she couldn't comprehend.

Holding the sword, she marveled once again at how light the damned thing was and how clean and flawless the blade looked. Glistening in the light, it was a true relic of beauty, something more mystical than she had never seen before in her life.

She nodded a silent affirmation, ran back into the front room, and stood before her brother, the sword raised and ready for battle.

"Fight me."

Dylan eyes grew wide. *"Put. That. Back."* He ran around the room, pulling the curtains to close all gaps where someone might see in. "Are you out of your mind? We're already in Trisk's worse-than-bad books, and you're bringing *that* out?"

Caitlin considered this a moment.

"Fine," she said, returning to the bedroom. A moment

later, she emerged with two bo staffs. "Here." She threw one at Dylan, who caught it instinctively.

"What are you doing?"

"You heard me. Fight me. If the governor is going to send me to possible doom, I need to learn some kickass shit to defend myself."

Dylan placed his bo staff on the chair. "Based on last night, you don't need any lessons. You managed to deal with those deadheads well enough—"

Caitlin swung her stick in a half-arc and smacked Dylan on the hip.

Jaxon barked loudly, jumping in the air, his mouth chomping for the stick.

"Ouch! That hurt."

Caitlin looked at Jaxon. "This is why we never got a pussy. Seems we've already got one living with us."

She swung at Dylan again.

"Sis, I'm serious."

"So am I." She held the stick between two hands and tried to twirl it around. It slipped between her fingers and clattered to the floor. Caitlin laughed awkwardly and picked it up. "See? There's only so much I can practice without a partner to fight back. I got lucky against the Mad, I know I did. If you hadn't come to help, I'd probably be with Kiera right now."

"No," Dylan said flatly.

Caitlin swung once more.

This time, however, Dylan was ready. He grabbed the stick in one palm, twisted his arm to the side in a smooth motion, and ripped the stick out of Caitlin's hand while forcing her off-balance. A second later, she lay on the floor with Dylan's boot on her neck and her hand twisted in a lock she couldn't escape from.

"If you're going to play with fire, you best be sure you bring the heat," Dylan said, a huge grin on his face. He released Caitlin and threw her stick back to her. "Now, go to bed. It's been a long night and we need our rest."

"Dylan…" Caitlin whined.

"There's not enough time, sis. At this point, it's better to rest up than it is to wear ourselves out by training." He glanced towards her bedroom where he could see the tip of the sword poking haphazardly out of the sheets. "Take the blade she gifted you. Keep it hidden. Should the shit hit the fan, you'll be sorted. At the very worst, you can take a swing with that sword and the vampire'll turn to dust."

Caitlin looked back at the sword in confusion.

"You really don't pay attention, do you?" Dylan said, rolling his eyes. "The sword is tipped with silver."

"So?"

"If we've learned anything from the old tales, it's that silver is the ultimate killer of all things…vampire-y. I can't say for absolute certain, but one poke from that should be enough to cripple her and leave her begging for mercy."

Silver? How could that be? And if that is true, then…

"Why would she give the sword to me if it's her weakness?" Caitlin picked the sword up again, looking closely at the polished silver that edged the body of the blade.

"Fuck knows." Dylan stretched and yawned loudly. "A lot of weird stuff has happened tonight, and there's only so much I can take. Now, get some shut-eye, sis. We have a long night ahead of us. We'll need all the rest we can get."

As Dylan headed into his room, he patted his thigh and

called for Jaxon to follow. The Shepherd paused a moment, his head cocked to the side, before turning and wandering into Caitlin's room. He hopped on the bed and rested his head on his paws.

Caitlin cast her brother a smug smile and closed the door.

CHAPTER FOUR

Carter Manor, Silver Creek Forest

Mary-Anne's nose twitched before her stomach rumbled.

What is this I smell? An animal? Perchance another human?

The manor was filled with darkness, but as Mary-Anne opened her eyes, she could see perfectly, as always.

Thanks to her heightened senses, she could still smell the gut-churning stench of the tainted blood of the Mad that choked her foyer. It would be a while before she found the strength and motivation to clean that lot up, even if it did disturb her slumber.

She thought about them all lying there, their blood spilled. *What a damn waste…*

But that didn't mean she could drink their blood.

Over the last seventy years, Mary-Anne had watched as her fellow vampires had struggled. The Madness was a killer of more than only humans. She had already gone far past the point of being able to count on her fingers and toes the number of companions she had watched fall to the plague.

The entire UnknownWorld had taken a colossal hit.

The vampire population had shrunk, and she couldn't remember the last time she'd encountered a Were. Humans were increasingly difficult to come by and, even on those days she did come across them, it was likely that they would be on the offensive.

Mary-Anne didn't mind removing those who harbored intent to kill her, but she had made the conscious choice years ago to not drink their blood. She had seen too many vamps drink what they thought had been clean blood, only to fall sick with the Madness within hours.

It seemed that faster healing and vampire strength did little more than fuel the Madness to act faster than it did in humans. The end result was monstrous.

Mary-Anne closed her eyes and pushed away the thought, her mind now turning to the girl—the one who had come by the manor last night, the one she began to think of as 'the honorable.' She had been fine. Mary-Anne had watched from the shadows, and the Mad hadn't even gotten close to her after she had handed over the sword.

Perhaps, if the girl comes back, maybe I could bargain a deal? Maybe I could use the sword I gifted her as leverage to taste some of her blood…

No. Mary-Anne shut down her thinking before it could spread. Her stomach roared in protest, a feeling that had never quite shifted. A hunger coded by evolution.

How can you guarantee that she isn't tainted? More than that, how can you guarantee that you'd be able to stop yourself before you drained her completely?

She pictured the scene, even now unsure that, if given the chance to taste human blood, she'd be able to stop her hunger from switching into overdrive and draining the body until all that was left was flesh and bone.

And besides, the girl she had saved ignited her curiosity. She'd shown no sign of fear at the sight of a vampire, and no intent to kill her.

A rare sight indeed, these days.

The unexpected encounter was a sad cry from several hundred years before. Then, vamps—and even Weres—could roam freely amongst the people.

It was a part of her history, ingrained deeply from generation to generation of vampires. The story told of how the world had almost ended in a fireworks display of nuclear missiles. How the survivors of what had come to be known as the "World's Worst Day Ever" had struggled and fought to rebuild the cities and towns of old. How the world had been on the brink of recovery before the light switch had been flicked—

And the Madness had come.

In one swift movement, Mary-Anne rubbed her eyes and ran through the manor. She didn't move at top speed. She simply couldn't anymore, her energy drained from the exertion of her intervention for the girl the night before.

She waited by the back door, her back to the wall, and listened. Something was rummaging outside. Something big. The door was slightly ajar.

She chanced a peek, greeted by the moonlit glow of her backyard, overgrown and falling to the forest around it.

A dark shape, the size of a car, sniffed the floor. The

bear let out a low moan, a sadness which communicated its own hunger.

Yeah. Don't worry. I know how that feels.

Mary-Anne let a small smile play on her lips, remembering a Were she had once met who could transform into a bear with shaggy, matted fur. He had been half the size of this one, though.

Her stomach rumbled once more.

Sorry, brother. Mama needs to feed.

She made death quick for the bear. She didn't even use a blade, merely leapt onto its back, sank in her own claws, and drank until the bear went woozy, stopped thrashing, and fell.

She wiped the blood from her mouth and panted heavily, feeling the warmth of it coursing through her body. It did little to sustain her.

Then, she caught the whiff of another smell.

A *human* smell which drove her crazy and made her mind cloudy. She looked down at the corpse of the bear, inhaled deeply, and identified that the smell was still somewhere inside.

She ripped at the bear's skin, her hunger driving her wild. Her instincts craved the true sustenance it needed.

And there, inside the stomach lining, was the source of the scent—several human limbs the bear must have ingested fairly recently. Human blood slimed the body parts like a coating of oil.

Mary-Anne stared at the limbs for a moment, her mind shouting at her to leave them alone. It wasn't worth risking the Madness for the small portion of blood she could lick clean from the bones.

What if the owner of that body had the early stages of Madness? The bear wouldn't have shown it at all. It would not even have been affected. How could she be sure that she'd be okay?

Her mind waged its internal battle for a moment longer, then she pulled herself away. Her stomach hurt at the idea of leaving it behind, but she had to do it. Survival in a world of Madness meant pain, and that was the world she now knew.

She returned to the manor, leaving the door ajar, and crumpled to the floor, feeling the warmth of the bear's blood inside her. That tiny amount of satisfaction made her feel like she was dying of thirst in a desert and had found nothing more than a couple of drops of water in an egg cup.

When was the last time she'd felt truly *full*? Would she ever feel full again?

She closed her eyes; she could see the girl now. A pretty thing with a fire in her heart. Maybe...just maybe...

Mary-Anne lay a while on the dusty floor, her mind full of memories of better days. She closed her eyes and began to doze out in the open.

After all, what did she have to fear? Anyone else wandering into her domain after the attempts of the last few guys would either have to be a lunatic or an animal with a longing for death on its brain.

Prison District, Silver Creek

Halrod Trisk kept to the shadows as he made his way along the parapets of Silver Creek. All activity down below in the main streets of his town had ceased some hours ago now. The curfew had been decreed under his orders which were, in fact, nothing more than a thinly veiled effort for him to show the people who was boss. There was no threat of anything coming from the outside world without his guards knowing about it.

No sirree.

He navigated the darkness, and his heart fluttered with excitement. He thought back to his old mentor, Jeremy, a man nearly twice Halrod's years who had been his guide for the best part of several decades. Jeremy had always held the firm belief that there were still others out there besides the Mad. Other creatures from the UnknownWorld. Closing in on nearly a hundred years of age before he passed, he was one of the few who had actually been around to see them before the Madness came.

Weres, vamps; even Nosferatu and lycanthropes. He had seen them all. Yet it was a secret knowledge he had only ever shared with Halrod and a handful of others.

Halrod was always careful to keep the truth to himself. The rest he had turned into fairy tales for the town. So many years had passed that he had almost started to believe that maybe Jeremy had been lying all along. Years of searching had turned up nothing.

Until his men had discovered the fabled vamp. How he had leapt for joy.

And now…

Well, now his heart raced with perverse excitement at his men's latest discovery.

It was dark out, the moon hidden by a thick layer of clouds. Torches burned on the lower levels, flickering and making the world swim. The odd sensation would make the average man queasy, but Halrod knew the layout of his town better than anyone else and walked the wooden boards with the confidence of a panther stalking its prey.

He traversed his determined route down a set of steps and through several long corridors leading away from the residential quarters. Soon, Halrod began to hear the moans. He nodded to a pair of guards who immediately moved to let him pass.

Oh, he loved the feeling of power. Of being an unstoppable force in Silver Creek.

Doorways appeared on either side of him, now, with bars that crisscrossed the entrances so that the prisoners couldn't escape but could be watched by the steady eyes of his own law enforcers.

He continued down another set of stairs and into a dark so black that even the torches failed to provide much light. Another set of guards stood to attention. This time, Halrod paused beside them.

"How is he?"

The one on the right—a man as short as he was wide—answered. "Quiet but still in containment. No sign of any shifts."

"Damn." Halrod swept past, the trails of his cloak flying behind him.

He stopped when he could go no further at a final jail cell filled with shadows and darkness. Without a word, he reached into his pocket and withdrew a dead mouse, stiffened and brittle. He tossed it through the bars and onto the floor.

Still and silent, he waited.

At first, nothing happened. Then, he saw the twinkle of a pair of eyes appear in the gloom. A voice spoke, casual and cocky, though with cracks between words and dry lips.

"That's not what I ordered."

"Tell someone who gives a shit," Halrod replied.

"I want to see the manager."

"You're looking at him."

The sound of shuffling ruffled the silence. Halrod grabbed a torch from further back and brought it closer to the bars. A man limped forward, naked as the day he was born. Thick hair sprouted in random patches across his body. His eyes glowed a keen green that seemed to absorb the torchlight, making it look like a fire burned around his pupils. His body, between the tufts of hair, was a mass of scars.

"Eurgh," Halrod exclaimed, recoiling slightly.

"You're not exactly a pretty sight yourself," the man replied.

The man was Kain Sudeikis. Earlier that day, Kain had stumbled across the borders of Silver Creek. Under Halrod's orders, Hank and a handful of men had been conducting a lap of the forests within sight of the town's walls—they liked to leave the more dangerous patrols to the ranger groups at night—and discovered Kain when one of the guards had heard a rustle in the bushes.

At first, they figured it might have been a fox or even a squirrel. When they approached the bush, weapons drawn, none of them had expected what they found.

A human leg poked out from between the twigs and leaves. When they grabbed the leg and pulled the man out, the upper half of his body looked to be more like the shape

of a giant wolf. The result was horrific, and as Kain transformed back into a naked man, as if in slow-motion before
their eyes, one of the guards had hurled on the floor.

"You don't like, you don't watch," Kain had growled, his
body contorted and twisted with the effort of the shift.

Hank Newman couldn't believe it. He had thought the
governor mad when he had first commanded them to keep
an eye out for anything that could be taken for a Were or a
vampire, yet there they were, watching one in the flesh.

Oh, how pleased Trisk had been when Hank had delivered his find.

Despite the story of his capture, Halrod had yet to
witness a transformation himself.

"I know what you're here for," Kain said, holding the
mouse up by its tail and licking his lips. He was thin and so
malnourished, his ribs stood out like blocks on a xylo-
phone. "That channel is no longer on the air, though, I'm
afraid. I'm a changed man now."

"What's a channel?" Halrod asked pleasantly enough,
hiding the anger that burned at the dismissive mockery
with which Kain addressed him.

People didn't deny the governor anything.

Kain didn't reply and merely teased his own lips with
the mouse's face.

Halrod pulled a chair up from the corner of the room,
turned it so its back faced Kain, and straddled it. His fat
spilled down the edge of the seat like dripping custard. He
rested his head on his chin, and when he spoke, his words
were soft. The kindest tone he could muster.

"I can see that you're hungry, Kain. There's a feast,
y'know? At the end of each month. A tradition that has

gone back since way before our humble beginnings. Food piled as high as you can imagine. Plates stacked with meats, with vegetables. Goblets of wine and ales all brewed here within these walls. Everyone here is invited, coming together to eat under the stars on tables which run the length of the streets."

Kain licked his lips. His stomach rumbled loudly.

"In fact, we often have so much food left over that it goes to waste. It's one of the saddest sights I know, watching the leftovers get discarded into our mulch containers to be used as fertilizer." Here, Halrod shook his head. "Such a shame. Such a damn shame."

Kain came closer, hands gripping the bars as his face pressed against the opening. "I can't do it, bucko. I know you know shit-all about my kind, so I'll say this nice and clearly for you to save us a lot of time. I can't...*shift*."

Halrod's eyes lit up at that. The first admission he'd had of what this man truly was.

"I want to make a deal with you."

Kain rolled his eyes. "Oh, here we go. It's always a deal with you people."

"Show me what you are. Shift—"

"I've just told you—" Kain tried to interject.

"Change into your true form, and I'll release you."

Kain paused a moment, staring into the depths of the governor's eyes. He exhaled slowly. "What's the catch?"

"You join my side. Become a law enforcer of Silver Creek. Help sniff out more of your kind and bring them to my cause."

Kain fell into thought. Halrod watched eagerly, his heart thudding a steady beat in his chest.

This was perfect. With a werewolf by his side, no one in the town would fuck with him. There'd be no more disobedience. No more betrayers. No more liars. He could use fear as his ally, and there'd be no more Monica Chapmans. With a Were there, he'd have the town under his thumb.

And what about the other colonies? The other towns which fell under Halrod's guardianship? The ones only his closest advisors knew of.

On the days when Trisk left to attend to matters in the smaller clusters, the Were could act as the ultimate enforcer. He'd be able to keep folks in line until his return, watch over his guards, and ensure that people knew and feared the governor's wrath.

He thought suddenly of the rangers and the guards currently walking through the forest towards the manor. A Were *and* a vamp? Now that would be a deadly combination to harness.

"What do you think?"

A horrible bubbling sound arose from Kain's throat. A second later, a thick glob of spit flew through the bars and landed on Halrod's cheek.

He felt his anger boil. Kain grinned, revealing a row of sharp, yellowing teeth. "I think you're about as trustworthy as week-old meat, and if I were to even consider—"

In a burst of movement, Halrod rose, kicked his chair away, and reached into his pockets. The sound of the chair echoed and magnified within the jail cell walls like a gunshot. He withdrew a small metallic parcel from his pocket, aimed it at Kain, and the room burst into the sound of pulsing electricity.

Kain fell to the floor, twitching and writhing. Halrod

held the button on the taser so tightly that his thumb turned white. His face a distorted mass of anger and rage, he reached into his pocket with his other hand and withdrew a muddied handkerchief with which he wiped the spit from his face.

He watched with delirious satisfaction as the man shook and trembled before him, noticing then that as Kain looked at him, his eyes began to glow a bright amber. The hairs on his back began to thicken and grow.

He waited a couple more seconds before releasing the trigger, feeling a warm feeling rising to his groin. Suddenly, his trousers felt too tight.

Footsteps sounded behind him as two guards rushed into the room.

"Sir, is everything—"

"Everything is fine, gents. I'm just teaching our friend here what it means to disobey his new governor. Take note, then return to your posts."

The guards exchanged a look which Halrod didn't see. "Of course," the shorter guard replied. They disappeared back around the corner.

"Kain, Kain, Kain... I see you've got a lot to learn here. Just because I'm a human without the supernatural powers that you *freaks* hold, doesn't mean that I don't have my methods of subduing those I need to subdue."

"Where... How did you..."

Halrod looked at the taser in his hand, his eyebrows rising in mock surprise. "Oh, this? A handy little relic of the old world. Did you know that just a few centuries ago, mankind invented a way to charge electrical items using nothing more than the *sun*?"

Kain coughed, clutching his stomach.

"They created loads of handy gadgets, most of which, unfortunately, have been lost to time. Though imagine my surprise when this little gizmo was pillaged some years back from an old city police station. I never thought I'd have a chance to use it but kept it collecting dust in a drawer."

Halrod crouched down.

"See, I have ways of making people obey. If you won't change voluntarily, then I'll just force it on you. One way or another, I'm going to get what I want. I *always* do."

He pressed the button on the taser again, instantly forcing Kain to go rigid. Once again, his eyes began to glow as the transformation began.

The shorter guard ran into the room, his words urgent and hurried. "Sir, I'm sorry to disturb—" Halrod released the button.

"What is it?" he growled.

"It's Walker. He needs to talk to you."

Sean Walker was the town medic. One of the only residents who held anything close to what could be considered medical experience in Silver Creek. An interruption from Sean usually only meant one thing, and one thing only. Someone had fallen with the Madness.

"Who is it this time?"

"It's Georgia," the guard said, his cheeks flushing. It always felt strange saying the name of one of the governor's whores.

Halrod's frustration emerged almost like a growl. He looked longingly back at Kain, who now lay still on the floor. Slow, shallow breaths sounded as his body rose and fell. As much as Harold wished to see the transformation, he couldn't help but hold a soft spot for Georgia. She could...do things that the other whores simply couldn't.

"Tell him I'm on my way."

The guard nodded and ran at a surprising pace out of the room and up the stairs.

"This isn't over," he grumbled back at Kain before whipping his cloak and leaving the prisoner to clutch his stomach in the darkness.

CHAPTER FIVE

Silver Creek Forest

"How much farther is it?" Hank called from behind them both, his voice grizzly and fierce. "I swear, if you're leading us the wrong way, Harrison, I won't think twice about gutting you like a pig and roasting you over a flame for dinner."

Caitlin turned to Dylan, who hid his determined expression beneath the shadow of his hood.

It wasn't exactly how Caitlin had pictured it, and she wasn't at all sure if that was a good or bad thing. By the governor's command, she and Dylan had been summoned to meet back at his quarters later that day. They found several other men waiting patiently when they arrived.

Hank stood with a sickening grin on his face as though he knew something that the others would never know—which, more than likely, was the case. With him were two other guards who both looked as though they were pretty new to the ranks—their faces fresh, their uniforms clean—and, to Dylan's surprise, Sullivan was there too.

"Hey, boss," Sullivan said, his voice deep.

"Sullivan? What are you doing here?" Dylan asked.

"He's coming with us," Hank answered as though it were the most obvious question in the world. "You think the governor trusts you two to drag the vamp back?" He shook his finger and tutted. "No, no, no. We're going to do what the others have failed to do on their own. Ain't that right, gentlemen? Time to bring out the big guns."

The two guards nodded enthusiastically, while Sullivan merely shrugged as if he had no clue what was going on. As if he hadn't heard or absorbed the word "vampire." He was happy to help Dylan, his leader, and that was all he needed to know.

Now, as they navigated around the twisting roots of the forest floor, Caitlin wished it had been only her and Dylan. The entire time, the guards had walked behind them, Hank flanked by the other two as they made crude remarks and wolf-whistled as her hips shook while she walked.

She could practically feel their eyes burning into her.

Still, she had Dylan to her left, and Sullivan on her right. That had to count for something, right?

The forest was cast in shadow, the moon hidden behind clouds. Despite the situation they found themselves in, Caitlin felt calm. She took deep lungfuls of the air and listened to the sounds of wildlife around her.

Something small rustled and ran out of sight in the foliage. Birds tweeted from somewhere above.

It was nice. Musical, even.

"How you holding up?" Dylan whispered.

"Just fine, boss," Sullivan replied, a little too loudly for Caitlin's liking.

"Not you," Dylan replied, unable to help the smile from growing on his face. "Not that I don't care."

Caitlin glanced down and managed to avoid a small hole that had been covered with leaves. "Fine, I think."

She glanced cautiously behind her to where the three guards were in their own deep, quiet discussion. Occasionally, their eyes caught hers and Caitlin didn't like the look they gave her and the others.

"You know, it's not too late to run," she said, grinning.

Sullivan's eyes suddenly widened, but before he could say anything, Dylan quieted him with a gesture of his hand that might have suggested he was petting a cow.

"Warriors don't run," Dylan whispered. "Warriors fight. Warriors survive. And the surviving warriors? They become revolutionaries."

"Why are you talking like that?" Caitlin asked.

"Like what?"

"Like some kind of brainy philosopher."

Dylan looked up at the sky, his face cast in thought. "I don't know. Maybe one day, when I'm too old to serve as a ranger, I'll become a philosopher. I'll scratch my knowledge into tree trunks and paint on dilapidated buildings. Leave a legacy behind in a way that others won't. It'd be nice to be remembered."

"Such a romantic."

"And, hey, maybe Sullivan could be my philosophical wingman. A sounding board to bounce my ideas and theories off. You're quite the thinker, aren't you, Sully?"

Sullivan's face melted into confusion, evidently struggling to understand what exactly philosophy was. Caitlin and Dylan both burst into laughter.

It was nice to know that Dylan was still thinking ahead to the future. It reassured her that he didn't think their late-night excursion and the mission they were currently embarking on would not be their end.

Kiera had been unfortunate. She hadn't had Dylan as a brother.

She hadn't had a decent sword.

She didn't have a vampire miraculously help her.

Running a quick equation of her odds and the things that had worked in her favor the night before, she considered the possibility that everything *could* be okay.

Somehow, it gave her strength.

"Hey! Keep it down," Hank whispered, the sound sibilant in the eeriness of the night. "This is supposed to be a *quiet* mission. I don't know about you, but I'd rather not create a load of disturbance and attract any nearby Mad to us, wouldn't you?"

His hands moved to the hilt of his blade. Caitlin held back a satisfied laugh when she saw the condition his sword was in. The edges were practically rounded, the color so dull and brown that it looked more like a stick in the light.

I guess even being a senior in the ranks couldn't make the blacksmiths perform any better.

Sword-maintenance, like so many other skills, seemed to have fallen into short supply in the days following the appearance of the Mad.

Hank waited for them to respond. Sullivan was the first to nod, then Dylan, then Caitlin.

"That's better," Hank's voice sounded condescending and deep. "Now, let's make sure that you guys can keep your word and shut the fuck up." He clicked his fingers. "Hendrick, you move up front with the chatty ranger boys. Caitlin, you come back with Victor and me. Maybe then we can keep our cake-holes shut and actually have a chance of sneaking up on the vamp, eh?"

They swapped over, albeit rather reluctantly, and continued on in relative silence. Hendrick—a guard nearly seven-foot in height with dark skin and teeth so stained that many had fallen out—accommodated the gap between Dylan and Sullivan, and Caitlin now walked in the middle between Hank and Victor.

She could smell Hank as they walked, a smell of body odor that reminded her of Trisk—stale and earthy. Her nose wrinkled as she tried to keep her thoughts distracted, knowing that every time she'd turn to look at Hank, he'd be watching her with a twinkle in his eye.

With every footstep, she felt her concealed sword tapping against her leg. She smiled, remembering the moment the vampire had given it to her. There was something comforting in knowing that she had a method of protection should the shit really hit the fan.

She had a lot to thank the vamp for, really.

"That's a pretty little smile," Hank said, slowing down enough to let the three in front take a greater lead.

"Thanks," Caitlin said bluntly.

"Don't you think she's pretty, Vic?"

Victor nodded, taking a second to eye Caitlin up and down. "Wouldn't mind spreading her on a slice of bread."

"You might have to wait your turn." Hank's gaze burrowed into Caitlin's. She despised the way they scanned her and could feel the thoughts hiding beneath.

It was no secret that Hank had a track record behind him of…well…taking what he wanted.

Caitlin had heard the stories and now thought of the countless women who had shared their tales of abuse and violation. They were people she had known and encountered, women who had all tried to go to the governor for some kind of justice but were waved away without a word.

It seemed it must be pretty comfortable for Hank, living in his master's pocket. Trisk loved his pet too much to see any kind of flaw in the man whom many feared.

Caitlin flushed at the idea of Hank laying hands on her.

Though, to her surprise, when she did actually feel a hand on her ass, it turned out to be Victor.

"Mmm…juicy." He leered at her, his face close enough for her to see it more clearly than she liked.

Adrenaline pumped through Caitlin's body. The world suddenly became a blur as icy fear shot through her.

"Fucktard," she snapped as, in one swift move, she grabbed Victor's wrist, pulled it towards her, twisted as she went, and threw him over her shoulder. His eye went wide as he flew through the air, a grunt escaping his lips.

As Victor thudded onto the dirt, she heard the breath leave his lungs. She stood back in shock, temporarily frozen, struggling to comprehend what she had just done.

Caitlin had never considered herself strong or particularly capable, but in her moment of anger had somehow managed to replicate the same wrist hold her brother had used on her the night before, only with her own spin. It felt effortless to use the guard's own momentum against him. A two-hundred-pound man now lay winded and on the floor because of a hundred-pound woman.

In her mind's eye, she imagined Jaxon barking madly, cocking a leg, and pissing on Victor's face. Now that would make a grand final nail in the coffin of humiliation.

The three in front spun, Dylan's expression torn between laughter and concern.

Caitlin froze, unsure what to do or say. She had to say something, though, and quickly, before Hank could get his words together and absorb what he was seeing.

"Touch my ass again, and you won't have any hands left to toss off your cronies," Caitlin said, straightening her back and taking a few cautionary steps away from Hank.

Hank stared back at her, his face turning from shock to laughter to anger.

He settled on that last emotion as his nostrils flared. His face turned red, and clearly, now decided that he needed to put his foot down and take charge.

He took a step towards Caitlin. "You stupid bitch—"

"Now, now," Dylan said, appearing at Caitlin's side. She was surprised to see that his hand was on the hilt of his sword. No one ever stood up to Hank and, while she loved her brother for jumping to her defense, she wasn't entirely sure that it was the best option in the long run.

At some point, we're going back to Silver Creek. At some point, Hank will tell the governor about this, and then what happens?

Dylan saw Hank's hesitation but seemed to also read Caitlin's thoughts. "We're all on the same side here." He raised his hands away from his sword. "What's the use of fighting amongst ourselves when we've got a job to do?"

Caitlin had always loved how diplomatic Dylan could be, a trait he'd learned from their father.

For a moment, Hank and Dylan simply stared at each other. The others watched in silence—except for Victor who still lay coughing on the floor.

Hank's rage shifted to an expression of mild contempt, a shift which Dylan had mentioned on occasion before and didn't like. Caitlin knew, as he did, that while they were outside the safety of the town, he was on an equal level with Hank. The minute they stepped back through the gates, however, Trisk would take Hank's side over Dylan's without a moment's hesitation.

"If that's the case, you ought to keep this bitch on a leash. If she touches another one of my men... Well...let's just say that it's been a while since I've had a playmate, and there's an itch I can't scratch myself."

The shit-eating grin was back on Hank's face.

Sullivan, in all his infinite naivety, stepped over to Victor and offered him a hand which he slapped away. Hendrick chuckled, offered his own hand which Victor accepted, then pulled his comrade back to his feet.

They took their positions once more, though this time, Hendrick and Victor swapped places. The tension spoke volumes as they continued through the darkness, the wind whispering through the trees as they walked warily through the undergrowth.

With each and every step, Caitlin thought about what had just happened. Where had she found the strength and skill to throw Victor?

Was it from her anger? Was it skill, nothing more than a technique she'd super-learned from Dylan?

She replayed the scenario once more in her head, trying her best to slow it all down as she envisioned tossing Hank over her shoulder. In this replay, as Hank hit the floor, she followed it by drawing her sword quickly, and ignoring the gasp from her brother, made a swift slice across Hank's neck.

———

There were a couple of moments along the way when Caitlin wondered whether they were headed in the right direction. After all, the last time she had found the manor, it had been accidental. The Mad had given chase, and the last thing Kiera or Caitlin had done was keep an eye out for memorable landmarks.

Now, however, every part of the forest looked the same to her. She trusted her brother with a confidence she couldn't explain and knew that he had spent many of his years wandering with his troop through the foliage beneath the canopies of Silver Creek. Still, as her legs grew tired and the time wore on, it felt like it would never end.

Even worse, the entire time, she felt… *exposed*, and not only because with every shadow and movement of a branch, she imagined the Mad leaping out from the darkness and attacking. Her unease and vulnerability lay in the fact that even now, she could *feel* the thoughts cycling through Hank's mind.

She could feel him undressing her with his eyes, and she *hated* it.

In all honesty, Caitlin had always considered herself desirable. She wasn't what anyone would call fat, either, and she liked to think her assets were well above average. A few times through the years, she had caught her reflection in a puddle or against some dulled steel and checked out the curves of her own ass. She thought her chest was small, but as her first boyfriend had once told her, "More than a handful is just a waste."

She had almost regretted socking a mean right hook to his nose after that. In hindsight, it was a compliment in itself, but she couldn't blame him for wanting to end the relationship. He'd done so with a hand cupped over his nose as blood seeped between his fingers.

She looked to her right, then rolled her eyes when Hendrick winked at her.

Sure, let them try and take me, she thought. *Next thing they know, they'll be bleeding on the ground having the world's most unhygienic circumcision with an unsuitably large scalpel.*

At some point along the way, Dylan raised a fist, and everyone came to a halt. Caitlin strained her ears, struggling to hear them at first.

Then, there it was. The tell-tale siren-song of the Mad, somewhere far off in the distance, a chorus of screeches and cries as they roamed endlessly across the world. Former humans, their entire will had been bent by the Madness to the insatiable hunt for human blood.

And I thought vampires were supposed to be bad.

It was difficult to tell which direction they were coming from, but there was almost something sad about the sound. It started as a melancholic wailing as the infected called out in pain to the stars and the moon. A moment later, another would join in, then another. The macabre melody drifted, distorted by the trees and thick undergrowth.

"Why are we stopping? There are none nearby," Caitlin said in a hushed tone.

Hank looked at Dylan for confirmation. He'd not spent a great deal of time actually out in the wild, and his anxiety, though controlled, was still very evident.

Dylan looked at the stars, studying the sky. "That's not necessarily true. Not all the Mad call or scream. Hearing several in the distance doesn't mean there are none nearby. Some rest in the shadows of trees. Some collapse on the floor, hidden in the leaf-strewn dirt, snapping teeth and rolling heads like animated bear traps." He pulled his sword.

Caitlin reached for her own, then cautioned herself against it.

Not yet...not yet.

She heard the sounds of the others withdrawing their blades.

"They can come at any time," Dylan continued. "Keep your wits about you, gentlemen. We're not too far off from Mossy Hollow now, and the last time we checked, this place was an anthill of Mad."

As Dylan again took the lead, he moved closer to Caitlin to whisper in her ear. "No running off this time, please."

Caitlin shook her head and smiled. "Ass."

"Bitch," Dylan replied.

She looked ahead, seeking instinctively for something familiar to remind her of the night before. At first, she couldn't see anything at all that suggested they were where her brother said they were. Not that she doubted his abilities. If anything, his skill was admirable.

She looked to the stars, then at the ground itself...

And there they were. Deep treads in the ground.

Dozens of pairs of footprints leading away from the far side of the clearing.

Dylan nodded, confirming his direction.

"We're close," he whispered to the others.

Caitlin felt the tension rise.

It spiked even more when, as they began walking again, they heard the dying cries of a bear cutting through the silent darkness ahead.

CHAPTER SIX

Carter Manor, Silver Creek Forest

"*Ho-lee-cow*," were Caitlin's first words as she stared at the savaged remains of the bear on the floor.

"More like, ho-lee-*bear*," Dylan whispered

Not ten feet away, Hendrick held up the shredded remains of an arm and hand he had picked up off the floor. He was busy playing with the fingers, fashioning the hand in such a way that, by the time he was finished, it was flipping the bird at the others.

Dylan, Caitlin, and Sullivan watched with a mildly sick look on their faces. Each of them clearly thought the same thing—the arm likely belonged to Drek Francis, their fallen comrade from the night before. It had no doubt spilled from the stomach lining of the bear which now sprawled on the floor.

Hank, on the other hand, struggled to hold in his laughter. There was something primal in him deriving pleasure from the idiocy of Hendrick playing puppet with the arm.

Victor laughed, though it seemed more out of necessity than his own humor. He had, in fact, gone rather pale.

An overwhelming desire to punch Hank and Hendrick and wipe the idiotic smiles off their faces washed over Caitlin.

The injustice of it all swept over her. How tragic that death had become a thing of laughter.

Dylan tried to hush them, snatching the arm from Hendrick. He seemed to instantly reach full alert, his eyes glancing at the back of the manor where overgrown ivy and weeds had made a good attempt at covering the entirety of the brickwork.

Hank suddenly grew serious and stepped towards the manor, his arms spread wide as if to soak in the beauty of the crumbling building. "Okay, here's the plan. We go in, we get out. Quick and painless."

"No wonder he's single," Caitlin whispered to Dylan.

"By all means, Captain. After you."

Hank considered for a moment, then ordered his guards to follow him.

They made their way to the back door.

They weren't in the least bit surprised to find the back door ajar. Since the Madness had plagued the world, there were countless houses, villages, and manors whose residents had fallen to the disease. Cars, blimps, and subways had all but been abandoned in the larger cities, and often, survivors would find buildings from the old world. All were ripe and ready for raiding.

That was if they could work out what they were. There had been times when Caitlin's father, a former ranger, had returned from patrol with gadgets and gizmos he had found. Often these were pieces of old weaponry but easily recognized, but half the time, they couldn't figure out how they were in any way useful.

Her father had explained to Caitlin and Dylan that there had been many things powered by electricity but were otherwise worthless when the power grids went down for good and electricity was no longer a household staple. Small contraptions with buttons and numbers and screens resembled nothing more than bricks now that their life source had ceased.

Hank led the way. He creaked the back door open, and they found themselves in a large storage room. They filed in one-by-one and paused to take in the crooked shelves lining the walls with miscellaneous boxes and containers all stained or half-rotted.

Sullivan closed the door behind them. They plunged into darkness.

"Sullivan? What are you doing?" Dylan hissed.

"I didn't want to let all the cold into the house," he replied a little too loudly.

"Shhh," Caitlin whispered.

"What does it matter if the cold gets in? The door was already ajar. Clearly, the vampire doesn't give a shit," Hendrick replied.

"I'm sorry. Manners are manners," Sullivan said.

"Can someone tell Pea Brain to open the door so we can see?" Hank asked. "And then can we please *shut the fuck up?*"

Before Sullivan opened the door, Caitlin felt another hand claw her ass—a small squeeze. Subtle, she acknowledged, but not careful enough. A moment later, a gentle wash of moonlight illuminated the room as the door swung open.

Caitlin wasn't surprised to notice that Hank was considerably closer to her now. He caught her eye, then looked around as if to say, "What? Me? No…that couldn't have been me."

Caitlin noted the increasingly familiar look on his face, saving it as fuel in her memory bank.

Over the years, she had never had any direct contact with Hank. But she had always wondered about him as she'd seen him strolling through the boulevards and streets of Silver Creek. Mostly, she'd wondered what it must be like to be the Captain of the Guards. A part of her liked to imagine that there must be some nobility in him outside all the rumors of harassment and abuse.

She was very quickly being proven wrong. The man was an outright spunk bubble.

Hank stepped away from Caitlin, apparently unperturbed at being caught groping her, and opened a door at the far end of the room. He recoiled, placing his hand immediately over his nose. The smell came in a thick wave. Caitlin wondered what it was until she remembered what had happened not twenty-four hours previous.

It was the smell of the Mad.

The smell of the dead.

"Woah, Victor. C'mon man, we're in the presence of a lady," Hendrick said.

'Are you okay?' Dylan mouthed to Caitlin.

Caitlin nodded and reached inside her coat. She felt for the hilt of her sword and clenched it in her fist, the sword's body remaining hidden within her clothing.

Guilt washed over her. Was she really going to use the vampire's own sword to threaten her and drag her back to Silver Creek?

It's either that or die. The decision is yours, baby-cakes.

Hank psyched himself up with a deep breath and stiffened posture, poked his head into the hallway. He most likely wouldn't see the blood in the foyer. It was dark inside with only small scraps of moonlight able to make it through the thick grime that covered the windows. Caitlin tried to imagine what he could see—at the far end of the hall would be the forms of the dead piled on the floor. Lines of them would lead up the stairs.

He paused. "Okay. New plan: Harrison one. Harrison two. Move up front. You know the way, yes?"

Dylan looked at Caitlin for confirmation.

Caitlin nodded. She brushed past Hank without making eye contact, muttering as she passed, "How's it feel relying on a woman to do your dirty work?"

Hank growled, grabbed a fistful of Caitlin's hair, and pulled her head back so fast it felt like it might snap.

"Watch your mouth before I find something of mine to fill it," he threatened, his face hovering above hers. He released her hair, then shoved her forward.

Caitlin rubbed her neck, took a deep breath, listened out for any signs of Mad—or vampire—and strode ahead.

Mary-Anne could smell them all a mile off. She wasn't exactly sure how many there were—that would need some further investigation. But even though her senses had lessened over the years, having a large group of humans trying to sneak through her house set her fangs into full salivation mode.

At first, she sighed, hoping it wasn't more of those damn soldiers come by to disturb her. But as she lay in her bed, listening to their laughable attempts to sneak around her house, a thought popped into her head.

The girl? Could she be here again?

Her mind flashed back to the night before, remembering the vulnerable position the girl had found herself in with a zombie behind her, and how Mary-Anne *wanted* to save her. That truth stuck with her because it was so unlike what she'd felt for the other men who had charged into the manor with weapons a-blazing. She had quickly dispatched those and made sure they never breathed another lungful of air again.

No, Mary-Anne had saved the girl. But...why?

Had it been a stupid move on her part? Mary-Anne didn't think so. The day had worn on, and she had attempted to sleep in the darkness. Instead, she'd tossed and turned as her stomach did what it always did after a mere whiff of human blood, roaring and growling uncomfortably. All the while, she had grown more and more curious about *her*.

Her last true encounters with humans had been years beyond count. Mary-Anne had traveled far across the country before finding herself back at her family home. Her friends fell one-by-one to the Madness, or slowly degenerated as they turned to vegetarianism as a basic means to survive. They'd found that, as time went by, their powers slipped. Their strength and speed began to fail until they were nothing more than simple human-strength vamps who wanted nothing more than to take their own lives.

Mostly, they did, although some of her friends had found alternate ways to survive.

Mary-Anne shook her head, remembering what she had found in a barn out in the wilds. Humans were strung up with rope, bite marks covering their bodies. They were all pale and as close to death as could be without actually dying.

The idea of it made her stomach twist in knots.

Then growl with hunger.

She was a vampire, after all.

But the girl…there was something about her. A vibrant strength that had somehow made Mary-Anne feel stronger simply by being around her. A strength that reminded Mary-Anne of a *much* younger version of herself in the days before she had been turned.

Mary-Anne rose from her bed, cracked her knuckles, and snuck through the house to get a closer peek at the action.

They paused out in the open of the foyer. There were bodies everywhere, those that had been sliced and destroyed the night before, now in segments for the flies to taste and devour.

The least she could have done was clean her corridor, Caitlin thought, holding her nose though she could still almost taste the stench of death.

"What the hell happened here?" Hendrick asked through his sleeve.

"What does it look like?" Caitlin asked, suddenly growing bolder as she reminded herself that she had taken most of these Mad down. "The Mad came, but they did not conquer."

"How poetic." Dylan crouched down to examine a body. "They look so peaceful when they're dead. Who could believe they're such monsters when they're alive?"

Hank was hit by an involuntary convulsion and covered his mouth.

"You okay, boss?" Victor asked, though his voice sounded strange. Caitlin glanced over and saw his hood had been raised and his face was now shadowed.

"Yes, fine. Fine," Hank said, waving him away.

Dylan put a hand on Hank's shoulder, concern on his face. "C'mon, let's move away from here. No one likes to see this many bodies dead on the floor—"

"*Don't* fucking touch me," Hank hissed, moving with speed and batting Dylan's hand away. "You think I haven't seen bodies, Harrison? You think I give a shit if there's three thousand bodies piled up in this room with maggots and rats crawling through the skin? No, I don't. So don't patronize me. You fucking touch me again, and I'll add your corpse to the pile."

Dylan raised his hands, "Okay, jeesh. Easy, easy…"

Hank ran a hand over his head. "Good. Now, can one of you lead the fucking way?"

Dylan turned to Caitlin and rolled his eyes. He took to the stairs and began climbing as quietly as he could.

Caitlin followed, but not without taking another look

at Victor. For the first time, she noticed his eyes shining through the shadow of his hood. She hadn't noticed before how bright and keen they were. A vivid green, twinkling in the stray rays of the moonlight.

He turned away and marched ahead of her up the stairs.

The house was bigger than she'd expected. She hadn't had a chance to look the night before, but at the top of the stairs, there were two long, wide corridors leading off in either direction.

"Split into two parties?" Dylan suggested.

"Oh, no. You think I'm letting you two out of my sight, you've got another thing coming." Hank pulled out his sword and pointed it at Dylan. "Pick one."

Caitlin nodded left—the same way she had seen the vampire emerge from the night before. Dylan walked ahead of the group. He moved slowly now, treading as lightly as possible. Not that it mattered, considering that Hendrick was so large, his footsteps were like muffled drums on the floor.

The boards creaked and some sagged with their weight. The house was a shit show, old enough to feel as though, at any moment, a whisper of the wind would tear it down.

And all the time, as they wandered down the dark corridors, poking heads into the doors that led to dark rooms, all Caitlin could imagine were red eyes shining from the dark. Eyes which glowed. Eyes that could, at any point, be a vampire's—or that of the Mad.

She closed her eyes and thought of them all lying out there. Zombies. That had been the hardest part so far— avoiding the empty stares of the faces of the Mad on the floor, vacant eyes looking up at the ceiling. Those same eyes which had once been a fierce glowing red had now become nothing more than a dark, empty black.

Caitlin couldn't even remember if it had been a quick transition from red to black, or if it had been like a set of batteries dying, the light fading gradually over moments.

Wait. What are batteries?

She thought of a book she had read once, then shrugged.

When they reached a room at the end of the corridor, Caitlin stepped forward and tried the handle. It was locked.

"It's locked?" Hank asked.

Caitlin nodded. *No shit, Sherlock.*

"Then it *must* be this one."

"How do you figure?" Dylan asked.

"Because if she wanted to hide, she'd lock the door. Duh!"

Hank turned to Hendrick for confirmation. He shrugged. That was enough for Hank.

"Well, we can soon fix this. Come out. Come out, wherever you are!" Hank sang, his words ringing like thunder through the house.

Before Caitlin could say a word, Hank raised his foot and gave the door a boot.

The door crashed off its frame, smacking onto the wooden floorboards and forcing up a storm of dust.

For a few seconds, they could see nothing beyond the dusty haze. They pawed stupidly at their eyes which burned from the powdered debris and dead skin particles of a family stretching back centuries.

"There," Hank said proudly.

"Good one. The door's open. But you might as well have fired a gun into the sky and cried out to every single Mad in the area. 'Hey! Hey! We're a walking *fucking* buffet. Here, have a nibble on our juicy thighs.'" Caitlin furrowed her brow.

"If they come, I'm using you as a shield," Hank said simply. He grabbed Caitlin's arm and threw her forward into the room.

Dylan moved to retaliate, but Hank's sword was already prodding into his back. "Uh-uh," he said, wagging his finger. "You first."

It took a few seconds for Caitlin's eyes to adjust to the dark of the room. When Sullivan walked instinctively to the curtains and pulled them wide, a torrent of silver swarmed into the room in muted tones. The moon was free of its clouds and did its best to shine through the grime-covered glass of the windows.

Caitlin raised an eyebrow in confusion.

The room was essentially empty. A cabinet stood on one side of the room and a sofa on the other. It looked like an ancient living room but devoid of anything that made it worth locking.

"Well...this was pointless," Caitlin said.

Hank's nostrils flared.

"Sullivan, don't touch that!" Dylan hissed as he saw Sullivan move to the corner where a small vase stood on a pedestal.

Sullivan jumped, turned, and his arm knocked into the pedestal. The vase wobbled precariously on its perch, and before he could move to stop it, it tumbled to the floor, shattering into tiny pieces.

"And you worried about *me* making noises," Hank muttered. "At least I'm not smashing family heirlooms. That might've been a nice gift for the governor to have taken from the vampire's home. He likes his souvenirs, ain't that right?"

Hendrick nodded stupidly at Hank, unaware that Caitlin, Hank, and Dylan were all now staring at where Victor had stood a moment before.

Victor had gone, now. Standing in his place was a woman with dark skin and black hair. Her green eyes caught the twinkle of the moonlight, shining with an eerie glow. She studied them each in turn.

She smiled at Caitlin, nodding ever so slightly. "We meet again."

"W-wha—" Hank stuttered, before clearing his throat and regaining his confidence. "Where's Victor?"

"Your friend is...indisposed." She cocked her head to the side. The room was tense and still. The woman looked at the pile of shattered china fragments on the floor. "That was my great-uncle's."

"I'm...sorry," Sullivan whispered, his throat gone dry.

The vampire shrugged. "No sense dwelling on the past." She turned to Hank. "And while I appreciate you admiring the beauty of my family's heirlooms, I'd highly advise that you tell your...governor...to keep his spunk-covered hands off my things, and maybe stay the fuck off Mary-Anne's land before she finds her way to your shitty excuse for a town and kills him herself."

Hank's face colored with rage. "Is that a *threat*?"

"No. It's a promise," Mary-Anne said.

Hank's eyes were thoughtful. Clearly, he considered

various approach tactics. Caitlin felt her brother crouch slightly beside her, coiling as if ready to strike. Hendrick slowly pulled out his own sword and moved into a fighting stance.

Caitlin felt for her sword. Mary-Anne's eyes flickered to Caitlin's hip, then her eyes. A slight flash of betrayal shone from the green.

"Five of us. One of you, *vamp*." Hank grinned, reached to his hip with his spare hand, and pulled out a wooden stake the size of a small blade. "I like those odds."

Mary-Anne rolled her eyes. "I see how it is," she said, fangs appearing in her mouth. "If it's a fight you want, then let's get started."

She cracked her neck and took a stance. "Okay, bitches. Who's first?"

CHAPTER SEVEN

Carter Manor, Silver Creek Forest

There was a moment of silent tension before Hank charged. He roared at the top of his voice and slashed at Mary-Anne.

She twirled, spinning out of the way of his advance. Hank stumbled forward and took a moment to regain his balance.

"Ah, humans. Such simple creatures," Mary-Anne said as her nails grew to sharp points.

"Don't just stand there, get her!" Hank shouted, his face twisted with rage.

Caitlin looked at her brother, feeling torn. Did she want to bring harm to Mary-Anne?

No.

Did she want to risk not helping and later being delivered to Trisk to be slaughtered because she hadn't held up her end of the bargain?

No. She had her honor.

Did she want to risk not being prepared to attack and having Mary-Anne kill her where she stood?

No.

Mary-Anne *was* still a vampire after all.

Dylan silently communicated similar thoughts, then took his own swing.

This time, she narrowly avoided the cut, stepping sideways as the rusted blade nicked at her skin.

Hendrick came from the other side. Sullivan joined the fray. Mary-Anne danced in the middle and swerved, ducked, and twisted away from each attack as it came.

At one point, Hendrick tripped over Hank's foot and toppled over, smashing into Sullivan, who groaned. He pushed Hendrick off him, and the two giants stood side-by-side, panting.

Mary-Anne found herself in a corner at the far side of the room. Her speed was impressive, though Caitlin noted that she now panted heavily, as though she had been running for several hours.

Undaunted, she cracked her knuckles and stretched. "That reminds me," she said, looking at her wrist as if checking something that wasn't there, "it's about time I booked another aerobics class."

Hank grinned, and a small cut at the side of his mouth oozed blood. He licked his lips. "Little vampire stuck in the corner, eh? Bad move all around, wouldn't you say, Hendrick?"

Hendrick nodded, his face dark and shadowed as he struggled to keep his anger controlled. As a giant amongst guards, he no doubt wasn't used to being dodged and thrown around. He had his pride, and his pride had been wounded.

"Why don't we make a deal?" Hank said as he signaled for everyone to gather closer and trap Mary-Anne in the corner. "You tell us where you've hidden our comrade, and we'll make this nice and easy on you. Come along quietly. Come along *willingly*, before this turns ugly."

Mary-Anne placed a hand on her chest. "Oh, I'm sorry. I thought it had turned ugly from the moment you walked into the room."

Caitlin struggled to hide her laugh.

"Here's the thing—" Mary-Anne began.

"Fuck this, bitch!" Hendrick called, seemingly pushed beyond the limit by the vampire insulting his boss. He charged at Mary-Anne, screaming in a voice hoarse with rage.

Hank laughed, waiting for the moment of triumph to see the vampire pinned to the wall by a sword. Like all of them, he'd no doubt heard the legends that vampires had healing powers. No doubt he assumed she'd be fine in the end, no matter what happened to her now.

Caitlin watched, mouth open, as everything moved in slow motion.

Mary-Anne ran forward, one leg rising off the ground to meet Hendrick's thigh. With unmatched speed, she kicked off into the air, grabbing his head in both her hands and somersaulting over his body, using her grip on his face as leverage to twist her back around in a delicious one-eighty. She landed softly on her feet and ripped the wooden stake from Hank's hand. Then, as Hendrick crashed into the wall, exploded forward and stabbed the stake through his trousers, stopping when the stake was so far up his ass that she couldn't shove it any further.

Hendrick screeched in pain. Hank stood open-mouthed.

"Ah, shit," Sullivan murmured, growing pale.

Mary-Anne stood, her chest rising and falling rapidly from the exertion of her attack. When she spoke, her voice was breathy. "Okay, fuckers. You've seen what I can do. Who still thinks they have what it takes to take me on?"

That was the moment it all changed.

As Mary-Anne finished talking, she doubled over, placing her hands on her knees. Caitlin watched with pity growing inside her.

In all the texts she'd seen and stories she'd heard, vampires had been noble creatures, full of vibrant life, strength, and power. Able to operate during the night for hours at a time, they had been the unchallenged kings and queens of the midnight hour.

That's was how it had been when Mary-Anne had saved her before. Until this point, Caitlin could have sworn nothing had changed.

Now, Mary-Anne looked ill, as though there was no fuel inside her to keep her going. Her attack on Hendrick seemed to have drained her considerably, and Caitlin didn't know what would help her. She was by no means weak—after all, could Hank, Sullivan, or Dylan move like that?

No.

But Hank must have realized it as soon Caitlin did. The vampire was on the back foot.

And now, Sullivan took his turn. He lunged forward

and kicked Mary-Anne in the stomach. A harsh sound of expelled air came from her mouth.

The kick moved her closer to Dylan, who pulled a length of rope from his pocket and jumped Mary-Anne, pulled her down, and straddled her, attempting to tie her up so they could drag her home.

Mary-Anne wriggled and writhed beneath Dylan.

"Don't fuck her. Tie her down," Hank roared, his face a painting of delicious triumph.

Mary-Anne spat at Dylan and screeched, her eyes glowing the brightest they'd ever been. She shouted and shoved Dylan backward.

He flew across the room, his back smacking into the window and sending cracks spiderwebbing up the panes.

Hendrick groaned in the corner. He tugged at the stake in his ass, moaning and sobbing.

Mary-Anne moved away from Dylan and Hank towards Caitlin.

Hank's eyes flashed as they met Caitlin's. "Well, what the fuck are you standing around for, bitch? Grab her!"

Caitlin, sensing danger now that she was within arm's reach of the vampire, pulled her cloak to the side and revealed the gleaming blade of the old world.

There was an audible gasp from Hank. The moonlight sang off the sword's body, and suddenly, Caitlin seemed to find her bravery. Her heart pounded in her chest.

For half a second, she saw the light in Mary-Anne's eyes fade as they exchanged a look. Was Mary-Anne trying to communicate something to her? Caitlin felt torn. What had the vampire ever done to deserve this attack?

"Harrison!" Hank called, running a finger across his neck to reinforce his point.

Caitlin hesitated, torn between two choices—To capture, or not to capture. Which one was worse? She fought in her head, arguing both sides until she heard Dylan's voice pleading and whispering behind her.

"Cat…"

She steeled herself.

"Okay, Count Bitchula. It's time to play."

"With *my* sword?" Mary-Anne asked. "Now, that hardly seems fair, does it?"

"Fair doesn't exist in this world," Caitlin said, swinging at Mary-Anne. The vampire dove across the room and retrieved Hendrick's rusty sword which he had dropped when he lost his anal-virginity.

Dylan came from the left, slashing and attacking, driving Mary-Anne back into the center of the room. Their swords chimed the music of battle.

Mary-Anne seemed to draw from some fuel reserves deep within. Sullivan joined in, then Caitlin, and before they knew what was happening, the room was filled with a blur of clashing metal.

The vampire was incredible. Though her grunts and gasps were loud as she struggled for breath, she never gave up. Caitlin threw a few slashes herself, but more from the fear of Hank seeing that she wasn't involved than from wanting to do any real damage.

At one point, Mary-Anne launched herself at Caitlin and ended up sitting on top of her. The move was so fast that it took a second for Dylan and Sullivan to realize that she was no longer standing there, an apparently easy target.

"You fight with honor," Mary-Anne whispered into her ear so quietly and with such speed that Caitlin wondered if she were hearing things. "I will not kill you this night, should you make the wise decision. These men are holding you back. Come with me, and I will train you. I will teach you. I will show you that the world is far more than just wooden walls and patriarchy. Just say the word."

"Cat!" Dylan cried as Mary-Anne rolled off Caitlin and avoided another boot from Sullivan.

Mary-Anne moved to the other side of the room and tried her best to gather her breath. Sullivan turned and pursued, lumbering across the room like a giant chasing a butterfly.

"Cat, are you okay?" Dylan said, appearing at Caitlin's side. He reached down and held out his hand, pulling her to her feet in one swift move.

Caitlin took a moment to evaluate the situation.

Hendrick was now up, stumbling along the wall with one hand held out like a blind man and the other wrapped around his ass. Sullivan was engaged in combat with Mary-Anne, and Hank was poised in the corner, watching everything unfolding before him, crouched and awaiting his moment to strike.

Letting the 'disposables' do the governor's dirty work? Is that your tactic?

"Cat?" Dylan pressed, deep concern in his eyes.

Caitlin turned, "Bet you're regretting not training me now," she said, winking at her brother.

Dylan rolled his eyes.

"What's the plan of action?" Caitlin asked.

Sullivan grunted across the room as Mary-Anne kicked him again. This time, the kick was feebler, only serving to shove him back a few steps.

"What else can we do? Keep fighting until she's exhausted, then drag her back," Dylan said. "It's either that or we die."

"Or we die fighting her," Caitlin added.

They watched as Sullivan moved to slash with his sword. Mary-Anne moved to counter it, but he managed to sneak in a jab with his left hand. His hammer of a fist connected with her face and knocked her to the floor.

Caitlin gasped.

Sullivan towered over the vampire, his sword in hand, poised to strike and stab her through the heart. Caitlin's hand moved to her mouth. She wondered at that moment if anyone had thought to mention to Sullivan that she was to be kept alive?

"Sullivan, *no!*" Caitlin shouted.

She had never seen this side of him. Outside of combat, Sullivan was a gentle giant. She had never understood why he was so valuable to Dylan on patrol, but now she saw the truth. He obeyed commands. He had power. He would do what needed to be done to protect them.

"Sullivan, halt!" Dylan commanded from beside her. His voice boomed with authority.

To Caitlin's relief, Sullivan stopped. His sword fell limply to his side.

Hank's nostrils flared. "Are you fucking kidding me?" He marched across the room to where Mary-Anne lay on the floor. He took his own sword, raised it high, and drove it down towards her.

Which was the exact same moment Caitlin came flying at him. Her mind had resolved into clarity, her decision made. She leaped through the air, her shoulder smashing into Hank's midsection. The sword flew off course, clattering against the wall.

Hank's weight slammed onto the floor, and she scrambled to climb off him, running as fast as she could to Mary-Anne's side.

Sullivan couldn't understand what was happening.

Dylan stood, frozen.

Caitlin crouched at Mary-Anne's side. "The word. Here. I'm saying the word."

No matter what happened in Silver Creek or what pressure she was under from the governor, she couldn't do it. She couldn't sentence someone who had saved her own life to that of torture and abuse by that man. It wasn't right.

Where was the justice in that?

Mary-Anne turned slowly. "Are you sure?"

Caitlin spared a look at Dylan. "Yes."

"Why, you slimy little cock-handling slut—" Hank began as he picked himself up.

In one final grunt of effort, Mary-Anne rose to her feet. "Climb on," she said, presenting her back to Caitlin.

Caitlin complied. A second later, they darted from the room.

Somewhere, Silver Creek Forest

Trees blurred past them as Mary-Anne sped clumsily

along at a pace that was alarming, given that she was clearly struggling to keep her strength. She navigated the darkness like it was floodlit but threatened to topple and fall at any moment.

"Are we there yet?" Caitlin shouted into her ear.

"Where do you think we're going?"

Caitlin thought. "Wherever the hell you're taking me."

"You sound just like my late nephew. He was as impatient as...*ooof*!"

Mary-Anne's words cut off as her foot caught on something hard on the forest floor. They both flew several feet through the air before crashing down on a dewy bed of leaves and moss.

"What the hell?" Caitlin spluttered. She tasted dirt in her mouth and clawed at her tongue until it was clean.

Mary-Anne rolled onto her back, staring at the sky. The moon was high, and the trees were tall. An owl hooted somewhere nearby.

Caitlin crawled over to Mary-Anne. "Are you okay?"

To her surprise, Mary-Anne began to laugh. Gently, at first, then rising and bubbling like a brook that became a river. The sound was beautiful but somber, and all too soon, Caitlin joined in.

It hurt to laugh, and Caitlin clutched her sides, feeling the tired muscles and the bruises from the vampire's iron grip as they had run.

When they eventually began to settle down, Mary-Anne sat up. "You fight well, flesh sack. Tell me. How did you learn to fight like that?"

Caitlin scoffed. "Me? Fight well?" She brushed the dirt off her shoulders. "Boy, you must really be tired. No. Hank,

Dylan, Sullivan, they fight well. Even you struggled to keep up with them."

"Ah, but if that's all it took to make someone a good swordsman, the world would be full of them. Men without technique. Men without finesse. Men who use their brute strength and not their heads, yet...you..."

Caitlin blushed. "I hardly touched you. I held back."

"For which I'm eternally grateful," Mary-Anne said, bowing as she sat, her hand clutched to the stitch in her stomach. "Yet, in all my years, I've never seen a human with such natural posture. You hold that blade as if it's a part of you. Even your soldiers can't match that."

Mary-Anne chuckled, then took in a deep hiss of breath.

Caitlin moved to Mary-Anne's side, wanting to help in some way but not sure how.

"I'm fine. I'm fine," Mary-Anne protested.

"You don't look fine."

"It's nothing, really," Mary-Anne said. "It'll heal soon enough." She lifted her top to reveal where Sullivan's foot had connected with her side. The blood had risen to the surface in a red weal. She looked at Caitlin, almost embarrassed. "I used to heal a lot faster than this, y'know. If you had found me ten, even five years ago, I would've been able to rip you all apart in seconds."

Well, that's an intense thought.

"He didn't mean it..." Caitlin said. Mary-Anne cocked her head. "Sullivan. He's a gentle giant. He's one of the good ones, just not too bright."

"Oh, you think I can't pick out the good guys and the bad guys from a mile off?" Mary-Anne said, waving her hand. "After several centuries of life, you think I don't know who is a prick and who just gets caught up in the chain of obedience? Trust me. There were three bad guys there tonight. One is bound and gagged in my basement in his underwear. Another has learned just how painful it can be to take a good stiff one up the back passage. And the other one...well, I'd love to have the chance to tear his head from his neck and paint my walls with his blood."

"Hank?"

"Mmhmm. Any man who stands and watches instead of engaging in the battle is a spineless coward."

"Why didn't you?" Caitlin asked after a second of imagining the scene.

"The same reason that made me save you. Honor." Mary-Anne pulled herself to her feet, wincing. "It's not my place to kill for the sake of killing. I gave him a chance to prove me wrong. Now, if I ever see him again, it'll be my ultimate pleasure to serve his head and body the divorce papers."

"Not if I get to him first," Caitlin said, unconsciously gripping the hilt of her sword. "But what about the other men Trisk sent to you before? You killed them?"

"If I hadn't, I wouldn't be talking to you now. Whatever your governor's instructions had been, those fellas seemed pretty ready to slice me to pieces and deliver me one chunk at a time."

They stood a while in silence, watching the sky. After all the action inside the manor, it seemed impossibly calm. Stars glittered overhead—the same stars that Caitlin had watched from the comfort of her bedroom window for as long as she had lived.

They seemed brighter somehow. Like they held more energy. Her head felt clearer than it had in…well…forever.

"Thank you," Caitlin said, almost inaudibly.

"I'm sorry?"

"Thank you for saving my life." She held out a hand, not sure what else to do.

Mary-Anne shook it. "You humans are strange creatures. Just when I think I've figured you all out, there's a gem that comes along that breaks the chain. For years, every man and woman I encountered wanted nothing more than to kill me or use me, to drain my blood for their own selfish gains, or to kill me through fear that I might turn Mad and go on a rampage. I took to hiding, sleeping away my years through fear that the world would never change—" Mary-Anne took a deep breath in, sniffing the air, "and then you come along…"

"I just want to fight for what's right," Caitlin said, looking thoughtful. "If I could rid the world of Mad, just one zombie at a time, I'd gladly take that journey. If it meant saving the people I love, of course."

Mary-Anne's ears pricked up. She pointed behind Caitlin to where a pair of red eyes had appeared in the darkness.

"Well…now might be your chance."

Caitlin turned and instinctively drew her sword. Another pair of eyes appeared.

"Do you want to take the left, or the right?" Caitlin asked.

There was no answer. She was suddenly alone.

She stood for a moment, confused by her companion's apparent disappearance. The owner of the first set of eyes screeched, running forward into the small clearing. Caitlin pushed aside all her questions to focus on a teenage girl with blisters and gashes along those parts of her body that were exposed to the air. She stumbled and hobbled as though she'd badly damaged her leg, paused, then ran for Caitlin.

Several more eyes appeared out of the darkness. A moment later, the air rumbled with the cries of the Mad.

Caught on her back foot, Caitlin slashed at the Mad girl, taking a nice chunk off one of her arms. She followed up by taking a leaf out of Sullivan's book and booting her in the hip. The girl spun off in a half circle, seemingly dazed for a moment, regained her orientation, then charged again, her limbs jerking and waving erratically.

"Mary-Anne? A little help here?" Caitlin asked the air as she slashed at the girl's neck. The zombie screeched as Caitlin pulled back for another hack.

"No, no, flesh sack. This is where your training begins." The voice came from somewhere high up in the trees.

Caitlin drew her sword back and stabbed it into the girl's chest. It was tough, but it went in deep, penetrating her heart. She yanked the blood-slicked sword from the body and prepared to face the additional five Mad which now ran toward her.

"Legs at an angle for balance. Toes pointed ahead. Bend your knees. Prioritize. The Mad run at different speeds, depending on how long they've had to degenerate. The difference may be infinitesimal, it may be huge. Breathe. Steady yourself. Go for the fastest first. Don't be scared to strafe and kick."

"Okay...okay..." Caitlin muttered between calming

breaths, doing her best to settle her mind and assess the advancing Mad.

A tall woman with a mop of dirty blonde hair seemed the fastest, her clothes nowhere near as tattered and blood-stained as the others.

Caitlin turned her attention to her first and yelled as the sword whistled and whined. A blood-curdling screech escaped the zombie's mouth as Caitlin ducked out the way of her arms and drove her blade into the back of the woman's calf. She collapsed to one leg, allowing Caitlin the chance to chop at the neck. It was thick, but she made some leeway, the neck beginning to flap and topple to one side.

"Behind you!" Mary-Anne's voice rang out.

Caitlin's heart raced, and her adrenaline flowed. Despite the terrible danger she knew she'd be in if any of her attackers bit or scratched her, she couldn't help but grin as Mary-Anne shouted instructions. One-by-one, she took them all on with a new sense of focus and growing confidence.

As she fought, she thought back to Dylan and his refusal to train her. She had asked her father, too, over the years for help in swordsmanship. Yet they had all refused, and she had been forced to hide away and practice in the secrecy of her home. Aside from the pervasive loneliness of those stolen hours, she lived constantly with a gnawing fear, never quite knowing if what she taught herself was right or not.

Now, finally, she was learning.

And it was from a motherfucking vampire.

CHAPTER EIGHT

Silver Creek, Silver Creek Forest

Dylan urged his legs to run faster. Every step felt like he was lifting lead. He looked behind him, checking the forest for any sign of Hank or the others. His heart pounded and his brow peppered with sweat as he calculated his next moves. They were in trouble. Well, *he* was. He wasn't sure about Sullivan at that point.

From the moment the vampire had run off with Caitlin, everything fell apart. Dylan could see in Hank's eyes that it was over. Now that his sister had joined forces with the vampire and ruined any chance they had of catching her, Dylan would now be the prime target.

Would he die?

Maybe.

But he didn't wait to find out.

"Get your ass back here!"

Hank's words had echoed through the halls as Dylan fled, leaving Hank with Hendrick and Sullivan. He knew Sullivan could take care of himself but still wrestled with guilt for somehow getting the loveable brute caught up in all this.

As long as he stayed with Hank, Sullivan would be okay.

Dylan hoped.

He wasn't sure what his plan was now, but he knew he had to get away. To grab a bag full of his things—maybe some food, too—holler for Jaxon, and head out into the wild.

That was the plan. Run and dash before Hank and the governor had the chance to catch him.

When the gates of Silver Creek came into view, he called to Clint and heard the grinding of the mechanisms. He slowed his pace, not wanting to draw extra attention to himself, and took the side streets home.

Was Caitlin okay? Dylan thought so. There was something between her and the vampire. A connection that he could sense. Why else would Mary-Anne have saved Caitlin? Why else would she choose to save Mary-Anne? He knew his sister as though she were an extension of him, and he knew she wouldn't risk everything without good reason.

Maybe he could find them out there? Join Caitlin and run away as she had offered? That didn't seem like such a bad idea now that he feared for his life. Silver Creek, the place he had grown up and where he had built his career and more memories than he could count, suddenly seemed cold.

Lifeless.

Gray.

Jaxon was already barking when he opened the door.

His tail wagged wildly. The two dark patches around his eyes reminded Dylan of a type of bear he'd once seen in a textbook. A black and white thing he couldn't quite remember the name of but remembered it looking cute as hell.

He'd even shown it to Caitlin, who took next to no interest. She wasn't quite like the other girls in Silver Creek. There was so much more to her than conventional responses.

Dylan darted around the rooms as he collected a leather bag and began shoving everything that he thought he needed inside.

He grabbed some food from cupboards and his bow and arrows and paused when he reached for a charcoal sketch of himself, Caitlin, and their parents.

Jaxon nudged his leg.

"Well, fluffs," he said, reaching down and petting his head. "Looks like I'm going to need your super sharp nose. Caitlin's out there somewhere, and we're sure as hell going to find her."

Jaxon cocked his head as if listening intently and understood each and every word that exited Dylan's mouth.

"That's right. Me and you. We'll find her, boy, won't we? We'll find her. Even if it's the last thing we do."

When Dylan was satisfied that he had everything he needed, he crouched low and tied the leash around Jaxon's neck. He held a shirt he had found in Caitlin's room to Jaxon's nose, and the dog took a big sniff.

"Does that smell like her?"

Jaxon barked.

"Good, then let's go."

It was as Dylan reached for the door handle that the knock came. Hank's voice followed shortly after. "By order of the governor, you need to open the fuck up."

Kain Sudeikis sat huddled up in the corner of his cell. An average man would probably be shivering and dead by now, but not Kain.

With one long, hard nail, he scratched at the wall, humming a song to himself. He wasn't sure at what point he'd picked the tune up, but he was pretty sure that it was from a band called King...or maybe Queen...or something like that. He only knew he liked it because there were a dozen changes of pace and melody. He remembered being shown a poster once of four guys with long dark hair.

"Nothing really matters...to meeeeee..." he crooned, almost in a low howl.

He looked down at the mouse that still lay on the floor. It was hard and crisp with rigor mortis. He felt his stomach rumble and wondered if it would taste as bad as he thought it would.

Until he saw a glint of something shiny further down the corridor. One of the guards leaned around the corner to try and get a better look at him.

They may not be able to see me in the dark. But I can sure as hell see them.

"*Psst.* Hey...you there."

For a moment, he was met with silence. And then, "Shhh. No talking."

"I thought that was only in libraries. So unless you've got a load of books hiding so far up your ass you can't move from your post, I think you might enjoy some pleasant conversation with your old buddy, Kain."

"What are libraries?" the guard returned.

"Shhh, don't pander to him, Ace. He's nothing more than a prisoner," the taller of the two replied.

"Don't hush me." Even through the darkness, Kain could see Ace's bald head, as smooth as an eggshell.

"The boss wants him quiet. Do you know what he'll do to us if he finds out we've let slip that there's a…that there's a…one of *him* down here?" The taller guard's voice shook ever so slightly. Maybe not enough for his companion to pick up on, but Kain was used to finding weaknesses and exploiting them.

"And you really think he's a *werewolf*?" Ace hissed. "They live in kid's books, Sid. Grow the fuck up."

"Not necessarily," Kain called.

He saw the two guards' heads turn, their eyes widening with curiosity. They began to whisper hurriedly to each other. It was cute. To think that they thought he wouldn't hear a thing with his heightened senses.

After a moment, the taller of the two—Sid—peeled away from his post and approached cautiously. He kept his hand on the hilt of his blade and stopped beside the cell but still out of arm's reach.

"You're right to be cautious. Our kind have built a reputation for our mood swings over the years," Kain said. Smiling inwardly at the open curiosity, he walked slowly across the cell and stopped with his hands on the bars.

"You admit it then?" Sid said in wonder. "You're really a..."

"A what?" Kain teased. "Oh...a werewolf? I don't know..." He turned away and paced a few steps inside the cell. Then, in a flash of speed calculated to take the guard by surprise, turned and slammed into the bars, his eyes glowing a fierce amber. Sid jumped back so far in fright that he fell to his ass on the floor, grunting loudly as Kain erupted in laughter. "You...should...have seen... your...face!"

"What the fuck is going on back there?" Ace called warily before he stepped out into the shadowed corridor. "What are you doing on the floor?"

"I've fallen, haven't I?"

"What did you do that for?"

"Don't mind him." Kain grinned. "He was just so stunned by my beauty that he passed out. It's not the first time I've been called a knockout over the years." Kain batted his eyelashes and licked his lips, enjoying the discomfort etched across the guards' faces. "Now, while you're both here, could you get me some real food? I'm friggin' starving. There's only so far a mouse can get me before I go..." His eyes began to glow again, a dull orange this time, but enough to stand out in the dark. "*Feral.*"

Sid picked himself off the floor and stood next to Ace. Their eyes squinted as they watched him with what seemed a mixture of fear and curiosity.

Sid shrugged. "I'll see what I can do."

"The boss said *no,*" Ace said, whacking Sid across the chest, his hand thumping against the leather of his armor.

"Look," Sid said, squaring off with Ace and once again

attempting to whisper, revealing little understanding of a Were's true powers. "The boss wants to see him transform, right? The boss wants to see a *werewolf* do his thing so we can use him around the Creek, right?"

"Right."

"What if *we're* the ones who make it happen?" Sid continued. "If we can send for the governor and show him that he's transformed, he'll have the proof he needs and we can get promoted. Think about it. More power. More *money*. I might even be able to buy Kate that dresser table she's been after for years."

"Kate does love that dresser…"

"Exactly," Sid said.

Ace's eyes lit up. "Do you think I could get Theresa that rug for our living room?"

"Anything!" Sid said.

Ace clapped his hands as Sid turned and disappeared into the dark. He waited near Kain for a few moments, thinking about his missus's reaction when he handed over the finely crafted rug she'd talked about for the last two months. That was, until he remembered that Kain was standing right behind him and the smile began to slip. Without another word, he returned to his post, a small spring in his step.

Kain waited patiently for Sid to come back, and when he did, he could smell him before he saw him. He carried a plate at arm's length as though it were a bomb that might detonate at any moment and set it down outside the cell.

"I can't reach it there," Kain said, crouching and reaching through the bars.

The guard bent down and slid the plate closer.

"A little more. That's it...nearly there..."

When the plate was but a foot outside the bars, Kain smiled and caught the guard's eyes. In one swift movement, he reached both arms out and pulled Sid tight against the bars. One hand wrapped around his body and stayed the guard's sword hand, while the other searched his body frantically.

Sid, held immobile by Kain's strength, found that words failed him at that moment.

"See, Sid. I don't need to transform to prove what I am. If you and your governor need solid evidence, then you might have to wait until the *next* apocalypse. Maybe you don't understand what's happening to Weres out there, but you're sure as hell not in a position to be making those judgment calls."

Kain found what he was looking for, released Sid, and pushed him away from the cell. He grabbed the plate of food—roasted chicken with distorted and mutated vegetables—*yum!*—and settled back in his corner, far out of reach of the guard's sword.

"You tell your boss about any of this, and I'll be sure to kill you first when I escape," Kain said, laughing as the guard stood frozen in the near darkness. After a long while, he must have accepted his reprieve because he returned to his post without a word.

"Oh, and thanks for the grub!" Kain called, stuffing the chicken in his mouth with one hand and fondling the keys he'd stolen from the guard's waistband in the other.

Even without seeing his face, Dylan could hear the glee in Hank's voice.

Fuck. Fuck. Fuuuuuck, he thought as Jaxon growled, threatening to bark.

"Shhh," he said, placing a hand over Jaxon's mouth.

Hank hammered on the door.

"Don't test my patience, Harrison. I know you're in there, and I've got a dozen good men out here ready to break in and seize your ass."

What to do? What to *do*?

He looked around the room for something—anything—that might help. He had his sword but knew that even he had limits to his talents. In one-on-one combat, he was great. Even against two, he figured he'd be able to handle himself.

But one against twelve?

Unless Hank was bluffing—which was a definite possibility. But could he take that risk?

"You asked for it," Hank called with a final fist pound on the door.

Without another thought, Dylan ran into the bedroom. Jaxon followed, hot on his heels. He looked around, saw the curtains blowing from his open window, and dove out. He executed a perfect roll on the floor to soften his landing, then suddenly remembered that he'd left his bag inside.

Shit!

He lingered a moment, weighing up whether there was any chance of climbing back in and—

"Where is he?" a voice said.

Nope.

"You've *lost* him?" Hank called. Dylan gleaned a certain amount of joy in hearing the anguish in his words. "Well turn the place over. Find Harrison and kill that fucking dog. That oughtta bring him out of his hole."

Good luck with that, Dylan grinned, edging around the side of the building as he silently thanked Jaxon for being smart enough to follow.

Dylan left the sounds of the troupe behind and tiptoed through the thin alleys between the residential district. These narrow corridors provided barely enough room for his shoulders to squeeze through when he hurried forward. Occasionally, he'd glance back to check the pooch was still following him. Jaxon stalked along, his head low, focused on his master.

Such a good boy.

He zigzagged and navigated the maze in a way that only someone who knew the town like the back of his hand could. Finally, he found himself six-feet away from an opening where the houses ended and the marketplace began.

People sauntered along at an easy pace. No worries at all. Making their way from point A to point B.

For a second, Dylan wished he was one of them.

He paused, closed his eyes, and listened for any sign of an ambush, but heard nothing. Realizing that no matter what he did, he would look out of place emerging from a side street still in his ranger uniform, he puffed his chest and walked out into the open. He prayed silently that he looked as though he belonged with the rest of the crowd.

"Just remember, Jax. Don't draw any attention to yourself—"

"Sneaky worm thought he could escape, huh?"

Dylan felt a heavy hand on his shoulder. He turned and was surprised to find Victor staring back at him. He looked disheveled. Red marks snaked around his wrists where Mary-Anne had tied him up.

Damn. Hank must've been quick to find him.

"Thought you'd be able to run away and leave us back there? I can't wait to hand you over to the Captain. Oooh, he'll be so happy to see you."

Dylan felt the cold metal of handcuffs clicking into place around his wrists.

"Hurry up, Vic." Hendrick appeared from around the corner, walking on tiptoes with a hand over his ass. He winced with every step he took. "It hurts."

"Oh, hush your face." Victor struggled openly not to laugh. "It's not like it's lodged in there anymore. Hank pulled it out, remember?"

"I think it's still bleeding."

Eurgh.

Victor shoved Dylan forward towards the street, almost tripping over Jaxon who raised his haunches and growled at them both.

"Oh, lucky. Extra points for the pooch too," he said, leaning down to Jaxon.

Jaxon launched forward, sank his teeth into Victor's hand, and shook his head.

"Why, you little fucker," Victor complained as he yanked his hand free. He pulled his leg back and went for the kick.

"Run, Jax! Run!" Dylan shouted, twisting to pull

Caitlin's t-shirt from his pocket. He leaned his body forward and threw it at Jaxon, catching him on the nose.

Jaxon sniffed, wheeled around, barked, and sprinted down the street.

"Good riddance to bad rubbish," Victor yelled, nursing his hand. Across the street, several women turned and stared at him, shaking their heads.

Dylan watched Jaxon dissolve into the distance, wishing that he had taken Caitlin's advice in the first place. Without a doubt, whatever the governor had in store for him now, it wouldn't be pleasant.

Go get her, Jax. Go get her, Dylan thought as Victor grabbed his elbow and marched him away.

CHAPTER NINE

Governor's Quarters, Silver Creek, Ontario

Trisk was spent. After at least seven minutes of fooling around with his concubines, he found himself out of breath, sweating from head to toe, and unable to hold out any longer.

And I was so close to beating my personal record—eight minutes!

"Good show, good show," he muttered, breathless.

He shimmied to the edge of the bed, pulling the sheets alongside him as the girls lay in bed, giggling behind their hands. They seemed to have enjoyed it as much as he did, though it could all have been an act—good girls being obedient simply to avoid his wrath. He'd long since ceased to wonder why their smiles never seemed to reach their eyes. What did it matter?

The governor donned his robe, reached for a large goblet on the far wall of the bedroom, and drank deeply. A trickle of dark purple liquid dribbled down his chin and dripped onto the folds of his stomach. He coughed, spluttered, then laughed.

"Makes a change to see *me* dribbling, eh, ladies?"

All three nodded and laughed, hiding their faces with the bed sheet. He liked them all, really he did. But still...he somehow felt emptier without Georgia to warm his sheets for him. He wondered if she had hated him at the moment he had administered the final blow, taking Sean Walker's knife and driving it through her heart as the final stages of the Madness took her.

It was only fair, really.

She was dying, and she was *his*. There was no coming back from the Madness.

He donned his dressing gown and exited the room.

Hank was waiting for him when he stepped into his reception room. "Ah, the finest of the governor's guards. How the devil does the day find you?"

He stumbled towards Hank and embraced him, oblivious to his own smell and the slick skin unhidden by the open gown. Hank recoiled momentarily, then recomposed himself when he was held at arm's length. "Good afternoon, Governor."

"Come now, it's Halrod to you. First, you bring me a Were, then you come back to tell me the good news."

"Good news?"

"You've caught the vampire, of course? Why else would you be back so soon?"

He looked at Hank expectantly but was met with silence.

He chuckled a hollow laugh and looked at the floor, his face shadowed.

"You're telling me that the bitch escaped? *Again?*"

Hank slowly nodded. "There was little I could do. The Harrison girl, she…she helped—"

"You're telling me that the Harrison girl aided her escape?" Trisk's wrath exploded. "Well, where are they now? Where did they go?"

"I'll have my best men out there looking for her come morning. Every one of them, if that's what it takes."

"Get them the fuck out there now!" the governor said as he hurled his goblet across the room. The wall exploded in a spray of purple liquid.

"Of course," Hank said, bowing low. He turned to leave.

"Hank. Wait," Trisk said, taking a seat. Though he was more disappointed than he'd been in a *long* time, Hank was still his number one. He took a deep breath and tried to collect himself. "Fetch me another drink."

Hank obeyed, walking to the corner of the room and pouring wine into a spare goblet.

"Get yourself one, too," the governor commanded.

Hank returned with goblets in each hand and presented one to his master.

"And with the Were in our hands…" the man muttered. "I thought we were on a winning streak."

"If you don't mind my asking, sir… Why are you so determined to capture the vampire? What guarantee is there that she'll work on our side?" Hank framed his query with the cautious respect that he'd learned early on in their working relationship. It bought him a little more leeway than the governor would ordinarily allow—up to a point, of course.

He waved a hand in an invitation for Hank to join

him at the table. A stack of books and old sheets of paper which Halrod had collected over the years littered the surface. A few of the loose leaves showed sketches of vampires standing proud on airships. There were variations of Weres who transformed from wolves to pumas to bears. And pinned on the wall was a large sketch of a handsome dark man next to a woman with dark hair and legs that seemed to stretch to her eyeballs. Both had fangs on display, and both were surrounded by men and women looking up at them in awe.

"The Dark Messiah and the Queen Bitch," Halrod explained. "They're of great fascination to me. Two of the most powerful vampires to ever have lived."

"I've heard the stories," Hank said bluntly, clearly unconvinced.

"Not just stories anymore, my friend. Can you believe it? After nearly a hundred years of uncertainty and doubt, Halrod Trisk might finally be the one who brings the Unknown back into the known world. With a Were on one side and a vampire on the other, I'd truly be unstoppable." Halrod chuckled, then downed his drink. "No matter what it takes, I need to see that vision realized. Can you imagine what we could do?"

"I'm happy for you, sir."

"Happy for *us*. If all goes well, you'll be by my side too, Hank. You've been loyal over the years, without end or reservation, and Halrod makes sure that he rewards loyalty."

The governor drained his cup in one long gulp, then slammed it on the table. He signaled to Hank to refill it, and the man obliged. When he returned, Trisk was lost in his thoughts.

Hank waited patiently.

"What about the Harrison boy? Where is he? Did he escape, too?"

"No, sir. He made a break for it once his sister ran off with the vampire. We caught him back in Silver Creek, trying to sneak away. Seemed he went back for some of his belongings. We found this on the floor of his house, alongside a packed bag." Hank handed over the charcoal sketch of Caitlin and Dylan's parents.

"Such a sentimental pair, aren't they?" the governor said, screwing the paper up and tossing it into the fire where it immediately curled in on itself, turning to ash in seconds. "Well, at least we've got some kind of leverage to use against the bitches."

Hank looked confused. "I thought they were not to return to the Creek empty-handed under pain of death?"

"And yet *you* returned empty-handed," Trisk snapped. He brushed a hand over his head and composed himself. "Think about it, Hank. If we kill the ranger, the girl has no reason to come back. But, if we keep him locked up and suffering, she's bound to come back to try and free him. And, if she really is in the pockets of the vampire, then we can draw two birdies back with one measly little worm."

"Sounds smart," Hank said.

"Someone has to be."

The door at the side of the room creaked open. Both men turned and saw a woman standing there naked, her skin glistening in the candlelight. She looked at Halrod, then saw the guard sat next to him. "Oh, the governor's brought us another plaything," she said to the room behind her.

A chorus of giggles and delighted explanations broke out.

Trisk raised his eyebrows and turned to Hank, "What d'ya reckon? You in?"

"I'm on duty, sir."

"Duty, schmooty. How about some booty?" Halrod said, jumping up with surprising speed and crashing across the room. He stood beside the woman and presented her to Hank. "Come on, lighten up. A quick bash on one of these speedsters and you'll be bringing your A-game to your duty."

Hank looked at the woman, who was arguably one of the finest women Silver Creek had to offer. He stirred in his pants as she swayed her hips seductively and rolled her finger towards him. He seriously contemplated the offer, thinking how long it had been since he had last lain with a woman...

Willingly.

Until Halrod belched.

That breaks that spell.

Hank suddenly envisioned Halrod's wobbling stomach crushing the ladies, his sweat dripping over their alabaster skin, and suddenly, it all seemed a lot less appealing.

"Maybe later, sir," Hank said, bowing low before leaving. "I've got a vampire to find."

"Ah well. More for me!" Halrod exclaimed and clapped his hands and dropped his gown. "Who's up for round two?"

. . .

Prison District, Silver Creek

The jail cell was cold, and the floor was hard. Though Dylan knew that it must be daytime now, there was no hope at all of ever seeing the sunshine.

He thought about Caitlin out there in the wild, and somehow wondered whether he had ended up with the worst end of the deal. While he was what he could consider to be safe in the cells of Silver Creek, she was out there roaming the Mad-infested woods with nothing more than a sword.

And a vampire. Remember, she does *have a friggin' vampire with her.*

At least Dylan wasn't alone down there in his cell.

"I see a little silhouetto of a man..." came that growling voice from the darkness.

Dylan had never actually been able to see the man singing, but they'd exchanged words since his arrival. Despite their situation, it seemed that jail agreed with him. It certainly did little to dampen his spirits as he crooned a song for which Dylan was fast learning the words.

"Morning, slugger," Dylan whispered. He'd already learned that the other man—Kain—had great hearing, way beyond what the guards up front could manage.

"Morning, sunshine. Did my singing wake you?" Dylan looked in the direction of the voice and could barely make out the shape of his companion.

Unfortunately, Kain had to speak louder than Dylan to be heard.

"Oi! Quiet in there." It was Sid's voice. Did they ever go home?

"What's the worst you think we're going to do? Talk our

way out of jail? C'mon, Sid, lighten the fuck up." Dylan heard Kain shuffling in his cell.

Footsteps sounded in the dark. A moment later, a hushed voice came from near their bars. "You won't be thinking like that when the governor comes later." If Dylan didn't know any better, he'd say Sid had developed a soft spot for the growling Kain. "Word has it that he's on a bit of a buzz at the minute. They say there's rumor of a vampire out in the wild, which makes him even more keen to see your...talent."

Talent? What did he mean, talent?

Kain replied in a voice that wasn't as steady as he'd hoped. "Well, he can try all he likes. If he can wobble his way down the stairs again without tripping, bouncing, and killing himself, I'd be surprised. Have you *seen* that man, Dill?"

"Yes. Yes, I have," Dylan replied without a hint of humor.

"If you say so," Sid said, returning to his post.

A length of silence followed. Dylan heard Kain sigh.

"*Shit,*" he grumbled to himself.

"What is it? What's the problem?" Dylan was already sure he wouldn't get an upfront response. He had no true idea who Kain was, but if the governor put Mary-Anne and Kain together in the same line of thought, could that mean there was some connection there? Could Kain be a vampire too?

"I'm sure you'll see soon enough, kid. You'll see." Dylan heard Kain return to his corner and fall quiet again.

It was several hours later when Trisk walked heavily down the stairs. Kain could hear his gasps for air and imagined his heart thumping at double speed to move the mechanisms that worked his massive body. How anyone could have gotten so fat in a world where food was so scarce and currency was tough to find was beyond Kain's understanding.

The guards parted, and for a brief moment, a sliver of light shone into the room. It diffused the darkness enough for Kain to notice Dylan sneak a peek at his scar-covered body.

Yeah, drink it in, kid. It ain't pretty, but it'll fuck you up in a heartbeat.

Ace lit a torch for the governor and handed it to him. Kain took the opportunity to examine the full extent of their captivity. Sawdust shavings strewn across the floor were damp and clumped from urine and God knew what else. Stone walls and iron bars completed the dismal picture.

Both prisoners blinked stupidly in the light, though Kain noticed the human was quick to adjust.

Trisk smiled and held out his arms as if addressing two old friends. "My two favorite prisoners...how are we both today? I hope you've not been causing my men any trouble."

Kain caught Sid's eye and watched as he turned quickly away.

When neither man replied, the governor's smile dropped. "Very well, abuse my hospitality. It means nothing to me, anyway, to see two monsters behind bars in my jail."

Kain growled and opened his mouth to talk but was interrupted by Dylan.

"If you're looking for a monster, look to your right-hand man. My sister did what she needed to do to survive."

"*Enough!*" Trisk said, his voice authoritative and booming. A dark shadow passed across his face and Dylan fell silent, shaking with rage. "Your sister betrayed the very town that raised her. She disobeyed a command, and will be killed the instant she's sighted. I don't care if she's with a vampire or a motherfucking Weredragon, she crossed the wrong governor." He turned his attention to Kain, though his words were still aimed at Dylan. "And besides, if you're looking for a monster, you've been sharing a bedroom with one for some time now." He withdrew the taser from his pocket and advanced on Kain's cage. "Isn't that right?"

Kain stood in the center of the cell and squared off against his enemy. He held his head high, knowing his ribs and hip bones stuck out, giving him the look of a sheet of elastic stretched over a matchstick skeleton. "You know nothing of monsters."

The governor smiled, clearly relishing the challenge presented him.

"I've ensured the guards don't interrupt me on this occasion. The last thing I'd want to do is get halfway through forcing your change, only to have to stop again. Was it painful? *Is* it painful when you turn?" Trisk looked greedy, almost hungry. He licked his lips, and his finger twitched over the button. "What creature do you turn into when you transform?"

"I turn into your mum."

"Wait...what's going on—"

Dylan's interjection was cut short when the governor laughed as he pressed the button. The prongs fired off the taser with a metal coil. Kain moved with such a speed that they hit nothing but air, plopping impotently onto the floor.

His would-be tormentor's laugh cut off and he took a step back. He looked down and stood transfixed as if he couldn't believe his luck. At the side of the cage was a wolf close to four-foot in height. Its eyes glowed amber, and its teeth were bared.

Trisk clapped his hands in delight. "How *wonderful...*" he muttered, staring in awe. Even Sid and Ace peeked around the corner to get a better look. "*Marvelous*. After all these years of searching, of second-guessing myself as to whether your kind truly existed...here you are."

"*Truuueeee. Truuueeee. Aaaand heeeere I coooome,*" Kain growled, advancing slowly on the governor.

"Oh, come now. Even a Were can't make it through these bars." The man knocked on the metal with his fists. "They're solid iron."

"*Iiiiif oooonly soooomeooooone haaad the keeeey,*" Kain replied, nudging against the door with his nose. The doors screeched on their rusty hinges. Trisk's eyes grew wide with alarm as he realized that the gate hadn't been locked at all since his arrival.

Kain knew he was terrifying in his wolf form. His hair raised on end as he reared up on his haunches. He wanted to tear the governor to shreds, to rip at his throat and destroy him. Over the years Kain had accumulated more than his fair share of blood on his hands. But dehydration and hunger had taken its toll, and there was a slight doubt in his mind that he'd have the strength to bring down the massive man before him *and* escape.

Trisk turned to the guards and began to run. Kain was faster, darting past the behemoth, weaving between the stunned guards in a matter of seconds, and disappearing up the stairs. The sun burned his eyes as he surfaced, but he could see the parapet guards all turn in alarm.

One way down, I guess, he thought as he launched himself off the wall and landed with a thud in the market-place below, disappearing quickly into the shadows.

CHAPTER TEN

Abandoned Airship, Silver Creek Forest

She heard her stomach rumble a long time before she was even aware that she was hungry. Despite the late hour, the forest was warm, and the sky was speckled with stars.

Caitlin took a seat beside the glowing embers of the fire and rubbed her hands. They felt raw, a sign of a hard few nights of training with Mary-Anne. Callouses had formed quickly, and a blister at the juncture of a finger and her palm looked fit to burst. It didn't seem to bother her none. For the first time in as long as she could remember, she felt...*powerful*.

They had taken refuge out in the woods. After a short conversation, they had agreed that there was no going back, at least for now. There was no guarantee that the governor, riled up from yet *another* failed attempt at capturing Mary-Anne, wouldn't send all his forces in one swift wave to apprehend them both.

As Caitlin was learning from a vampire who refused to drink human blood anymore, there was only so much they could do in a fight. The governor would be sure to send his men in droves the next time he attempted to ensnare Mary-Anne.

Caitlin supposed she should be worried or at least concerned that she now had a mark against her. She would undoubtedly be a target for the man whose authority she had flouted.

Yet she wasn't.

Something had changed, now. Even in simply taking time away from the Creek and seeing more of the outside world, she found her mindset shifting. Life beyond the walls wasn't half as scary as she'd been taught to believe—well, maybe not with a vampire at her side—and she couldn't help but marvel at the beauty of the things they had already found of the old world.

Take now, for instance. Caitlin looked around and marveled at the corpse of the old airship. At some point during the Second Dark Ages, the thing must have fallen from the sky. Maybe from some great battle of pirates, Weres, and Vamps, in a time when the world was different. When people traveled, relocated, and moved without fear.

The ship had smashed down on its belly, opening a hole in the wooden frame that yawned like the mouth of a cave. Over the years, the forest had done its best to claim the structure, now covered in moss and insects, but it was actually the Mad that Mary-Anne and Caitlin had to clear before they could use it as an adequate shelter. Their fire burned within this protective shield, warming them without drawing attention to themselves.

That had been a training session unlike any other.

Mary-Anne had joined in on that one. The two had made quite a pair.

"Any word on food yet? If I get any hungrier, I'm going to take to chewing tree bark, and a mouth full of splinters is the last thing I need," Caitlin called as if to no one. She knew Mary-Anne was off hunting and would hear every word but had no idea how far she had gone.

As if on cue, Mary-Anne returned with a rabbit held by the ears in each hand. She was panting and out of breath.

"Will this suffice, *your highness*?" Mary-Anne said, taking a sarcastic bow. "Or should I see what further delicacies I can find that fit her tastes?"

"They look perfect," Caitlin said, giving the embers a blow to stir up the fire. She picked up some sticks and began trying to fashion a spit, but every time she attempted to skewer the rabbits, the sticks broke. "What took you so long?"

Mary-Anne took the hares off Caitlin, picked up a stick, and stabbed it effortlessly through from butt to brain.

"Jesus, bet he's never taken anything that far up his ass."

Mary-Anne chuckled. "Have you?"

"Nope, but Hendrick has, thanks to you," Caitlin replied.

Mary-Anne wiped a tear of laughter from her eye and turned the carcass over, watching the blood spill onto the forest floor. After a long sniff, she seemed satisfied and revealed her fangs. She chomped into the rabbit and began sucking.

"Why do you waste so much blood?" Caitlin asked, fascinated—and a little queasy.

Mary-Anne wiped her mouth. "Force of habit, I guess. I

want to be sure that there's no Madness in the blood of the animals I eat."

"Animals can catch the Madness? I've never seen that before," Caitlin said.

"Neither have I, thank the Queen Bitch." Mary-Anne rocked back her head and looked at the stars. "Lucky, really… But even though it's never happened, I don't trust that it never could. There was a time when I could snack on humans with little consequence. But these days, it's worth neither the risk of humans discovering my existence nor the risk of draining blood tainted with the Madness." She sniffed the rabbits once more and her nose wrinkled. "These should do just fine."

They cooked the meat over the fire until it was crispy, the fatty juices spilling and spitting into the fire.

When she'd finished the first rabbit, Caitlin licked her fingers and cocked her head.

"What? What is it?" Mary-Anne asked.

"You're not exactly what I expected from a vampire, y'know?" She watched Mary-Anne carefully in the fire-light, the flames throwing shadows over her face which danced and frolicked in the night.

"You're not exactly what I've come to expect from humans," Mary-Anne replied, a softness in her voice. "Courage, boldness. A burning passion to do what's right. You don't see that a lot these days. It's been so long since I've last seen any glimpse of honor." She paused, contemplating her next sentence. "Even if you're hardly aware of it yourself."

Caitlin grabbed her sword off the floor beside her and placed it on her lap. She stroked the blade idly. Just a few hours before, it had been covered in the blood of the Mad who had adopted the airship as home, but now...well, it had cleaned up rather nicely.

"Who says I'm not planning on killing you?" Caitlin winked. She caught her own reflection in the sword and didn't recognize the woman staring back at her. "Who says I'm not using you for your training so that I can find a way to deliver you back to the governor?"

"I wouldn't doubt that's a factor that may have crossed your mind. After all, that was your brother who was fighting alongside you, no? The handsome man with the dark hair?"

Caitlin nodded. "How could you tell?"

"I've been around long enough to know these things. The fearful sideways glances. The way you both stand. The way you both look. It's textbook." Mary-Anne took a deep breath. "But, no. You wouldn't kill me, there's more to you than that. I can't explain it, but there's so much more in you than that. There's so much of myself that I see in you too—well, a young me, anyway."

Caitlin sat up straight, throwing her empty skewer back into the fire. "You keep saying 'honor.' You keep talking about 'honor this' and 'honor that,' but I can't see it. What is so honorable about abandoning your brother and running off with a vampire?" Her head lowered.

"Because I know that we'll be going back there."

Caitlin's eyebrows lifted.

"Oh yes, Caitlin. What do you think I'm training you for? So that we can frolic out in the wild and live carefree amongst the Mad? No. Your decision in my home was tough, but that's what honor is. It's making the tough decisions even when you know it could turn those you love against you. Your brother is a strong man, he'll be able to look after himself. You believe that, right?"

Caitlin thought about it a moment. At the time, it had seemed entirely instinctual. Ultimately, somewhere deep down, she knew that the governor's eye of death was on her, not her brother. Whatever happened, *she* was the disposable one. Dylan was the head of the rangers and therefore offered more value to Silver Creek. Sure, his return might ruffle some feathers, but had Caitlin returned empty-handed, she would have died, not her brother.

Mary-Anne stared at Caitlin from across the fire and smiled. "Though you don't see it now, you have honor in you, Caitlin Harrison, and I plan to draw that out and dawn a new age of change in this Mad-infected world. My family is dead. All my people are hiding or dying. We cower in fear from humans, every vamp scared to death of accidentally ingesting the Madness through human blood because, believe me, it's far worse for a vamp to turn than a human. The Madness affects our nanocytes differently. Makes them rage and burn like a firework. We're a dying breed, and it won't be long before vampires and Weres truly fall into myth."

"Nano-*what?* Caitlin asked, trying to take all this in. "How do you know all this?"

"Because I have lived for hundreds of years. I have seen cities grow and empires topple, and with every fall, there comes a rise. Your governor's men awoke my slumber after decades of watching the world fall into Madness, and I think it's time that that Madness comes to an end." Mary-Anne stood then, rising taller than Caitlin had ever seen her. At that moment, she looked like a queen of legend, a beacon of power and terror.

Caitlin smiled, feeling inspiration flooding through her, positivity and hope that things could get better; that they stood at the dawn of the rebirth of humanity. "But how do I fit into this? You're a *vampire*. Surely you've got more chance of accomplishing this than I do? I've seen you tear the heads off the Mad as if they were toys. Why can't you just run around at night and destroy all the Mad until the disease is gone?"

Mary-Anne looked once more at the sky. "Because you think one vampire can lead the charge? You think that eradicating the Madness is the end of it all? No, my dear. It's much more than that.

"The Madness is just a part of the disease. A conduit which has allowed evil and dictatorship to spread. Bandits, thieves, *governors* have all used the fear tactics of the Mad to keep people like you and your brother in hiding. To step on the little man. To dominate and to abuse. If we want to end all this, we *must* bring civilization back into the world by ending the injustice. Ending cruelty. Ending famine. Ending it all."

Mary-Anne grabbed Caitlin's shoulders. "And it's *you* who is going to lead the people into the light. It's you."

"Me?" Caitlin said.

Mary-Anne nodded. "The age of vampires and Weres is fading, Caitlin Harrison. It is you who must end this Age of Madness."

Caitlin wasn't sure what to think at that moment. Sure, she had lived most of her life feeling as though there was more out there that she could be doing. More than living the daily routine and following in the footsteps of her mother while Dylan followed in the footsteps of their father.

She had watched people out in the street with their ragged clothes and their mud-covered skin. Beggars alongside the streets of Silver Creek, desperate for food and change, leapt back into the shadows through fear of torture and death the minute the governor's men appeared.

She had seen the injustice of Trisk's quarters and his store of fine trinkets and ornaments. He lived a life of luxury as the people of Silver Creek fed off nothing more than the basics.

And now, she had a chance to change all that. To not only work with a vampire to clear the woods of the Mad but to liberate the town and help bring in a new era, one in which their world could be filled with something more. Perhaps, she reasoned, one in which she could deliver the one thing she'd begged for her entire life.

Hope.

Caitlin stared into the deep pools of Mary-Anne's eyes. The centers were as dark and deep as a well, the irises a vibrant green. At that moment, she understood what she was being asked to do and let go of any reservation that she might have had. If they were to go down this road, then they sure as hell needed to become a team.

Caitlin needed all the help she could get.

"Well, then," she said, her resolve set. "What the fuck are we waiting for?"

CHAPTER ELEVEN

Abandoned Airship, Silver Creek Forest

They made something of a base out of the fallen airship.

At first, they had spent a night looking for more stray Mad to further Caitlin's training, remaining alert for anywhere else that might constitute a good hiding place out in the woods. But there was nowhere satisfactory, and every time, they ended up returning to the ship.

Mary-Anne made a home out of the hull, plugging up any holes or gaps that had been made that might have let sunlight leak in during the day. She slept in a wardrobe that had fallen to the floor—presumably when the damned thing had crashed some years back.

During the daytime hours, Caitlin caught what sleep she could but found herself so curious and driven by the things she was learning, and by the need to find out more of what she didn't know of the world, that she couldn't settle. She explored the ship, finding guns and weapons far beyond repair but with fascinating shapes and markings. She'd hold a gun—rusted and slick with moss—and aim it straight in front of her, pretending that the ship was being boarded by Nosferatu and feral Weres and that it was her job to take them all down.

Mary-Anne told Caitlin of legendary battles and of a vampire queen who had traveled from overseas to protect New York from an invasion led by her brother. This feat which had earned the vampire respect and an unimaginable gift from the Dark Messiah himself.

Kids' stories, Caitlin had thought as Mary-Anne told the tale. Though a big part of her had always wondered, until a short while ago she hadn't believed in vampires. What else did she not know?

"Keep your mind on the task at hand," Mary-Anne said, interrupting Caitlin's thoughts. A sharp jolt of pain shot up her arm.

She looked down and saw the mark Mary-Anne's sword had left—a thin gash with blood now dribbling freely from the wound.

"Hey! If you wanted a suck job, all you had to do was ask." Caitlin joked but felt slightly uncomfortable as Mary-Anne licked her lips at the sight of her blood.

"No. I do not feed on friends. It is my one rule. Especially now, when food is scarce and I can't trust myself to hold back." Mary-Anne lowered her sword, suddenly looking more tired than she had in days—if that was even possible.

"Then we need to find you some food."

Mary-Anne nodded. "Agreed."

They traveled far that night, with Caitlin riding on Mary-Anne's back again. She used the stars to navigate, imagining the small villages which Mary-Anne had told her might still be dotted around the forest. These small outposts paled in comparison to Silver Creek but were full of sturdy men and women who could hold their own against the attacks of the Madness.

Caitlin had hardly believed her at first. The governor had made it seem that Silver Creek was the last remaining defense, possibly one of the only places in which to live a civilized existence. Could there really be more out there like them?

While Caitlin used the sky to navigate, Mary-Anne used her senses. Now, she sniffed and turned slightly left and right to weave between the trees at speed.

"There. Just ahead."

It took a few minutes for Caitlin to believe what she was seeing.

Mary-Anne placed Caitlin down by a tree close to the edge of a large clearing. In the center was a handful of small houses with vegetable patches and a small pond dotted between. The lights were off in all the houses but one, where they could see the silhouette of a man and woman in the window. The man's voice was raised, though they couldn't make out his words.

"Where are we?" Caitlin asked, taking a step forward.

"*Careful.*" Mary-Anne tugged at Caitlin's shoulder and forced her back.

"*Hey,*" Caitlin whispered.

When she looked down, she was thankful for Mary-Anne's guidance. Threaded between the trees around the clearing was a fence—waist-high—wrapped with barbed wire, now so rusted and dark that it blended in with the shadows. Caitlin had been only an inch away from piercing her skin on the barbs before she had been pulled back.

"Thanks," Caitlin said.

"Don't mention it."

The voices in the house raised. They could hear the anger in the man's words, and the woman now cowered in fear. For half a second, Caitlin flashed back to the moment she had hit the governor and he had retaliated.

Whatever was going on in there, it wasn't good.

"We should help," Caitlin said, jumping over the wire and tiptoeing towards the building. She took a few steps and stopped, realizing that Mary-Anne hadn't followed.

"Aren't you coming?"

"No. This one's all yours," Mary-Anne replied.

Caitlin turned to the house, then back to Mary-Anne, noticing then that, once again, the vampire had disappeared from sight.

"Eurgh. I hate it when she does that."

As she crossed the clearing, she watched the figures with interest. They were animated, clearly caught in a row of sorts. Whatever it was about, the argument was very one-sided. The man appeared to be close to seven-foot, and his companion was no more than five.

They disappeared from her view through the window, and Caitlin heard a slap followed by crying. She began running.

New Leaf, Silver Creek Forest

'Big Bill' Tompkins was drunk. Hammered. Plowed. Off his *fucking* face again. After a long, hard day of chopping wood and repairing the damage on several houses—just a few days ago a horde of Mad had found their way through the fence and attacked their hamlet—he wanted nothing more than to sit on his ass, drink, and relax.

But had he been able to do that?

No-sir-fucking-ree.

Not even another beating would put Alice in her place.

It had been Frank's wife, Mabel, a pretty young thing with an hour-glass figure and boobs that held her chin up who had told Big Bill what Alice had been up to in the daylight hours while he was away.

"It's hard not to hear them. Screaming and rolling around like a couple of piggies as they do the nasty business. Can't believe no one's told you sooner. Alice and young master Abraham can't keep their damn hands off each other. It's unsightly. It's hard enough to get work done around here without a soundtrack of passion drawing all eyes to your house. Can't you keep your woman in check?"

Big Bill had grown so red in the face that Mabel clearly thought he might pop. She had pulled Big Bill close to her chest and calmed him down in the only way she knew how —with a nice long kiss to his nether regions as comfort.

When Big Bill came home that night, he had watched Alice with a curious eye. No words were exchanged beyond grunts and mutters. She was red-faced and flushed. He imagined that would be the result of Abe's prowess replaying in her mind, the ghost of his libido as he pounded Big Bill's wife again and again.

It was only after dinner had been eaten and Big Bill sat in his favorite chair, a large goblet of murky brown mead at his side, that Alice finally addressed her keeper.

"Long day, sweetie?"

Sweetie... Sure, play nice housewife now. Is that how it's going to be, huh?

"Sure. Not as good as yours, though, I hear."

"Huh?" Alice replied, bringing a hand up automatically to cover her face.

"Think I don't know what goes on in this house when I'm not around?"

And it was from there the argument had spun. For the next hour, they went from room to room, with Alice in tears and Big Bill launching verbal assaults followed by physical assaults. Was he this cruel when he wasn't drunk? Yes, absolutely. But the alcohol-fueled his rage and Alice could do nothing but try to swim away from the tidal wave. No amount of words would convince him otherwise.

Late into the night, with Alice's face red with frustration, the final slap had come. Not the kind that covered her arms and legs in bruises, but one that delivered a fresh jolt of hot pain across her face.

For a moment, Alice simply stared at him and held her cheek. It was as if, even after several years of his abuse, she couldn't believe it.

Big Bill shrugged. "Tell another soul, and you'll be setting yourself up for more than just a slap. Bitches need to learn to keep their mouth shut, know their place, and keep their legs closed to other men. Got that?"

Alice had been about to reply when—

Boom.

They both turned towards the door that had crashed open to reveal a tall, slender woman in a dark cloak with a determined expression written across her face. Alice stepped back against the wall as if trying to melt into the shadows. Big Bill, however, grew to a level of rage he had never experienced before. He spoke, and spittle flew.

"*Stupid* bitches. Who the *fuck* do you think you are?"

The woman took a step forward. "Just your friendly neighborhood keeper of the peace. Now step back and leave this poor woman alone, or things are going to get ugly. And if you want to see just how ugly, then find a mirror and look at your own reflection." She turned to Alice. "Am I right?"

Alice couldn't help but laugh.

The giant roared and dove for Caitlin. She had to admit, she wasn't expecting anything so fast, and she slammed into the wall with a painful expulsion of breath.

They tumbled to the floor, the giant ending up on top of her. His face was a twisted image of red as his anger flooded his features, clearly catalyzed by alcohol.

He punched Caitlin in the face. White stars appeared in her vision. "Who the *fuck* do you think you are?"

As the next punch came, Caitlin used all her energy to push against the wall. She slid under Big Bill's legs and jumped to her feet. The sound of his fist connecting with the stone floor followed by a loud epithet revealed his pain.

The giant shook his hand in a futile attempt to wave away the agony.

But that didn't mean he was done.

He glanced sideways to a knife on the worktop as he thrust to his feet. He grabbed the weapon in a second and slashed at Caitlin, who drew and parried with her sword. He was sweating, his eyes unfocused and pupils dilated. If she didn't do something quickly, it would end badly—for her, that is.

It seemed humans were a lot tougher than mindless zombies.

He licked his lips.

Caitlin poked out her tongue.

That did it for the giant. He seemed to reach boiling point, a volcano about to erupt and spit lava all over the house. He slashed again and caught Caitlin's arm. A white-hot pain spiked through her as she saw the skin part and blood trickle out.

Without another thought, she smacked the knife out of the giant's hand, bent to retrieve it, and stabbed forward.

The giant swung for her, and the knife drove into his side. He gasped and groaned, falling to the floor but grabbing at her clothes on the way down.

"*You—*" The giant's words cut short on a bellow of pain.

He crashed to the floor but summoned an unexpected burst of energy and chomped at her ankle. Had she not moved a moment earlier, she would have been missing a good chunk of it. He grasped at his side for the knife, withdrew it with a horrible wet sound, and made one last effort to drive the blade into Caitlin's flesh.

That was enough for her, whose heart now raced with the adrenaline coursing through her veins. She saw the knife coming for her, and in instinctual defense, she attacked. In a single flash of silver, she raised her sword at incredible speed and stabbed it through the giant's back.

He looked down in dreamlike surprise before the final whisper of air escaped his lungs.

Caitlin took a deep breath, then turned her attention to the woman who still cowered on the other side of the room with her hands over her mouth.

"I'm sorry it ended that way," she said, though she wasn't sorry at all.

When the woman removed her hands, Caitlin was surprised to see a beaming smile on her face.

"Who...who are you?" she stuttered.

Caitlin shrugged, twisting the blade. "A new age of hope." She looked down at the giant. "Just not for scum like him."

"Thank you," the woman named Alice said as she sat at her table and drank from the goblet that had formerly belonged to her keeper. "I don't know what he would've done if you hadn't arrived. He thought I was cheating on him. How stupid would that have been to do in a hamlet as small as this?"

"Men think crazy things when they've been drinking. Actually"—Caitlin paused to rephrase her words—"men just do crazy shit, full stop. You should see what the men do where I come from," Caitlin said, taking a sip herself.

Alice studied her. "Where did you learn to move like that? I've never seen anyone move so quickly with a blade. Even our best fighters would struggle to keep up with your speed. It's almost as if..." She trailed off and fixed her gaze on the table.

"As if what?" Caitlin said, reaching across the table and taking Alice's hand.

"It's stupid, really. We keep a stock of ancient books here in a cabin just down the way. While Bill works, I do my chores, but that still leaves me with a lot of the day to fill. So I read. Just a few weeks ago, I stumbled across books that talk as if from a history text about... well...*vampires*." Alice bit her lip.

Caitlin pulled back and burst into laughter. "Me? A vampire? I think that slap may have rattled a few pieces around in your head."

Alice stiffened and pulled away, her face red and openly defensive. "Why not? What else explains your sudden appearance in the middle of the night? Your speed? Your... pale complexion—"

"Clearly, you've not read your books properly. If you really want to know what a vampire looks like—"

"Then here it is," Mary-Anne said, materializing from the shadows. Alice turned around and suddenly recoiled, running to stand behind Caitlin.

Caitlin had to admit, the effect of a person appearing from the shadows with eyes glowing bright red was rather intense. Had she not known Mary-Anne as well as she now did, she might even shit herself too. But instead, she found herself laughing.

"Okay, cut it out now. Alice has been through enough tonight."

Mary-Anne's eyes extinguished. "Sorry. Even vampires like to have their fun."

"So you're a...you're a... It's true?" Alice babbled.

Mary-Anne opened her mouth, and two fangs grew. "As true as anything."

"But...how? The textbooks say that your kind are extinct. That when the Madness came, it brought with it a degenerative virus which affected vampires and..." She paused and gasped. "Does that mean that Weres are real, too?"

Mary-Anne cast a brief glance at Caitlin as if deciding this was a conversation for later. "One thing at a time, I think."

"The books say that something in Unknown blood broke down, killing all vampires and forcing Weres into permanent states of either their human form or their animal form. It says there are none left out there anymore, and that the world now belongs to the Mad." Alice looked saddened at this last part.

"Your textbooks are partly true," Mary-Anne said, "though there is far more to the story than I have the time or wherewithal to bestow upon you. Truth is, there are still Weres and vampires in the world—of that I'm sure. I think... I hope, at least, though with the Madness there is something at play which has taken its toll on my kind. Forcing them into hiding or even forcing them into taking extreme actions to fight for their own survival. A sickening turn of events from a world where not more than just under a hundred years ago, all species got along." Mary-Anne looked out the window at the sky now turning to a deep purple, a sign of the rising sun.

"But there will be time for this later. I must find somewhere to sleep away the day. Caitlin, are you ready to run?" Mary-Anne presented her back for Caitlin to hop onto.

"Wait!" Alice said, suddenly alarmed at the idea of their departure. "There's a cellar below. You can sleep down there. I can't thank you enough for arriving when you did, and I'm pretty sure there's going to be some difficult conversations tomorrow. If the governor's men discover that Big Bill is dead, I don't know what I'm going to do."

Caitlin's ears pricked up. "The governor? As in 'Governor Trisk?'"

"Yes. They come around once a week to check that the villages and hamlets are providing the resources needed for Trisk's cause." She stopped when she saw the look on Caitlin's face. "Why?"

Caitlin ground her teeth. "Because it was he who forced me out into the woods. It was the governor who threatened my brother and me with death if we didn't deliver this vampire to him. This same man failed to tell any of us common folk in Silver Creek that the world was bigger than our own walls." She clenched her fists, her hands shaking by her sides. "To tell you the truth, the more I learn about Trisk, the more reasons I'm finding to rip out his fucking throat."

CHAPTER TWELVE

New Leaf, Silver Creek Forest

Caitlin stayed up for the best part of the morning, talking with Alice. They moved Big Bill's body to the bedroom, rolling him under the bed to hide him.

"Another one bites the dust," Caitlin said, throwing the bed sheet over the edge to shield the body.

Alice laughed at that. If she hadn't already unloaded all the nasty things Big Bill used to do to her, Caitlin would have been surprised by her humor. She already wanted to forget some of the unspeakable details Alice had shared that night.

As the morning wore on, Caitlin discovered more and more about Alice, her former lover, and New Leaf. It seemed that Caitlin was the first person, aside from Trisk's men, who had ever come there from an outside village. New Leaf had made its reputation by sticking within the safety of its borders and provided wood and fish for the governor's use. Once a week, the men would come from Silver Creek—never their leader himself, of course—strip them of the goods they had collected and earned, drink excessive volumes of their locally brewed mead, and rape several of their women.

"There's normally ten of them on horseback, but not always. They come, they leap the fence, they demand what is rightfully ours," Alice explained. "There's little in the way of manners, and the women don't even resist anymore. There's a saying here in New Leaf, 'If you're born ugly, you're lucky.' The guards don't touch the ugly ones unless they're excessively drunk because they mostly have their favorites."

"Why? Why does no one argue or fight? Why don't the men stand up for their women?" Caitlin asked. Outside the house, she could hear people moving about now. The bright sun offered little cheer as it shone through the window.

"It's the way of things here. Some of the men admire the guards, want to be like them. Others have seen what happens when they try to resist. It doesn't help that the guards have better weapons and greater numbers. We think of them like the Hydra." When Caitlin returned a blank expression, Alice explained. "A beast of myth. The stories tell that for every head that was cut off the beast, three more would grow back in its place. If we took any of the governor's guards down, we don't know how many more would come." Alice sighed.

Caitlin noticed scars lining Alice's arm and wondered if they were the work of Big Bill or of Trisk's men. It didn't matter, she supposed. At the end of the day, they were all capable of the same shit.

Alice continued, "I'm told of a time when our ancestors

used to wander free and chose to do whatever they liked. A time when, if you wanted to be a soldier, you signed up and trained. If you wanted to marry and settle down with kids, that was a *choice*, too."

Alice glanced at the bedroom.

This was all difficult to process. Caitlin had thought that she had problems at Silver Creek. That life there had been tough enough having to watch the patriarchy and the men go out and do the dirty work. But here…

Talk turned to Silver Creek and Caitlin's life there. Alice asked questions and her eyes widened at every mention of how big the town was and the large community within its walls.

"I'd love to see it."

"Nah. You wouldn't. To be honest, it's the same shit show as here, only with more people, and you get to actually see the governor once a week."

"What's he like?" Alice asked, eyes in wonder.

"Imagine a newborn pig, only ten times larger." Caitlin held her arms wide and puffed out her cheeks.

Alice burst into laughter.

A banging sounded on the door.

"Oi! What's so funny in there?" came a deep voice.

Caitlin studied Alice as she suddenly became alert.

"Shit. Right on time." Alice flapped her arms and placed a finger over her lips. "Don't. Say. Anything."

"The governor's men?"

Alice nodded.

Caitlin couldn't believe the fear that suddenly manifested in Alice. All blood drained from her cheeks. She looked panicked, completely uncertain of what to do. She imagined the men outside the door with their grimy faces, licking their lips. Was Alice right? With Big Bill indisposed, would these men try their luck at taking another helpless maiden?

"Hey, we know you're in there. We don't like being ignored," the voice boomed as several more fists pounded on the door. The wood bowed in its frame.

An idea struck Caitlin. The guards didn't know that *she* was there. She had the element of surprise...

"Let them in," Caitlin whispered.

Alice's mouth dropped. "Are you crazy? Caitlin, the last time a gang of the governor's men came into my house when Big Bill was gone I—"

She trailed off, a tear gathering in the corner of her eye.

Caitlin took Alice's shoulders. "Look, I know they hurt you. I know you're terrified right now. But trust me. I'm not going to let anything happen to you."

"You promise?" Alice wiped her eyes with the back of her hand.

"I promise."

With the next knock on the door, Caitlin grew resolute. She felt the burn of injustice in her gut and formulated a plan. This had already gone on long enough, and Alice would not suffer anymore. Not while Caitlin was able to do something about it.

She disappeared into the bedroom and hid behind the door. Through the narrow crevice formed by the door's hinges, she watched as Alice composed herself.

She had barely turned the handle when the men piled in—four of them. The door opened so violently that Alice was pushed back against the wall, the air knocked out of her lungs.

She backed away while the men looked around wildly, expecting an attack of some kind. Swords glinting in the early morning light.

The man leading the guards—Caitlin knew his face but had no idea of his name—looked Alice up and down, a hungry gleam in his eye. "Took long enough. Where's Big Bill? We've had reports he was supposed to be out with the other woodcutters an hour ago."

Alice shrugged. "I've not seen him all night. I've been worried sick."

"She's lying, boss," a runt of a guard called from behind. "Mabel says he came back last night blind drunk and stumbling."

Caitlin watched as the lead guard's eyebrow raised.

"Is that so?" he said. He moved closer to Alice, towering over her tiny frame. Caitlin could see her shaking. "Well, that begins to make me wonder why a pretty thing would lie to our faces, doesn't it? I'll ask this again: Where. Is. Big. Bill?"

"I don't—"

In a move so fast that Alice had no time to counter it, the guard spun behind her. One hand wrapped around her waist, the other hand clamped over her mouth to stop the scream. Caitlin still heard it muffled beneath his glove.

She could only imagine what his breath smelt like, his cheek touching hers.

"I tell you what, gents," the guard rasped. "I believe this bitch. Big Bill isn't home."

"How can you tell?" one of the guards asked.

"Because, if Big Bill were home, he would've made himself known by now. *Ain't that right, Bill!*"

Though Caitlin knew Big Bill was dead under the bed, she still looked at him as if half-expecting a response.

"And if Big Bill ain't around, then that means…"

The runt guard clapped and licked his lips. "Oh, goodie…"

The lead guard grabbed a handful of Alice's clothes and was about to rip them off, but Caitlin'd had enough of waiting. She could see these shit-eating turd-bags for what they were.

And now it was her turn to play.

"You're not going to get started without me, are you?" she said, pushing the bedroom door open in a slow reveal. She cocked her head to the side and turned on her best smile. "I wouldn't want to miss out on all the fun."

Caitlin could practically hear them all grow erect.

The lead guard released his grip on Alice slightly. She tried to wriggle free, but he pulled her back, scrunching her hair in his fists. "Well, well, well, gentleman. Looks like things have just gotten interesting. Who do we have here?"

The guard ran a hand through the grease tracks of his hair.

"Do names really matter?" Caitlin said, inviting them in with a wag of her finger. "I've always wondered what it would be like to lay with a guard. Alice tells me such stories."

A flicker of doubt crossed the guards' minds, then seemed to be immediately overwritten as their biology led the way.

The lead guard shoved Alice ahead of him, then booted

her in the back. "Go on. Join your friend. Looks like there's plenty to go around, boys."

The guards behind him chuckled.

As they walked, they all began to remove items of armor. The lead guard threw the top layer of his at the wall, then his top, revealing a chest thick with hair and peppered with battle scars.

"What if Big Bill comes home?" the blond guard asked, pausing as he unbuttoned his tunic.

"Well, he can either join us or fucking die, can't he? Though I'd rather get this moving before we have to kill anyone. Wouldn't want to have to get the floor dirty with his blood before we wrestle like horny pigs."

Pigs was right.

Alice looked worried. *Terrified.* She turned to Caitlin and wordlessly asked, *Well...what now?*

Caitlin took a seat on the bed. She leaned forward and pushed her arms together so that her cleavage was fully on display for all those in the room. "I hope *I'm* the one you like," she said, throwing a wink at the lead guard, hoping to distract him away from Alice.

His words seemed to catch in his throat and his tongue lolled out his mouth.

Fucking idiots. How do men make it so easy?

"Me first, gents," he said, advancing without looking. She could see the bulge in his pants already and inwardly rolled her eyes. "I bet you've never been with a proper man, have you, princess? I'll show you such a good time that you'll wish you'd die then and there, because life doesn't get much better than with me."

Caitlin could smell him as he approached, a musty stink of sweat that boasted of limited hygiene.

When he was only a couple of feet away, Caitlin reached into the bedsheet where she had hidden her sword and pulled it out in one quick flash.

The guard stilled, his eyes wide. His hand froze around the crotch of his pants where he had been a second away from revealing his member. His face grew red.

"*You bitch—*"

"Uh-uh," Caitlin said, placing a finger over her lips. "One wrong move and I'll skewer you like a fucking kebab."

The other three guards watched from a safe distance, their mouths agape. They went to reach for their swords.

"And I wouldn't do that if I were you," Caitlin said, bringing her sword up so that its tip prodded their leader's throat.

The men looked at each other, considered for a moment, then spun on their heels and went to run.

"Where're you going in such a hurry?" Alice said, holding a knife in each hand and advancing on the guards so that they had to step back into the room.

Caitlin was impressed. Putting aside Alice's housewife attire, with a dagger in her hand and a mean expression on her face, she actually looked like a steady warrior. Her hand shook a little as she held the knife, but she was hardly to blame for that. Not when four men had been ready to bend her over and take her how they wanted to.

Caitlin wondered if Alice was putting it all on for show, or if somewhere deep down, there was something akin to courage in there after all. Had this Alice been hiding inside all along? How many women in the nearby towns and villages were like Alice, oppressed through fear and crushed under the power of the governor's men?

They tied the three guards together with rope Alice fetched from the basement, placed them in the center of Alice's bedroom, and led the leader back to the front door. Caitlin gave him a swift kick on the ass, and he fell forward onto the grass.

Jesus, that was satisfying.

"See, Alice? Strip away their weapons and backup, and they all crumble. Men are nothing without their toys." Caitlin stepped into the sunlight, realizing then that there were other women around the camp now staring in her direction. The men, presumably, were all out in the wilds doing the 'hard' work. The women stared from dirty faces, their hair shaggy and unkempt. Many of them held their backs as they stood and watched what was happening at the door with interest.

Caitlin could hardly believe it. Every woman there looked to be around middle-age, but that wasn't possible. Had the hard work and dire conditions of this life aged women prematurely? How many of them had grayed and wrinkled through fear and worry alone?

The only exception to the rule was a woman Caitlin noticed peeking out from behind the shade of a house. There was a bruise across her cheek, and the minute Caitlin caught her eye, she squeaked and ducked away.

That's it, Caitlin thought, feeling her resolve settle in like an old friend.

Caitlin raised her voice. "Women of New Leaf, your servitude is at an end." She pointed at the guard, half-dressed and on the ground, with her sword. "There is no more power in men than there is in women. We give them power out of fear. Your governor has you all thinking that the world is dangerous. That we are alone in our villages and towns. That there is no way we can live outside our borders and be free."

"How do you know this?" a woman shouted. "Why should we believe you?"

"Because Trisk is out to kill me. He used my friend and me as nothing more than fodder for his own gains. I refused to endanger another's life so that they could be turned into a slave, and for that, he wishes me dead. He wants nothing more than a world in which we bow to his every whim. It doesn't matter who he kills or hurts in the process. This guard before my feet is nothing more than a symptom of that sickness, and I, Caitlin Harrison of Silver Creek, send this man with a message to deliver to his master."

She turned to face the guard who was now on his knees, casting sideways glances at his horse. Clearly, he wished to be anywhere other than there.

"Tell Governor Trisk that fear is coming to him. A revolution is brewing, and should he not step down from his duties and pass over leadership to the people, then all the people, and all the world that he knows, will come for him." The guard's eyes burned into Caitlin's. He grunted as she kicked him once more. "Now. Go."

The guard spat at Caitlin's feet. "You don't know what forces you're dealing with."

Caitlin chuckled, thinking of Mary-Anne currently

snoozing in the basement of Alice's house. "No. *You* don't know the forces on my side. Now, go."

The guard flinched, narrowly avoiding another boot. He scrambled to his feet and ran to his horse which had been grazing happily at the side of the house. With a swift *"hyah,"* the horse hopped the barbed-wire fence and they faded into the shadows of the trees.

A moment of silence followed as Caitlin felt all eyes on her. Then a clap from behind that made her jump. She turned around and was surprised to see that it was Alice. Seconds later, the women around joined in a ripple that turned into a round of applause.

"What are you clapping for?" Caitlin asked Alice, her voice barely audible above the sound now. Women around dropped what they were carrying to join in the chorus.

"You, Caitlin. They're clapping for you and what you bring to these women."

Caitlin waved. "And what is that?"

"Hope," Alice said with a slight chuckle. "For the first time in their lives they're seeing hope."

And she was right. Though a few women had their reservations, the majority of them now walked towards her. The closer they got, the more bruises and scars Caitlin could see on their flesh. The sight of them made her angry, but their smiles made her warm inside.

Maybe, just maybe, there was something in this town she could use to help her fight for justice. Maybe, just maybe, these women could join her and help start the revolution.

And, of course, any men who wouldn't be stupid enough to stand in her way.

Caitlin spoke to the women as the sun beamed down and a gentle breeze rocked the trees. She helped wipe tears and shook hands until her own felt raw.

It was as the talking began to die down that Caitlin heard the most unlikely noise. A sound which Caitlin recognized in an instant but couldn't quite believe.

"Can you hear that?" Alice asked, looking around for the source of the sound.

Other heads turned, looking towards the trees as a dark shape streaked towards them.

Caitlin's eyes widened. *It can't be...*

All heads turned in the same direction as a black and brown dog with heavy dark rings around both eyes launched over the barbed wire and sprinted through the village. Its fur was matted and caked with mud, but its eyes gleamed a bright green as it beelined for its master.

Caitlin fell to her knees and opened her arms wide. Jaxon leapt into her chest and she squeezed him tight, feeling the sticky mass of blood and dirt on his fur and not really giving two shits as he lapped at her face with his rough tongue.

Her smile was so wide that it hurt. The townswomen flocked around to get a better look at the hero-woman and her furry companion.

CHAPTER THIRTEEN

New Leaf, Silver Creek Forest

"What is *that?*" Mary-Anne asked after dusk fell and she rose from the basement.

Jaxon growled and reared back on his haunches, his teeth bared. He was actually a shit-scary sight when he wanted to be, all hackles and teeth.

"Now, now, Jaxon. It's okay," Caitlin bent low and tousled Jaxon's fur. She pursed her lips. "It's just a wittle scawy vampire."

Alice began laughing until Mary-Anne scowled.

"It can't stay with us," Mary-Anne said bluntly, crossing the room and taking a seat. "There's already enough danger out there without having to look after a pet."

"*It?*" Caitlin gasped. "*He* will be no problem. He's a smart boy, aren't you? Yes, you are."

Mary-Anne looked down her nose as Caitlin stroked and praised Jaxon.

She might have been pissed at her mentor's attitude towards Jaxon, but she thought she understood. Mary-

Anne slumped in her chair, her face paler than a vampire's ever should be. It was a pitiful sight, really.

"You're just cranky because you're hungry."

"Hungry?" Alice asked.

"Yes, dear. Hungry." Mary-Anne rolled her eyes. "Even though vampires are *monsters* to most, we are still creatures of the world who need to eat and feed."

"And shit," Caitlin added, Jaxon now scooped in her arms, licking her face.

"And shit," Mary-Anne agreed.

Alice thought for a moment. "Why don't you eat *them?*" She pointed to the bedroom where the door stood slightly ajar. They could see the three guards, their eyes suddenly alight with panic.

"Now there's an idea," Caitlin said, her head turning to Mary-Anne.

"I can't," Mary-Anne said, her eyes betraying her temptation and hunger as they burned a dull red. "It's too risky. What if they have the—"

"Madness?" Caitlin tilted her head to the guards. "Do any of you gents have the Madness at all? Encountered some Mad? Been bitten by some Mad? Been scratched, licked, prodded, or in any way come into contact with the Mad on the way over here? Do any of you have a slight fever? Boils growing at all? Feel the need to bite into your friends or hurt anyone in the nearby vicinity?"

The men shook their heads warily, aware that in admitting that they weren't going Mad—in which case they could be killed—they were opening themselves up as a buffet for a vampire, which could also lead to a nasty death.

Mary-Anne stared coldly at Caitlin. "That was unnecessary."

"What's the problem?" Alice asked.

Caitlin replied before Mary-Anne could. "The *wittle* vampire is scared that if she feeds off a human body, she may turn Mad. That there might be a tiny bit of it in the blood that's undetectable and which will accelerate in her own vampire blood and create a super-mad-bloodthirsty-vampire of epic proportions. That about right?"

"I really hate you, sometimes," Mary-Anne said, though her small grin suggested otherwise.

"Good," Caitlin said, returning her smile. She grabbed Mary-Anne's hand and led her through to where the guards were tied up. "Look, I need you to be at full strength so you can help me change the world, and you're not going to be able to do that if you're sipping off rabbits, bugs, and forest creatures for the rest of your life. Vampires need to feed off *humans*. So, there are three humans. Take your pick."

Mary-Anne's eyes narrowed, clearly toying with her desire to finally feel full after so many years of vampire vegetarianism and the concern of what could be hidden within the blood.

Her concern was warranted, of course. Though Caitlin had no idea how bad it would turn out if a vampire ingested Mad blood, she certainly understood her worry. There was no surefire way to know if a person had been tainted, until it was far too late—at least not without technology that had long since vanished in Caitlin's society. But if the guards had made their way there and had worn their armor, then that meant that they'd be clean.

Right?

"Well?" Caitlin whispered as the guards trembled and moaned beneath their gags.

Mary-Anne jerked her head back, and two fangs suddenly appeared in her mouth. Without another word, she dropped cautiously to her knees, held the head of the middle guard still, and bit into the skin.

The sounds were gross, without a doubt—a gentle sucking at first, quickly turning into a slurping. The guard's moans soon began to fade and quieten.

"Not *all* of it," Caitlin jabbed, prodding Mary-Anne in the back of the head and eliciting another moan from the guard. "There are *three* of them after all."

Mary-Anne turned, her mouth stained with blood. She nodded, then drank from the other two in turn, gasping and moaning like a nymphomaniac who hadn't had sex in several decades.

It was quite disturbing, really.

When Mary-Anne withdrew, her face was half red. The blood was streaked and dark, and for the first time, Alice saw the figure that most people feared when they thought of vampires. The bloodsucking monsters who attacked at night and cared for little more than killing.

Mary-Anne coughed, hocking up a hair that had made its way down her throat. She stuck two fingers down there and retrieved a long blond hair that had somehow escaped the guard's head.

Alice shuddered.

"Classy…" Caitlin said, maybe a little too judgmentally.

Mary-Anne wiped her mouth with the corner of the bedsheet, then looked up and gasped, pointing at the window. In the corner of the glass, someone was watching —a long rat-like face staring back in surprise. They heard an exclamation, then the face was gone.

"Who was that?" Caitlin asked.

"Who cares? If it's that big a problem, we can deal with them later," Mary-Anne replied, piercing a pin-prick hole on the end of her own finger. A small bubble of her own blood rose to the surface. She leaned back down and rubbed it over the marks on the guards' neck. The wounds instantly began to heal until there was nothing there at all aside from dry pink stains.

"Impressive," Alice said in awe.

"How are you feeling?" Caitlin eyed Mary-Anne with concern.

The vampire stood now, her eyes closed, and took deep breaths. A smile grew wide on her face. She looked satisfied and energized, probably the effect of the power of the human blood coursing through her. Her expression spoke of satisfaction, as if she savored every moment of the energy fueling her body. It wasn't hard to imagine that she hadn't felt this good in years, not on a vegetarian diet that denied her primal need.

Caitlin and Alice watched and waited, noting how the color returned to her face. She immediately stood taller. When Mary-Anne opened her eyes, they were brighter than they had ever seen, her two fangs a proud feature on her face.

"Well?" Caitlin prodded.

Mary-Anne looked at them both. "For the first time in a long time, I feel *fang*-fucking-tastic!"

And then she was gone, a blur as she sprinted and ran

loops around the room at a speed they couldn't follow. Her laughter trailed behind her, and pretty soon, Alice and Caitlin joined in too.

Mother Wendy's Tavern, Silver Creek

"Sir?" Tyrell asked sheepishly.

Hank could feel himself shaking with rage. His face turned a dark crimson. When he had swung by the local tavern—a moderate-sized building within Silver Creek's market square with upturned barrels for chairs and a pretty little thing behind the bar—the last thing he had expected was to be told this.

Victor and Hendrick sat frozen around the table with beers in their hand, waiting for a response from their captain. Hendrick shuffled on the cushion he now had to bring with him whenever he went somewhere to sit down for long periods.

Hank exhaled slowly. "You're telling me that four of my men arrived at New Leaf, and *one* came back."

Tyrell nodded.

"One?"

Tyrell, one of the stronger guards on Hank's forces who traveled between villages and collected the debts and resources of the weak-willed towns, lowered his head. "Yes, sir."

"*One!*"

Tyrell nodded. Hank leaned back, ran a hand through his hair, and grumbled, his teeth rubbing together. He reached forward, took a long draught of his beer, closed his eyes, and counted to ten.

"And it's all because of *one* woman," he said, more to himself than his audience. This time, he kept his words low, already noting a few people in the tavern looking over at his table. Now was not the time or place to explode, not until he had the situation handled. The last thing he wanted was any of the governor's spies to see that he was losing his shit. No one must know that there were more women out there rising up and causing problems, and he wasn't doing anything about it.

That wouldn't do at all now, would it?

"Well…technically it's because of two. Big Bill's wife—Alicia, I think? And another I don't recognize, but she seemed to know Trisk well enough to want to send the message." Tyrell picked up his own beer and took a large gulp.

"And Big Bill is where?"

"I don't know." Tyrell hung his head. "Wherever he went, he wasn't there."

Hank flinched. He had known Big Bill personally, having met him once when he had accompanied his messengers to the distant towns that were held under the governor's rule. He had been much younger at the time, and even then, Big Bill had been fearsome. A tall man with broad shoulders who could hold his own, he'd stood out as a man who others feared. Over the years, as Hank had risen up through the ranks, he had always planned to recruit Big Bill to join the elite guard, but he had never put it into action.

But still… It seemed strange that he hadn't been there. Had he finally bitten the bullet and gone solo? What if the Alicia girl had done something to him?

Impossible.

"And you couldn't protect your men against two measly women? What good are you on the force if all those years of training can be undone by two simple females?" Hank felt himself growing red again and did his best to control it.

Thankfully, Victor chipped in and changed the subject. "What was the message? What did she say?"

Tyrell sighed, glad to move on from his failure against the girls.

He told them what Caitlin had sent him to say—maybe not word for word, Hank realized, but as close as he could remember. He might be strong, but he wasn't the brightest, after all.

When he was finished, he addressed Hank directly, hoping to earn some brownie points with the next part. "She said for the message to go straight to the governor, but I thought it would be best coming from you, sir. I don't know that I've got the stature to tell Trisk myself, and I also know how hard it is to gain an audience unless you're...well...you."

Hank drank again, the flattery bringing a grin to his face.

"Describe the girl," he said.

Tyrell described Caitlin with her long brown hair and the dark green cloak that flowed behind her as she walked. When he got to the description of her sword, he saw Hank's eyes widen, if only briefly, because his expression looked hopeful. Maybe he thought this information would earn him forgiveness after all.

Hank sat for a moment, deep in thought. Or at least,

that's what he chose to show to the others. Inside, he was pissed off and a little bit afraid.

How in the name of holy hell did that bitch manage to survive? Wasn't it bad enough that she had stolen his vampire? But now, she was working her way to the villages, threatening to shatter Trisk's regime and give people hope? How long had it taken for them to manipulate the societies to believe that there was nothing more than danger and death in the woods? If that twiglet bitch was out there, spreading the truth...imagine the chaos she could bring.

"Sir?" Hendrick asked.

"*What?*" Hank replied, a little louder than planned. Several heads turned in their direction, including one man whom Hank recognized as that Sullivan fellow who had accompanied them to the manor. He stared blankly at Hank, then returned to his plate of slop.

"I was going to ask if you wanted a refill," Hendrick said, barely audible.

"Oh. Yes. Two." Hank shoved his glass Hendrick's way, then turned his attention back to Tyrell. His left eye began to twitch.

"Should I not have said anything?" Tyrell asked, unable to help watching Hendrick hobble over to the bar, his legs bowed.

"Not at all," Hank said, doing his best to instill his 'nice guy' tone—whatever good that would do. As much as he hated the news, he was glad that it was at least his to do with what he pleased now. "Thank you for coming straight to me with this. Your loyalty is greatly appreciated, and I'll be sure to find a way to reward you kindly.

Leave it with me. I'll be sure to report directly to the governor."

After that, they sat a while longer, drinking and watching the night grow darker outside. Soon, there were only a few left in the tavern and Hank left the other gentlemen to their drunken games. Their attitude shifted to mirth and silliness, and as much as Hank had matched them in drink, he certainly wasn't in the mood to play.

He stood outside, looking up at the moon, imagining the Harrison girl out there surrounded by a hundred angry men and women.

If they were to storm the gates, what could his men do? Sure, they had numbers on their side, but Hank had no *real* idea how powerful a vampire could be if unleashed in battle.

"Everything okay, boss?" Victor asked, appearing behind Hank.

Hendrick and Tyrell stumbled out too, arms around each other, though they stopped when they saw the glare that Hank gave them both.

"That girl. The one who sent the message for the governor…" Hank said, so quietly that they had to lean in to hear him.

"What about her?" Victor said.

"Yeah, what about her?" Hendrick added with a hiccup. "Should we be worried?"

Tyrell was silent.

Hank looked at them each in turn, his eyes cold. "No. No, we shouldn't."

Hendrick scratched his head. "How come?"

"Because we're going to go out there and find that

bitch," Hank said, feeling for the sword at his side. "And when we do, we'll mount her head on a fucking spike."

Sullivan sat a while longer in Mother Wendy's. He liked watching the people, and though he hardly touched a sip of his mead, he enjoyed the ambiance of the tavern. From where he sat in the center of the room, he could hear almost everything. The rangers of Silver Creek were trained and attuned to listen to the quietest of sounds and to use their senses to maximum ability.

Despite what many of the others thought, Sullivan wasn't as dumb as he appeared.

And now, several hours into the night, Sullivan had grown curious.

He had heard every word of Tyrell's message and had himself wondered whether the girl might have been the one who had accompanied them a week ago. Dylan's sister, somehow out in the wilds now, a survivor of the vampire attack.

Sullivan shuddered, remembering the vampire's glowing eyes, the struggle and fight he had, and how close he had come to capturing her. She had been strong, but he had been stronger—at least until Caitlin had saved the vampire and they had fled.

What had that all been about?

Sullivan set his drink aside and stood up. He breathed in tight, doing his best to weave between tables without his massive size knocking them over. Patrons were busy talking to their peers about their days, nibbling food, drinking their drinks.

Something caught his eye.

Some*one* in the corner. His raised hood ensured that shadows covered his face, but something glinted where his eyes were.

Sullivan took a breath and wandered over. He took a seat beside the stranger, unable to quell his curiosity.

"It's rude to stare," Sullivan said.

"Who says I was staring at you? Don't flatter yourself, buddy. The wench behind the bar is enough to feed my eyes." The voice was rough, and though the words seemed brash, his tone was friendly.

"Oh," Sullivan said. He watched Mother Wendy serving drinks, flashing her winning smile with lips red and bright. He'd always appreciated those tits so big, they reached almost to her chin. "My mistake."

Sullivan went to stand up. The stranger held his arm in place.

"Doesn't mean you have to leave. Stay. Finish my drink for me, if you like."

Sullivan shrugged, reached forward, and drained the cup.

The stranger chuckled. "You're a trusting one, aren't you? What if that had been poison? What if that had glass in it? Or urine? Or shit?"

"Did it?"

"Well…no…" the stranger said.

"Well then, we don't have a problem." He flexed his bicep. "Do we?"

Sullivan's eyes latched onto his face. The stranger

studied him, lingering on his cloak, "You're a scout, right?"

"Aye. Why?"

The man rose to his feet. He began walking towards the exit, half-turned so that Sullivan could just see the skin damage on his cheek. "Come with me," he said, then carried on ahead without looking back.

Sullivan considered whether it would be the smartest move to follow a stranger. His shift was due to start any minute now. But with Dylan gone, there was no one to tie the rangers together. Over the last few days, the guards had done their best to force the rangers out on patrol, but what was it all for if their captain had been taken and imprisoned without providing a sufficient replacement?

Sullivan headed outside and found the stranger down a side street. He was nearly impossible to see until Sullivan heard a *pssst*.

"What's your game?" he asked suspiciously.

"I need your help," the man whispered.

"Got a name?" Sullivan replied.

"Kain. Yours?"

"Sullivan. But my friends call me Sully."

Kain sniggered, catching himself before the laugh grew too loud. "Sullivan? What kind of name is that?"

"One that my mother gave me. If you've got a problem with it, take it up with her." Sullivan held the hilt of his sword in his hand but noticed that Kain didn't even flinch.

Not one bit.

"Okay, we'll start with Sullivan and see how we go. Who knows, before the night is over, we may work our way to Sully," Kain had to look up at him now. "Here's the deal. I'm in a bit of a sticky patch here, and I think we could both benefit from helping each other."

Sullivan put his sword away. "And how do you figure that out?"

Kain lowered his hood revealing his sharp features. His cheekbones stuck out, and his face was gaunt. He clearly hadn't fed properly in weeks, and his skin was more pocked and marked than a gravel road. Despite his ghoulish appearance, Sullivan didn't find himself in the least bit afraid.

"I know where your captain is."

"Dylan?" Sullivan gasped.

"Yes, and here's my proposition: help me escape from this hell-hole of a town, and I'll give you his freedom."

Sullivan thought for a moment, eyeing Kain up and down. He looked the furthest thing from trustworthy he could possibly imagine, but the idea of rescuing Dylan… now that was tempting. Dylan had been good to him over the years.

"How do *you* know where he is?" Sullivan asked.

"Because I occupied the cell next to him. Down in the darkest recesses of the town. Lovely chap. Can't sing for shit, though." Kain reached deep into a pocket and withdrew the key he had stolen from the guard. "And this…this is his ticket out of there."

Sullivan thought for a moment, imagining what it would mean to break into the prison building and break Dylan out. "What use is that key by itself? Even if you handed it over, how are we supposed to get Dylan out when there are guards left, right, and center?" Sullivan said.

"*We?*" Kain replied, scoffing once more. "Who said anything about 'we?' No. *You* get me through the gates. *I* give you the key. What happens after that is your business. I'm out of here. Ciao. S'long. Sayonara!"

They heard footsteps around the corner and the chatter of drunken guards. Both tucked tighter into the shadows, perfectly still and silent. A group of seven guards wandered past, talking loudly. Some laughed, but one at the end remained unengaged in the conversation.

There were mentions of "governor," "Hank", and "escape of a wild creature" mixed amongst the babble, but their spirits didn't seem to match the content.

Drunk. The lot of them. What kind of corrupt system lets their elite guards drink in uniform and parade around the town?

When they were gone, Sullivan turned back to Kain, a question springing to his mind. "What is it that *you* did? Why are you trying to escape?" He paused for a moment, thinking things through. "Why were you down in the extra security prison?"

"That's none of your business," Kain snapped.

"It is if you want me to help you," Sullivan retorted bluntly. "What are you trying to hide?"

For a moment, Kain simply stared. Then, a dull amber began to throb in his eyes. "Trust me, kid. The last thing you want is for me to tell you what I truly am." A slow growl began to rumble from his throat. Sullivan drew back.

"You're a...you're a..." He leaned forward conspiratorially. "*Vampire?*"

"A vampire? What do *you* know of vampires?"

"Only that they're real. I saw one, out in the woods. A woman with dark skin, fangs, and glowing red eyes."

Sullivan placed his fingers over his mouth to create fangs, looking like a five-year-old at a Halloween party. He looked Kain up and down, his eyes wide. "I can't believe I've met *two* in one week."

"Well, clearly, you didn't get a close enough look before," Kain spat on the floor. "A *vampire*... Pah! I'm the furthest thing from a vampire."

"Then what are you?" Sullivan asked, seemingly deflated.

Kain grinned wide. For some reason, Sullivan recognized a kind of shared affinity without fully understanding it. "I'm even better than a goddamn vampire. I'm the best thing you'll ever meet. I'm a motherfucking werewolf."

Sullivan gasped.

"That's right. So, here's the add-on to my proposition. Help me escape, or I'll bite your fucking balls off."

CHAPTER FOURTEEN

New Leaf, Silver Creek Forest

"We have to get moving, and soon," Mary-Anne said, standing in the doorway to Alice's bedroom. Jaxon lay in the corner, his head resting on his paws. His eyes watched Mary-Anne without blinking.

Alice was busy in another room. Sounds of rummaging through boxes and the closing of drawers and doors were the only other noises in the house. "What's the hurry?"

Caitlin sat at the kitchen table, spitting on a cloth and running it the length of her sword. "Yeah, what's the rush? The guard we set free must only be arriving at Silver Creek by now, surely? Take a breath, Mary-Anne. It's almost like you haven't slept all day."

Mary-Anne cringed at the shortening of her name but decided to let it pass.

She looked down at the three guards tied together and gagged on the bedroom floor. Her mouth filled with saliva as she watched them snooze. They had fallen to sleep not long after she had fed from them, and now, they snored peacefully.

"Because if we don't go soon, I may have to suck these fellas dry," she said, remembering the sensation of her last feed. She was still full, but that didn't mean she couldn't snack for taste, right? They were the first humans she'd tasted in years, after all. The first source of *clean* food she'd dared to taste.

One of the guards rolled over in their sleep.

"Ooo-er. I'd bet they'd love that," Caitlin said, crossing the room to Mary-Anne. Alice chuckled from the other room. Caitlin threw her arm across her companion's shoulder and pulled her away like a drunk man trying to veer his friends towards the next bar. "How about we just don't look at them for now?"

"What does it matter if they're dead?" Alice called, appearing a moment later around the corner of the door-frame now wearing her traveling gear—a dark green cloak with riding boots on her feet. "The governor's a prick. The guards are pricks. I say slay all men."

Caitlin raised her eyebrows.

"I mean all of *his* men," Alice corrected.

"The governor may be a prick, but that doesn't mean that all his men are bastards. They may just be following orders. Ain't that right, gentlemen?" The guards answered with the heavy breaths of sleep. "Besides, my brother is… was…the captain of the Silver Creek rangers. All his duties operate under Trisk's orders. You think he and his men should die too?"

Alice's head sunk. "I didn't mean—"

"That's right. If we were to take down all the men,

there'd be hardly anyone left to defend our people. I still believe that honor, loyalty, and bravery exist. All we have to do is remove the oppressors and chaos will no longer reign. In its place will be honor."

Caitlin finished polishing her sword and threw the cloth onto the table. A second later, she noticed one of the guards suddenly wake and struggle against his bonds. He was trying to shout, though the gag did a great job of muting any sense from his words.

"What does he want?" Alice asked.

Mary-Anne bit her lip. They could hear her stomach rumbling again. "Eurgh. And I'd just forgotten about lunch."

"Did you not get enough the first time?" Alice asked.

Caitlin ignored them both and wandered over to the guard. She held the gag in one hand and whispered, "Any shouting or funny business, and I'll find another excuse to get my blade dirty." She removed the gag when he nodded frantically.

"You're the ranger captain's sister?" the guard managed, trying to catch his breath. The man beside him woke at his words, realized where he was, and had a moment of panic. He looked at the guard now talking to Caitlin and shook his head, indicating that he should shut up.

Caitlin rolled her eyes and said, "I am. What of it?"

"Let me free, and I'll tell you what I know." His eyes were fearful, already knowing that he was pushing his luck.

"You're hardly in a position to make a bargain," Caitlin said, kneeling beside him and pressing the tip of her sword against the guard's spine until the skin dented inwards. "Now, what about my brother?"

. . .

Prison District, Silver Creek

Dylan woke with a start, though he wasn't sure why.

In his dream, he had been free. He had returned to his place as the ranger captain, only the guards did not exist. Silver Creek was *his* town to rule, and he did so with the opposite attitude to the present governor. The streets were full of smiling individuals. Trade routes had been established with far-off towns and villages and were monitored and protected by his people.

The world looked set to rebuild in a blazing demonstration of glory.

Not like the shit reality of what life really was. Dylan didn't know much of what lay beyond the boundaries of his patrol, but dear Lord, did he wish he did. Maybe somewhere out there was a true governor—one with honor. A real leader with the ability to show compassion and trust the men who served him. A governor who didn't flaunt his riches and his women or stay tucked away aside from the occasion once a week in which he emerged from behind his wall of guards.

Guards led by Hank Newman.

Haaaaank.

Oh, the power one guard could have over Dylan's honor.

As day passed into night into day, Dylan had no idea of the turning of the world outside. All he could do was stew in his anger, plotting for the moment he could do what Kain had done and break free. Not only had he seen a vampire in the last week, he had now also seen a werewolf.

What the fuck was the world coming to?

What was real?

During the hours spent drifting between sleep, talking to the guards—who seemed to have livened up somewhat since Kain's escape—and eating the tiny morsels of food given to him, he plotted his escape. He kept himself in control by planning what he would do the moment he emerged into the sunshine and confronted the governor, likely killing Hank along the way.

Yeah... That'd be perfect.

And then there was his sister. Somewhere out in the wilds was Caitlin, with the vamp. He wasn't sure how he knew she was okay, but he didn't feel too worried about her. Something deep inside told him that she knew how to hold her own. Something in the encounter with the vampire in the manor told Dylan that she wasn't out to kill.

Why else would she have given Caitlin the silver sword?

Yep. His sister was a strong one, though he couldn't entirely imagine what she'd be up to right now. Whatever it was, the only thing he knew for certain was that it would be better than this. Anything was better than wasting away in the dark, waiting in the stink of urine, hay, and vomit without knowing whether it was night or day outside.

Dylan closed his eyes once more, rested his head back, and drifted between the darkness of reality and sleep.

New Leaf, Silver Creek Forest

"Imprisoned?" Spittle flew from Caitlin's lips. Rage burned inside her as she threw her hands behind her head and marched through the town. She had no idea where she

was going, only that what the guard had told her seemed nearly impossible to comprehend.

"Caitlin, calm down. You're going to wake the town up." Alice ran along beside her, casting furtive glances at nearby windows as if afraid of peeping eyes or lights turning on. Despite the noise Caitlin made, it was oddly quiet.

"So what? Maybe this town needs a little wake-up call." Caitlin simply couldn't get her head around it. So, Trisk had locked Dylan away?

How was that fair?

Did that mean that he would live up to his promise? That it would only be a matter of time before they sent Dylan to the chopper?

Something didn't quite add up. Caitlin knew that the man had ordered them to return with Mary-Anne under pain of death, but she had figured that he might be more lenient towards Dylan after finding out that *Caitlin* had saved her.

There was nothing he could do. Dylan knew that. Sullivan knew that. Hank...

Hank.

Caitlin felt her teeth grinding against each other.

"So what are you going to do?" Mary-Anne asked. "Shout and roar until you draw the Mad to the town? Until the governor's men know exactly where you are and what your weakness is?"

Caitlin spun on her heels. "The guard will already have told them where we are by now. And besides, I have no weakness."

To her surprise, Mary-Anne laughed. "Yes, you do."

"No, I don't."

"Your weakness is your family."

Caitlin's face dropped. She looked down at Jaxon, her heart stirring. Mary-Anne was right. If Trisk's guards were to suddenly arrive now, they would know that the one way to get to her would be through holding her brother as a bargaining chip. If she wanted to get him back and overthrow the town, she'd not only need help, but she'd need to keep her emotions as contained as possible.

"What is it that you suggest?" Caitlin asked, staring at her unexpected mentor for answers.

To her surprise, it wasn't Mary-Anne who answered.

"We suggest you get the fuck out of our village, little girl." The voice came as if from nowhere. Then a figure emerged from around the back of a nearby house.

The man was stocky with a bald head. He wore nothing but shorts and a vest top. He patted a length of two-by-four against his palm in a gesture that needed no translation.

Another man emerged, this one small and thin with a rat-like face. "Yeah, I think you've caused quite enough trouble here. Why don't you zip up your vagina and return to the woods, little nymph?"

A third appeared, his face hard and sullen. "Yeah...so... fuck off."

The first man rolled his eyes and whacked the third man's shoulder. "Jesus, Chris. Real fucking smooth."

"Hey..." Chris complained.

"Leave him alone, he's only trying," the rat-man muttered.

Jaxon growled.

Caitlin squared her shoulders and planted her feet in

the way Mary-Anne had taught her in training. Rule number 101. Or 106…or something.

Mary-Anne stepped up to her side, followed shortly by Alice. Three men against two women and a vampire.

Caitlin grinned. *I fucking like those odds.*

"What seems to be the problem, fellas?" Mary-Anne asked.

"She's talking to us as if she's people." The bald guy cricked his neck.

"Don't act like you've got nothing to hide. I saw you…*vampire*," the rat-man said, flinching as he spoke.

"I told you we'd deal with the problem later," Mary-Anne said to Caitlin.

Caitlin grinned and turned her attention back to the three men.

"Look, you've picked the wrong night, gentlemen. I'm already all kinds of pissed off with a reserve tank of ass-kicking waiting to unleash on whoever gets in my way." She pointed at the men and counted, "One. Two. Three. Haven't really got too much of a leg to stand on now, do we? And, as you so politely pointed out, one of our three is a vampire, too."

Andy chuckled and furrowed his brow. "Oh, if only it were three."

More men, and even a few women, emerged from the shadows. Women who Caitlin didn't recognize from earlier, burly, hardened women with scars across their bodies and stakes and kitchen utensils in their hands. By the time they all moved close enough to be seen, around twenty people were hemming them in, all with evil smirks on their faces.

They were a strange bunch, Caitlin thought. There she was, looking to head out on the road and leave the town anyway so she could get back to Dylan, but they were stopping her from leaving *to make her leave*.

"Ladies," Caitlin muttered, just loud enough for Mary-Anne and Alice to hear her. "Formation."

They stood back to back. Caitlin drew her sword and locked eyes with the bald guy, his men, and the several others now at his side. Alice held two small knives in her hands. Though she had yet to test her skills as a bladeswoman, something told Caitlin that she'd be more than okay.

Mary-Anne turned her attention to a group of women. Caitlin looked them over quickly—butch-looking in their appearance, with pots, pans, and some silverware in their hands. She held no weapon herself, but then, with fangs like those, who needed weapons?

"Last chance to back down," Caitlin said with terrifying certainty. A couple of people encircling them shuffled their feet and glanced sideways.

Caitlin whispered to the others. "Remember. Do nothing unless they make the first move."

Alice and Mary-Anne nodded.

Suddenly, everyone turned when a woman to Caitlin's left roared loudly and threw what was in her hand. It glinted in the moonlight, spinning over and over to land several feet in front of Caitlin on the grass. She looked at the nine-inch fire poker, then back at the woman.

Caitlin sighed. "I guess that's it, then."

"Bring it on, fuckers!" Mary-Anne roared, ducking as a rock flew towards her face. A second later, three men charged at her. Her eyes burned bright red in the night as she sprinted towards them. They only had a chance for, "What the—" before Mary-Anne had them by the hair and tossed them against the side of the house.

There was an audible sound of their heads hitting wood before they each slumped unconscious on the floor.

A large woman with bright red lips gasped, then grabbed the fork that was in one of her hands and stabbed it instinctively into Mary-Anne's arm. The vampire grunted as it drove into her skin, then saw the pan in the woman's other hand, tore it from her grasp, and smashed her over the head with it.

She grinned and looked down at the dazed woman. "Maybe you should've come up with a better *pan?*" Mary-Anne said, chuckling.

She turned her attention to her arm where the three prongs of the fork stuck into her skin. Without hesitation, she grabbed the fork's handle and yanked it. A small trickle of dark blood fell and clotted on her clothes.

"Vampire blood?" a small man who looked of around sixteen years said in awe. "I've read about that. The healing properties. Isn't that supposed to—"

"No," Mary-Anne said sharply. "If you even think of drinking this shit, I'll sneak under your bed in the middle of the night and make it so you can never tug yourself off again. You hear me?"

The fellow nodded, then ran away.

Alice, meanwhile, was struggling. Her daggers were already slick with blood, but where Mary-Anne had the strength that came with the vampiric nanocytes in her bloodstream, Alice did not.

"A little help here?" She choked, a thick arm around her neck as the man attempted to throttle her. Her scream turned to a hoarse whisper, and out of sheer panic she drove her dagger down into man's leg. He roared in her ear, his grasp weakening. But still, he held her in place.

The man's eyes widened at a loud bark. Brown and black fur blurred as Jaxon leapt, sinking his teeth into the man's throat.

The assailant let go, his screams a gurgle of horror. Jaxon held on, growling and twisting his head side-to-side until a nice big chunk of the man came with him and he dropped back onto the ground with ease.

"Cheers, pooch," Alice said, her chest rising and falling rapidly as she drew back the air she had lost.

Jaxon barked as if in response, then dodged as a woman with thick blonde hair dived at him in a fashion that made Alice think of what she had seen of people wrestling pigs. The woman splatted onto the ground, breathless, leaving Alice to drive a boot into her face and make the bitch see stars.

"I think we make a helluva team," she smirked at Jaxon, immediately turning her attention to another guy now charging for her.

"Back off! He's mine!" came Caitlin's call across the battle. She looked back at Alice with a smile before turning and swinging her sword in an impressive arc that split the block of two-by-four the bald guy had tried to hit her with.

He looked at his hands in alarm, then at the sword. When Caitlin first drew the weapon, he had obviously thought of it as nothing more than a plaything.

Chris and the rat-man's faces dropped as quickly as the

bald guy's. They looked at each other, silently communicating some kind of signal before they both advanced on Caitlin.

Whether it was fear or loyalty driving them, Caitlin didn't know. She thought perhaps stupidity, above all. Who would attack her after seeing her sword?

She sighed, finding this fight harder than any fight she'd had with the Mad. These were *real* people, now, not mindless zombies. She wished she could talk sense into them, but the three advancing on her were gunning for the kill.

She walked backward until she felt the house behind her. She was trapped with the three now feet away from her. Behind them, she could see Mary-Anne, Alice, and Jaxon engaged in their own fights.

"Aw, the itsy-bitsy spider is now trapped against the wall," the bald guy said, pulling a rusty knife from his pocket. Chris chuckled at his side while the rat-man watched.

"This is your final warning," Caitlin said, standing straight and holding her sword in both hands. "Back the fuck away, before I teach myself how to play golf with your head."

The bald guy laughed, turned to the others, then slashed at Caitlin. She was fast, managing to parry the hit.

A second later, Chris stabbed viciously. She twisted to avoid the hit.

"Son of a bitch—" she shouted, watching now as the rat-man came at her. With three of them on her, it seemed impossible to parry everything. She saw the flash of the rat-man's knife and couldn't quite move fast enough—

A flash of silver caught her eye as the harsh screech of metal on metal distracted her attackers.

"Back the fuck away!"

Caitlin turned and saw the guard she had set free after he had divulged the information on Dylan's whereabouts. At the time, she had been dubious about releasing him, fighting her instincts telling her to leave them there until they were far, far away. But at that moment, she couldn't have been more grateful.

Caitlin looked impressed.

"You seem surprised to see me," he said.

Caitlin shrugged. "I figured you'd run back to your master as soon as we released you. Thought you'd be halfway to Silver Creek by now…"

She paused, trying to remember the name he had told her.

"Ash."

"I know."

The bald guy grimaced and took another charge at Caitlin, which she batted away with barely a hesitation. He fell to the floor, mud splashing over him as he slid several feet with his own momentum.

"And miss all this fun? Now where in Silver Creek can we party like this?"

The rat-man growled and took another desperate swing. Chris followed swiftly behind. Ash hardly turned in his direction as he tapped the blow aside, then booted Chris in the chest. There was a satisfying *goooph* as he flew through the air. "Besides, as much as I *love* the benefits that come from being under the governor's orders—"

"Sarcasm?"

"How could you tell? I'm beginning to think that maybe there's someone else who I'd be better to serve in the grand scheme of things."

Taken back a little by the kind words of one of Hank's men, Caitlin lowered her sword.

Then raised it again immediately, twisting it beneath the crook of her armpit in a panicked attempt at defense as she heard the scream from behind. The blade now stuck out behind her.

She heard the wet sounds of blood as the sword made its way into Chris' stomach. He had been ready for the kill, ready to launch on her back and slice her throat.

Caitlin closed her eyes, feeling nausea rise to choke her.

"I see you're not a fan of the kill?" Ash said with a look of concern, batting away another attempt from the bald guy.

"Let's just say I can deal with killing mindless Mad. I'd rather not kill fellow humans if I can help it."

"Hey. *He* jumped into *your* sword." Ash shrugged. "The way I see it, you're innocent in all this. It's not like you started this fight either, right?"

The bald guy roared and began throwing slashes at them both, turning between each in a frenzied assault. His face screwed up in a twisted red of anger, his teeth bared.

"Though that's not to say that some people don't deserve it." Ash planted his feet and swung, taking a big chunk out of the bald guy's neck. "Some people are just monsters."

There was a moment of quiet as Caitlin collected herself, hardly believing the hatred that had been inside these people. It seemed that no matter what her intentions were, some people were simply downright cock-nuggets.

It was as they were about to re-engage in the battle beside Mary-Anne and Alice that they caught the rat-man trying to crawl away. He stopped, cowering on his knees by the bodies of his friends, disbelief written on his face.

They both advanced, towering over him.

He dropped his knife and held his hands up in the air. "I surrender! I'm sorry, I'm so, so sorry," he whimpered. He bowed low to the ground, sobbing. "I didn't mean it. I'm sorry."

"What do you think?" she asked Ash.

Ash shrugged. "Not my decision. Why not ask the others?"

"Good idea." Caitlin cupped her hands and called to Mary-Anne. The vampire's face was now covered in gore. "Is sorry good enough?"

Mary-Anne looked over, her eyes ablaze. Her own chest rose and fell rapidly as she sat atop a man's chest who had clearly just pissed himself with fear.

"We should probably make a decision sooner rather than later on that. This guy says he's sorry, too. But only after trying to stab a pitchfork into my shoulder." She grabbed the man's cheeks and squeezed so tight his lips pursed. "Ain't that right, little morsel?"

The man spat in Mary-Anne's face.

She punched him in the nose.

It was his own fault really.

It was then that Caitlin heard the kid's cry and the padding of feet. A second later, a boy appeared, no more than five summers old.

He sprinted across the grass towards the man that Mary-Anne straddled, his arms held out wide. "No, Daddy. No, no, no."

He was so focused on running towards his father that he didn't see the man leaping at Mary-Anne from the shadows. The man was so focused that he didn't see the kid until it was almost too late. Caitlin spotted the rock in the man's hand ready to bash Mary-Anne's skull in and yelled a warning. Mary-Anne moved with incredible speed, picked the kid up, and ducked out the way. A fraction of a second later, and he would've killed him.

Mary-Anne stood with the boy in her arms, covering his eyes as the brute pulled back at the last minute, landing clumsily on the body of the boy's father.

"Idiots," she whispered.

The men rolled over in shock, not quite believing what just happened.

"You...you saved him?" the boy's father said, shoving the man off him and running to Mary-Anne to collect his kid. He turned to the others in awe. "A *vampire* saved my kid!"

Those now left fighting seemed to notice her for the first time.

Alice, who had been in the middle of clashing weapons with a lean man of a similar build to herself, lowered her weapon as he lowered his and stared. Jaxon kept his hackles raised, growling loudly.

Caitlin seized the moment of pause to regroup. She left rat-man on the ground and took Ash with her to join Mary-Anne. Alice came over now too, the four of them a fearsome quartet.

"That's right. A vampire saved the life of a child and likely spared a lot of you tonight," Caitlin said. "If you're looking for a monster, look no further than the man who has you all thinking that this is as big as life gets. Look for the man who has trained you all into a life of misery and servitude."

As she spoke, she saw the heads of some of the women who had been around earlier in the day pop sheepishly out of their windows.

"I should know," Caitlin continued. "My brother has been taken by the governor and is being held prisoner in Silver Creek's dungeons for doing nothing more than his job. He is an honorable man, rotting in a cell under the orders of a fat slob who has tried to have me killed, did have my friend killed, and would likely kill all of you before he had a chance to look at you." She wiped her sword and sheathed it. "This fight is over. Before daybreak, we will be leaving to kick some governor ass and release my brother from his cell. Silver Creek is a big town with many guards. We'll need all the help we can get. Those who are willing to journey with us and fight for a greater cause than your day-to-day lives, show yourself and come forth."

"And what about those who aren't?" a voice said. Caitlin turned and saw the man Alice had wrestled with a moment ago. His black teeth and fierce expression gave him a savage look.

"Well then, stay here and carry on as you were. There's little I can do about that. I'm going with or without you. It's your choice."

At first, no one moved, and Caitlin couldn't help but

feel a little disheartened. Then a young woman stepped forward and fell to one knee.

"I'll stand with you until the end," she said.

"And I," another added.

Soon, there was an echo of agreement as the men stepped forward in turn and pledged their allegiance to Caitlin. By the end of it, she had a group of men and women around her, each with steel determination locked on their faces. All were ready to fight and stand up to the governor, to reclaim their lives and their freedom.

CHAPTER FIFTEEN

Silver Creek

Kain wasn't entirely sure he liked this.

Though it was late at night, the streets seemed to be more crowded than ever. He felt it with every step. With every movement, he was conscious of the threat of discovery. Sullivan seemed more at ease, like he was tired and just wanted to get home without being stopped by a friend or nosy neighbor.

Or maybe harboring a fugitive brought out a fatalistic calm.

A fugitive who also happened to be a werewolf. Kain tried to put himself in his companion's shoes and failed.

"Fuck me," Sullivan grumbled as they snuck between some houses and peeked around the corner.

"No thanks. I prefer my men with vaginas," Kain muttered behind him.

"Not exactly what I meant."

They sidled into the shadows. After a careful look around, they crossed the street, ducked between more houses, and eventually, Sullivan led them to a small house which squatted unobtrusively near the large wooden walls. He knocked three times—once loud, once quiet, once loud —and when he was satisfied there was no response, made his way inside.

It was dark. The smell of extinguished lanterns still lingered in the air.

"Good. We've missed them," he said, crossing the room where the silhouette of a large wooden chest could be seen in the corner.

"Missed who? We crashing a birthday party?" Kain laughed at his own joke, then stopped as he tried to remember the last birthday party he had been to. It had been havoc. Partying with Weres—Weres who hated you— was never the most pleasant of affairs.

Sullivan ignored him. "Here, put these on."

Kain saw clothes flying at him in the dark. He caught them with ease. "What are these?"

"You want to escape, right? You'll need to look like a ranger to be able to pass for a ranger." Sullivan began to straighten out his own fatigues, pulling his hood low across his face. Had it not been for Kain's heightened senses, he would've blended in with the shadows. "Silver Creek's a small town, by all accounts."

"Larger than any place I've seen in years."

"But small enough that everyone knows everyone," Sullivan said. "You try and head through the gates wearing that, suspicions are going to raise. You need to blend in. Otherwise we'll both end up in the shitter."

Kain chuckled. "You should smell my cage, man. But if

Silver Creek is such a small place, surely the guards will notice that I'm not one of the regulars?"

"You give the guards too much credit," his companion said. "If you look enough like a ranger, they won't bat an eyelid. I don't think you realize the distaste rangers and guards have for each other."

When they left the ranger's quarters, Sullivan instructed Kain to walk with him in the center of the road. Now that they were both fully equipped, it was less conspicuous for them to walk out in the open rather than clinging to the walls. At least, that appeared to be Sullivan's opinion, anyway.

"Tell me," Kain said as the gate came into view. He couldn't remember them from the last time he had passed through. Though, of course, that time he had been carried in a cage. "If the rest of the rangers have already gone off ahead, what's to stop these guys from wondering why the fuck we aren't with them?"

Sullivan shrugged.

"Oh, good. I was worried that we didn't have a plan."

Sullivan smiled beneath his hood—a dozy smile which suggested it should all be really simple. As long as they didn't act suspicious, Kain reasoned, hating that he was dependent on a complete stranger. Sullivan was well-known amongst Silver Creek as the dozy ranger, that much was obvious, but the fugitive guessed that many didn't know that there was more going on behind the curtains than met the eye. His instinct might have served him well when it had honed in on Sullivan. Time would tell.

"Good evening, gents," a guard said, stepping forward

with one hand out in front and the other on the handle of his sword. "Where might you fine gentlemen be heading to at this late hour?"

"Good evening, Clint," Sullivan said, doffing his hood. "We wish to embark on our rangerly duties under orders of our master, the governor."

Clint's eyebrow raised. He looked behind him at a second guard who stood near the chains which operated the gate. "A little late to be playing catch-up with the rest of your group."

"Aye, it's my fault. A day full of drinking and games can sometimes make it difficult to get out of bed." Sullivan shrugged.

Kain was impressed. Despite his clumsy size, Sullivan was smooth.

"Very well," Clint said, laughing as he nodded to the second guard. "If there's one thing I know well, it's the affection of dear Lady Booze. Say...you wouldn't happen to have anything warm and naughty on you now?"

Kain brought a scarred hand to his mouth in an attempt to stop himself from laughing.

Sullivan carried on as if nothing had happened. "I'm afraid not, though I'll be sure to buy you a round for your troubles next time you find yourself in Mother Wendy's."

Clint studied Kain. "And who's your friend?"

"New recruit from one of the outlying towns. First in years," Kain said, drawing out a hip flask from the inside of his cloak. "Here. I'll bet my last dollar that you haven't tasted anything like that before. It'll finally put some hairs on your chest."

"I think what my friend here is trying to say is thank

you for your help." Sullivan pulled Kain by the elbow and wandered towards the gate. "Please, enjoy the brew from the foreign lands and have yourself a nice evening."

Clint sniffed the flask, then took a swig. He coughed the instant the liquid hit his lips, then went for another sip. "Hey, Mattis, give this a whirl. Tremendous stuff."

He tossed the flask to Mattis as Kain and Sullivan exited the gates.

Silver Creek, Silver Creek Forest

"This here is where we part ways, kiddo." Kain stopped at a fork along the forest path. "Cheers for the help."

Sullivan looked suddenly afraid. Kain couldn't blame him. If he were human and were about to be left alone in a dark forest where the Mad were known to roam, he'd be afraid too. If they could jump back some eighty years or so, it might not have been half bad. But Kain had seen a lot of things in his life, and the descending of the Madness was one of the things he wished he could forget.

The worst part was that it did much more than drive those affected into a state of zombie-like lunacy. Kain had seen it first-hand with his own pack. He'd seen members of his pack struggling to change into their animal forms, and struggling to change back. He wouldn't forget watching the Alpha resort to fear tactics to keep the pack safe.

And, unfortunately, that was a pack Kain felt he could never go back to—not after the way he left.

"Can't I stay with you a bit longer, at least until I find the rangers?" Sullivan said, lowering his hood for the first time since leaving the town.

Kain closed his eyes and took a deep breath through his nose, savoring the scents of the forest. Dirt, leaves...*human*. When he opened his eyes, he pointed down the path to Sullivan's right. "Down that way. Keep heading straight. If you're fast enough, you'll find them."

"And if I don't?"

"That ain't my problem anymore. Here." Kain pulled the key out of his pocket and handed it over to Sullivan. "Through the district. Bottom dungeon. Heavily guarded. However, if you think you're going to get into that place alone, you best think twice. I doubt I'd have gotten away at all if the guards weren't half surprised to see a wolf sprinting off."

Kain grinned, remembering the looks of shock and the shouts that followed him as he had sprinted into town and found a place to lie low. The governor's smug fucking face had wobbled as he ran and chased him up the stairs, stumbling and heaving with every breath.

"Before I go..." Sullivan paused, unsure whether to ask the question. "Can I see it? The change?"

"Not this time," Kain said. "There's a lot you don't know about Weres, and a lot that has changed since the good ol' days. Maybe someday, you'll find out. Maybe you won't. To be honest, at this point, I couldn't give two shits."

Sullivan smiled and held out his hand. Kain took it and shook. Not two moments later, Kain headed off into the blackness of the forest.

He had smelled another scent, and there was someone he wanted to find.

. . .

Somewhere, Silver Creek Forest

"You know, for a town as small as ours, your conversion rate is rather high," Alice said, walking at a steady pace at the front of the group. Caitlin led the way, riding atop a moderate chestnut horse that had been hiding around the back of one of the houses. It turned out to have been Ash's, but he donated it eagerly.

"His name is Silver," Ash had said, stroking the horse's nose.

"That's a dumbfuck name for a brown horse. Why don't you call it something closer to its hair color?" Caitlin said, stroking her chin and thinking.

"What about shit nugget?" Mary-Anne offered.

Alice chipped in. "Or stallion?"

"Or combine the both?!" Caitlin said, clapping with excitement. "I dub thee: Shitallion!"

They had all laughed then, though Shitallion had seemed unimpressed. Maybe that was the new name choice, though it probably had something to do with the horse's unease at a vampire standing a few feet away from him. Caitlin had heard that animals could sense the differences between creatures. They could sense fear. Jaxon certainly could.

And from what Caitlin had seen, Mary-Anne was something to be a-fucking-fraid of.

Now, riding along at least an extra person's height above the rest of those following, Caitlin looked down with questioning eyes at Alice. She had really come out of her shell quickly.

"Conversion? What were you talking about?"

"Don't pretend you can't see it, Cat," Ash said. For

someone who had been one of Trisk's guards until very recently, he certainly seemed to fit in well with the crowd. "Look behind you. Your following. You entered a town with one vampire and came out with twenty people willing to follow you and fight for your cause. Or has that escaped your notice?"

Okay, maybe he had a point.

Not only did she have over twenty women and men from New Leaf following her through the dark of the wilds at early dawn, but she had also accrued a guardsman and a sidekick along the way.

It felt funny, that. To think that these people felt her cause and could see the downright indignity of how people lived under the governor's rule after so short a period. It was as though his regime was a pimple ripe for the popping.

Caitlin felt a surge of warmth and closed her eyes. For half a moment, she was back in her house with Dylan. He had just come back from his duty, and Caitlin was sorting the clothes and tidying the house—and wishing yet again that she could be out there with him, serving the town on a bigger scale instead of staying inside. The only perk of staying at home could be found in Jaxon's company.

"Cat?" Mary-Anne's voice through her memory. "Caaat."

Caitlin turned sharply. "Don't call me that."

Mary-Anne looked on, unfazed. "But it's fine for you to abbreviate my name at every opportunity?"

"What's wrong with Ma?" Caitlin said, catching Alice's eye as they both tried not to laugh.

"It makes me sound old."

"You are old!" Ash declared, though not without a careful look to gauge Mary-Anne's reaction. "You're a vampire."

"That doesn't mean I need constant reminding, least of all from children such as yourselves. You agree to stop calling me Ma, and I'll agree never to call you Cat. How's that sound?"

Caitlin considered this a moment. "Nah. Not worth it. Now, lead the way, Ma!"

Alice and Caitlin shared lighthearted laughter. Even Ash had to try his hardest to fight it. Jaxon whirled and wove between Shitallion's legs, causing the horse to rear and buck.

Once Caitlin had regained control, they continued through the forest at a steady pace. Her following grew more and more quiet with every step. They were tired and used to traveling and walking during the daytime. Caitlin pitied them and sought comfort from Mary-Anne who was eyeballing the sky, the black canvas already beginning to turn to purple.

"I must find somewhere away from the sun, and soon." She sniffed the air and looked around as if trying to gauge her direction.

"Oh, no." Caitlin sighed.

"What's wrong, Caitlin?" Alice asked.

"I've just realized that if Mary-Anne's going to be our leading weapon on this mission, we're pretty much fucked. What kind of soldier only comes out at night? Might have to look at trading you in for a badger. Or a hedgehog." She watched Mary-Anne carefully, feeling braver and braver every day and loving how easy it was to wind her up.

"A soldier that could rip off your head and drain the blood so quickly you wouldn't even be able to say—"

"Ma?" Caitlin interjected.

Even Mary-Anne laughed at that one.

"Exactly," Mary-Anne said. "But in all seriousness, I must go on ahead. I won't be able to keep your pace without exposing myself to the sun, and as much as the world bites big donkey scrotum right now, I'm almost positive I want to stick around and see what you'll end up doing with it."

"Where are you going to go? You know you're my compass, right? I don't know the way," Caitlin suddenly realized she sounded panicked and did her best to bring confidence back to her voice for those following close enough behind to hear their conversation.

"It's easy," Mary-Anne said, pointing ahead and slightly to their left. "Keep on straight in that direction. Don't falter, and you should be at the old airship within less than an hour. I may or may not be there at that point, depending on how fast I can run and how much I can carry at once."

"Carry?" Alice chirped.

"What are you up to, Ma?" Caitlin said, her mischievous grin growing wide.

"I've got a plan, Kitty Cat," Mary-Anne responded as she turned and dashed straight into the trees. There were audible gasps behind from certain members of the group who caught her running away and were stunned by her speed.

"Okay, Kitty Cat is much too fucking far!" Caitlin shouted after her.

A bone-chilling screech called back from somewhere

far off in the distance. The group began to shuffle in panic. A sudden realization dawned on Caitlin. They were still in the thick of the Mad-infested woods, and their vampire protector had fucked off to Lord only knew where.

It was now down to her, Ash, and Alice to protect the herd.

As she kicked Shitallion's side and got him moving again, she couldn't help but notice Ash glancing sideways at Alice's cleavage, which admittedly pretty much hung out of her traveling garb.

Caitlin rolled her eyes. *What the hell am I going to do with these children?*

CHAPTER SIXTEEN

Abandoned Airship, Silver Creek Forest

Mary-Anne wasn't at the husk of the ship when the group arrived, but that didn't mean she hadn't left presents.

Lots and lots of presents.

Putting aside the gasps of awe that had escaped their lips when they saw the colossal shipwreck emerge through the forest trees, the folks of New Leaf—now Caitlin's mini-battalion—all marveled at the gleaming pile of swords and weapons that glinted in the golden rays of the morning sun.

Caitlin realized immediately where they had come from. Mary-Anne's plan must have been to sprint as fast as possible back and forth between her manor and the ship itself to provide everyone with enough weapons to at least protect themselves should a horde of Mad attack—or even just a little baby one.

Hold on. Were there babies somewhere out there? Crawling around, mindlessly hunting for flesh?

Caitlin pushed the thought away. It was far too gross to even think about.

Still, she couldn't believe it. Mary-Anne must have had an armory or store of some kind at her place. The same place from which she had fetched Caitlin's sword on the day when she had nearly been chow food for the Mad. How many more of these did she have lying around? It was a wonder that the governor hadn't discovered the store and looted them yet.

"Where did she find these?" Ash asked, marveling at the blades. "These are unlike anything our blacksmiths could craft. They are from the old world." He ran a finger along the edge and recoiled as a line of blood rose to the skin. "Still sharp, too."

"Make sure you get on your knees and thank her when she's back," Caitlin said, comparing them to her own blade. Thankfully, none matched the craftsmanship of hers. "Hopefully, she'll be back soon so we can."

But Mary-Anne didn't manage to complete her final journey back to the wreck before the sun began to burn hot in the sky. That left Caitlin, Alice, and Ash to watch over everyone to make sure that they all behaved themselves.

"Get yourselves rested. There are sleeping quarters in the back, though they're pretty basic," Caitlin announced. "And no touching anything sharp or capable of killing anyone until I say."

There was a chorus of "Aw. man!"

"What do you mean by basic?" A portly woman with fiery red hair and freckles painting her cheeks stood with her hands on her hips. She looked weary but still feisty.

"It means there aren't any beds, but you can at least shut the door and escape the daylight."

Not everyone went to sleep straight away, of course. There were a few there who explored the ship, wandering along the vast deck which stood at a crooked angle, making the whole thing more of a climb. There were some who stayed awake simply to talk to Caitlin and share their thanks and enthusiasm for being able to join her on her journey.

They shared horror stories of the governor's men. They spoke of rumors and tales they had heard which, by all accounts, seemed too nasty to even contemplate. Stories of babies fed to the Mad, stories of rape and famine, and stories of heartache and pain reminded her of all the reasons why she had made this choice.

Caitlin listened with attentive ears, but by noon, she was exhausted. She set up a watch schedule with Ash and Alice, and they alternated throughout the day. Caitlin was the first to sleep, suddenly overcome with tiredness.

She whistled for Jaxon to follow as she headed towards the ship.

At the back of the hull, beneath a panel with a rusted iron ring which Caitlin pulled with greater ease than she had managed the first time she had found it, she eased herself below deck and found herself in the cellar. She passed through a room that was dark apart from the silver cuts of light which made their way through the boards above. There were empty kegs to her left and right which she wandered past until she found her way to a door almost camouflaged with the walls. She entered and found herself in the remains of the old captain's quarters.

The room was a luxury she still couldn't believe was possible, the only room on the ship with linens and pillows for the bed. She curled up on top of the sheets and spent a good fifteen minutes doing her best to pull the dried blood and muck from Jaxon's fur.

Eventually, they both slept.

Silver Creek Forest

Kain could smell it a mile off—the scent he was looking for. Something which he still couldn't believe his nose could detect from this distance, and after so many years, too.

Where are you hiding? he thought to himself, strolling at a leisurely pace now that the sun was out and he could see his way. He wasn't hungry anymore. Had found a nice selection of forest critters to kill, cook, and munch earlier that morning. Now, all he could think of was finding them.

He made his way through a clearing and stopped when he saw a deer. The sight was beautiful, really. He couldn't remember the last time he'd seen something so magnificent simply standing there in the sunlight. Kain was used to living in the carcasses of the old cities. They provided places where there were plenty of shadows in which to hide, and so everyone did. Every street and every road was a booby trap for some kind of vamp, Were, or human.

It's a dog eat dog world out there. He laughed.

God, he was funny.

He left the deer to its own agenda, sneaking around the clearing so quietly that the creature had no idea anything had been watching at all.

As the sun rose and began to fall, Kain made steady progress towards the scent. By early afternoon, he saw it ahead. A large manor loomed up out of the trees. Several parts of its roof had caved in, and the garden was incredibly overgrown.

Just like a vamp not to trim their bush.

He made his way to the door. It creaked as he pushed it open. Inside, it was dusty and cobwebbed, and there was something else now, a smell which made his heart beat faster.

The smell of Madness.

Not fresh Madness, mind you. No. He could tell that from miles away. That didn't mean he shouldn't be careful.

Kain took the stairs one at a time, making extra effort to avoid any spots that creaked. He vividly remembered the last time he had snuck up on a vampire and how that had gone.

Carter Manor, Silver Creek Forest

Mary-Anne felt better than she had in months. So good, in fact, that it had been hard to fall to sleep when she had arrived back at the manor. Her body still buzzed from the fresh injection of blood she had drunk from the guards, and she felt like she wanted to rediscover her powers. She desperately longed to smash through walls, run at speed, and go on the hunt.

She had almost forgotten how much fun it all was.

But eventually, she had slept. Though she hadn't had time to make her way back to the others at the airship, she had piled a load of what she considered to be her "silverware" by the back door, ready to journey out the minute she was able.

Swords, katanas, daggers, axes, and more—her relics from times long gone now. With each one she'd plucked off the wall, she had been thrown back to a time when she had first encountered it. A dagger she had collected on a journey to New York, back when the airships hovered, and the vampire blood business was rife. She had only been a young vamp then but had managed to avoid being caught and drained by humans for sport and nourishment.

An axe from a time she had found refuge in the back of a woodcutter's house out in the forests.

A katana from an overly confident human drug lord with tattoos and several scantily-clad women at his side.

That was a fun one.

They were all there in her weapon collection, like a photo album of gore that only she knew the stories behind.

Mary-Anne thought about it all as her eyes flickered and her breathing went deep. It would take a lot to wake her from this slumber. This was the deepest she'd now slept in years, thanks to Caitlin and her friends.

Which was probably why she almost didn't hear the werewolf walking into her chambers.

Almost.

Kain's heart raced. He couldn't believe it. He'd heard rumors vamps had fallen into extinction. They'd either been killed off by the blood trades of the Second Dark

Ages or destroyed by the Madness. He hadn't seen it first-hand, but Kain had heard stories of the destructive forces of Mad-infected vampires. The affliction coursed through their blood faster than any human, affecting their nanocytes and forcing the vamp to go on a rampage so deadly that they might as well have set off a bomb in the center of a town.

But this one wasn't dead. Nor was she Mad. This one was…peaceful.

Kain crept over to the edge of the bed and watched her in the dark. Though he had never been attracted to vamps before, he couldn't help but scan his gaze over the curves of her body as they rose and fell.

She was pretty. Slender. He almost scolded himself for staring, then stopped.

He was a hot-blooded male after all.

He leaned closer, listening for her breath. Wondering how long she had been asleep for—

The vampire's eyes shot open. Two orbs of glowing red. "*Boo!*"

Kain jumped back, and in that second, the vampire had him pinned against the wall by his throat. Her grip was like iron.

God, he had forgotten how much he hated vamps.

"Wait. *Wait!*" he croaked, struggling to breathe.

"You know it's never smart to sneak up on a lady like that." Her gaze burrowed into Kain's. "Especially in the middle of one's beauty sleep."

Kain held her wrist with both hands. "'Lady'? Is that what you're calling yourselves these days?"

"Something like that." The vampire released Kain, and he stumbled as his feet touched the floor.

He rubbed his throat, his own eyes pulsing a mild amber as he tried to hold back his automatic response to being threatened.

"Now, who are you? Tell me what it is you are here for. The last encounter I had with a Were was...how do I say this? Unsavory. To tell you the truth, I believed you all gone." The vampire's eyes calmed, suddenly curious. "I thought you were all gone."

"That's kind of the reason I tracked you down." Kain stood as tall as he could, though he knew that his skinny frame—compared to this vampire's body—would never win any contests. "My name is Kain Sudeikis, and I am a nomad. A wanderer. I've traveled far with no place to call home, avoiding danger and keeping to myself at all costs." He studied her once more. "I couldn't believe it when I heard that there was a vampire living somewhere out in the woods. I had to try and see it for myself."

"And who told you of my existence?" the vampire demanded.

"Uh-uh. You know my name, you give me yours first."

Her eyes blazed. For a second, Kain felt he might have gone too far until he saw the corner of her lips tweak up into a wry smile. "I forgot about the personalities of Weres. Stubborn fuckers."

"Speak for yourself," Kain said, rubbing his neck idly. "You nearly squeezed my throat so tight my head would've exploded into crimson confetti."

"Force of habit." The vampire shrugged. "Name's Mary-Anne."

Kain held out his hand in an offer of a handshake. Mary-Anne looked at it and shook her head.

"Suit yourself," Kain said.

"Now, tell me what you know."

"I don't know much," Kain started as he explained what had happened to him over the last few weeks. He revealed how he had been asleep in a hollow in the forest when he had been taken by a large group of men in leather armor and dragged back to Silver Creek. Mary-Anne listened intently when he spoke of the governor and his fixed agenda for the UnknownWorld—a voyage of discovery to try and collect as many Weres and vamps as possible to work on his side. He finished with the ranger he had shared a jail with and Sullivan who had helped him.

"And so, when I finally did escape, I figured I'd try to find you. Trisk has put a target on your back, and I thought it only fair that I find you and give you the heads up. Loyalty amongst the UnknownWorld, after all. Especially in these mad times."

To his surprise, Mary-Anne started laughing.

"What?" Kain said, scratching his chin.

"I appreciate the concern, Were. But I'm just fine. My manor is already full of the governor's intruders I've dispatched. The humans who live near here, unless they rise up together, don't stand a chance."

They laughed together then, chatting idly about the world they both knew. Eventually, the conversation turned to Silver Creek. They both took a seat on the floor, Kain with his back to the wall and Mary-Anne against her bed.

"Tell me, what is this governor like?" Mary-Anne said.

"I've heard so much about him that I feel like I should at least have a picture in my head by now."

Kain laid his head back against the wall. "Imagine a flabby little baby that can barely stand because of the rolls around its feet and arms."

"Mmhmm."

"Now imagine a six-foot version of that, only no one ever wiped this baby's chin or taught him any manners." Kain paused, remembering the wicked grin on the man's face as he had held the trigger down on the taser. He shuddered as he recalled the electricity rocking through his body, forcing out his inner wolf.

If only he could've had him then and there. He almost regretted not ripping out his throat as he sprinted past him in that moment of surprise.

One day, he thought. One day...

"Sounds like a delight to be around." Mary-Anne fought back a yawn and stretched her arms.

"Am I keeping you up?" Kain chuckled. "I know how much you vamps like to sleep away the beautiful sunshine."

Mary-Anne yawned again. "We do. So, if you'll excuse me, you've disturbed my slumber long enough, and I need at least another hour of beauty sleep if I'm going to be of any help to anyone come dark. The guest room is free if you wish to lay down your own head, though I suggest that whatever it is you plan on doing now, you should probably get to it sooner rather than later. The governor's men know of this place's existence. They're probably already planning a raid as we speak. I can handle the heat and run if I need to. I know it's been a few years, but I'm not sure exactly what a Were is capable of these days."

"I can hold my own," Kain said, puffing his chest until he realized that he didn't know what his next move would be.

What had his plan been after finding Mary-Anne? He'd been on the road by himself so long now that he wondered what was next. He had almost given up hope of finding others like him since leaving his pack, never quite sure who to trust in this world. But now, maybe that could change. It almost seemed a waste to abandon a vampire after so many years of almost being certain they were gone.

Much worse, to abandon one with such a sense of humor seemed a damn shame.

The sound of china breaking came from downstairs. They both turned to look at the door.

"I'll go with you," Kain blurted in an effort half to demand and half attempt to not offend Mary-Anne.

She eyed him cautiously, looking him up and down almost insolently. "You're a little skinny for a Were. But you could be a large sight better than the rest of them out there. Tell you what—you help me clear the vermin from downstairs while I sleep, you can tag along. Deal?"

Kain took a deep breath through his nose and smiled as he identified the intruder downstairs as merely another human suffering from the Madness. "You're kidding, right? Give me a challenge."

And with that, he was off.

Abandoned Airship, Silver Creek Forest

Caitlin awoke to the sound of metal on metal. Birds chirped outside, and she could hear voices.

What in the name of shit-eating-fudge-nuggets is going on out there?

She rose sharply from her bed and exited the captain's quarters. When she emerged into the sunlight, she blinked and raised her hand. In her head, she had images of her followers engaged in a battle against the governor's men, or *worse*, a horde of Mad.

That's the last thing I need right now, to be playing stabby-stab with the Mad folks.

But now, she could see from the deck of the ship that at least a dozen former New Leaf folk held swords and weapons, running through drills as Ash called out commands and gave direction. Alice stood not too far away, her own daggers in her hand as she practiced moves with another man who kept eyeing her up and down between rounds, losing his concentration and almost losing his finger.

"Focus!" she heard Ash call and wondered whether that was more for the man's benefit or for his own.

Caitlin strode over and stood beside him.

"Morning, sunshine," Ash said, beaming.

"I said no touching the weapons. What is all this?"

"Ah, relax. A few of the guys figured they wanted to make the best use of the time we were here and asked me to teach them some stuff. You were asleep. I've trained people before. And, before I knew it, the guys were at it and I'm standing here playing grandmaster coach." Ash scanned back over his pupils and shouted at a pair who were out of breath and sweating. "Back to it, maggots, you can rest when you're dead."

"No need to be so harsh, it's just practice," Alice called, sticking out her tongue.

"You say that now but wait until a ten-foot werebear comes for you. Then you'll really be wishing you'd paid attention." Ash held his arms up in the air and imitated a giant bear.

Several people stopped and laughed.

"A werebear? That's not a thing." Alice scoffed.

"When's my lesson, then?" Caitlin asked, drawing her sword and taking her place beside Ash.

He looked taken aback. He had seen her fight back in New Leaf, of course, and she seemed to recall that he'd looked at her with raw admiration more than once.

"Are you sure you can handle one of the governor's guards?" Ash raised a cocky eyebrow.

"Oh, please. It wasn't that long ago that you were hogtied and lying on my bedroom floor."

Caitlin had him there. Ash burned bright red and turned to those close enough to hear. "It's not what it sounds like. It's not!"

Caitlin turned to Alice and held the back of her hand theatrically to her mouth. She spoke loud enough for everyone to hear. "It's okay. He took it like a real bronco. Ain't that right, Shitallion?"

The horse whined in response as Caitlin placed one hand over her ass and the other over her mouth.

Laughter erupted around the clearing. Several folks who were still sleeping poked their heads out from the ship.

"Okay then, big shot," Ash said seeing no better option than joining in with the laughs. "Show us what you got." He turned to address the group. "Hey, who here would like to learn some sword-swinging skills from the Chief Cat?"

Caitlin's smile dropped as every single hand shot in the air, including Ash's. Just over a week ago, she had no real idea about swordsmanship. Now, she had been trained by a vampire and was being looked at by over twenty hungry eyes who all wanted a lesson directly from her.

Well, fuckety-fuck. How things can change.

"Okay, bring it on." Caitlin walked forward, her back to the ship and sword in front, poised and ready for battle.

Ash grinned and steadied himself. He had been a guard for most of his life, trained and ready for any battle situation.

The only problem was that he had never really encountered an enemy that knew swordsmanship. Most of his kills had been on Mad, and he had never had a reason to fight with another guard. They would never admit it, but over the years, most of the guards' sword skills went sloppy.

Fuck it. Let's dive in.

Caitlin took the first swing. Ash brought his sword up to meet hers, grunting as the metal clanged. The swords locked in an "X," and they looked at each other through the middle.

Ash shoved her sword away, stepped in, and took a jab which Caitlin blocked, using the momentum and force to bring her sword up and over.

He raised his sword above his head, batted the attack away, and stepped back.

The gathered crowd cheered and clapped. Some laughed, and many offered words of encouragement.

"Go on, Ash!" Alice cried.

Ash winked her way as Caitlin cried, "Hey!"

Alice mouthed an apology. The combatants turned back to each other.

They took turns stepping forward, their blows singing in the clearing as they slashed, hacked, and twirled. With every hit, their intensity increased until their chests rose and fell with heavy breaths. Out in the sun, fighting was sweaty work.

"Surrender yet?" Ash asked, wiping sweat with the back of his hand.

"Never!" Caitlin responded, shouting and leaping forward, driving him back with a series of blows until he was almost at the line of trees.

Ash roared, swung the sword in loops around his back, and jabbed at Caitlin. The blade caught her hip and cut the cloth. A moment later, it was sticky with blood.

She drew in a sharp hiss of breath and clutched her side. Her face suddenly grew dark. The crowd behind her quietened.

In a moment of madness, she lunged forward. Ash, panicking, raised his sword which Caitlin batted away so hard that it fell to the ground.

"Caitlin? Wait! What are you doing—"

Someone screamed behind them.

Ash folded to the floor and held his head.

Caitlin missed him by inches. He waited, half-expecting

the final stab to come while he was on the floor, until he heard the gurgles and growls from behind.

He turned around and saw then what Caitlin had seen —two Mad. One now lay chopped in half on the floor. The other sprinted straight at Caitlin, his cloak shredded and his eyes red.

Ash laughed in disbelief. She hadn't been attacking him. She had been *saving* him.

CHAPTER SEVENTEEN

Abandoned Airship, Silver Creek Forest

Caitlin took the fucker down in seconds, her sword finding its way through those vital body organs that the Mad needed to operate.

Heart. Brain. That sort of thing.

But the thing was like the hydra Alice had talked of. The minute she killed one, several more appeared, stumbling into the clearing until their red eyes locked onto the human bodies gathered beneath the ship's shadow like an all-you-can-eat buffet—then they'd run.

Despite the imminent danger that the Mad cast on them, Caitlin couldn't help but enjoy herself. Her blade sang as it whistled through the air, and she was impressed by how many of her people had grabbed their weapons and come to her aid as well.

Not that she needed any help.

For every one they took down, Caitlin was on her fifth. She was exhilarated. She was on fire.

Just like teaching a girl to dance. Only instead of twirling and frolicking to music, I get to save lives and destroy evil.

Fuckety fuck, this is awesome.

When a teen girl with a foaming mouth and blistered sores came at her, she lunged at her, grabbing her with both arms. She side-stepped so quickly the zombie fell forward in a daze. She picked herself up quickly, found her again, and took another charge.

"Oopsy-daisy!"

Caitlin booted her square in the chest. The girl fell back on her ass.

"You! Toss me your blade," she commanded an older gentleman who was being overly cautious considering the fight happening around him.

He obliged.

"Thanks. Now, keep an eye on this one for me for a second." She drove the man's blade directly between the Mad girl's shoulder blades, then tossed the knife back to him.

She caught up with Ash at the edge of the clearing. Alice had joined him, staying close as they worked together for both defense and attack. Occasionally, they'd stand back to back and Ash would cop a feel of Alice's ass.

She didn't seem to mind.

He drove his sword into the throat of a zombie to his left, withdrew it with a haunting sound of a boot pulled out of a thick slick of mud, then turned and focused on the guy creeping up behind him. With a sweet figure-of-eight maneuver with the sword and a grunt as Ash used all his strength, both the zombie's arms were gone.

Note to self. Get Ash to teach me that sweet-ass move before I die.

Ash noticed Caitlin. "Thanks...for saving me back then. I haven't had a chance to—"

"Don't mention it," Caitlin said. "Behind you."

He turned, his eyes widening as he stepped in to take down a zombie about to chomp into Alice's back. "Watch your six, girl!" he admonished Alice, rolling his eyes.

"Sure!" she replied, sticking her butt out at him. "The minute you *stop* watching it."

"Just focus, will you?" Caitlin said, though the smile on her face was enough for him to know she wasn't totally serious. "I'm not ready to lose you guys yet."

"Aw, is Cat getting sentimental?" Alice chirped. "I haven't seen that side of her."

"It'll disappear just as quick if you're not careful."

Eventually, the Mad stopped coming from the trees.

Caitlin looked at her people and saw that there were now only three Mad remaining—and they were certainly in the losing camp. For each Mad left, there was now four of her own group hacking and slashing and working together to bring them down. Their blade-work might not have been that sophisticated—in fact, they almost reminded Caitlin of cavemen with clubs—but dammit, it was a sight to see.

"You need a name for them," Ash said, wrapping his blood-slicked arm around Alice's shoulder. "Something badass we can use when we tell this story in years to come."

Caitlin considered this. She liked the idea of finding a name for what she was creating. The pride in her stomach grew as two Mad remained.

Then one.

"How about the Kitty Cat club?" Alice smirked, looking up at Caitlin.

If Caitlin could have made her eyes glow red with rage, that would have been the moment. She kind of envied Mary-Anne in that way.

"Nah, not badass enough," Ash said. "How about 'The Catastrophics?'"

"Catastrophics make us sound like a bunch of clumsy killers!" Alice replied, smacking Ash in the arm. "And you thought my idea was dumb."

"At least my idea doesn't make us sound like a petting zoo. The Kitty Cat club? Sounds like something I'd take my kids to, if I had any."

Ash and Alice went on bickering as Caitlin watched the last zombie get taken down by her collective team now gathered together and working as one. The zombie screeched once more then went silent as sword and dagger tore the thing apart. A nasty business, really, but in a kill or be killed world, what other choice did they have?

Caitlin knew then, smiling like a mother watching her children play together for the first time, that they were on to something huge. Something different. Something that would take the survivors of the world out of hiding and towards something greater.

"The Revolutionaries," Caitlin said.

Alice and Ash stopped arguing

"The Revolutionaries?" Ash rubbed his chin, leaving a red smudge there.

Alice watched the folks now heading back towards them with smiles on their faces. They stopped as they noticed the zombie Caitlin had left spiked to the ground wriggle and thrash to try and tear itself free.

A couple of them looked up at Caitlin as if for permission. She nodded. They drove their swords into the zombie's body until they were sure it was dead.

"The Revolutionaries." She pondered the idea a little more. "Yeah. I like the sound of that."

New Leaf, Silver Creek Forest

They had walked for so long that Hank had begun to think they were now lost. His patience was shrinking, and he wanted nothing more than to settle the score and destroy the girl who had caused him so many problems.

The message that she had given to Tyrell to deliver to the governor played round and round in his head. If he played his cards right, it was most certainly a message that would never be delivered. He could envision himself popping off her head, shitting on her body, and setting the damn thing on fire.

Just the thought of it made him smile.

When the village came into sight, his heart began to thump excitedly in his chest. It had been years since he had journeyed so far from his town, and much had changed. There were new houses, the borders of the barbed wire fence had grown wider...

And there were body parts all over the place.

Holy fucksticks.

"What the hell happened here?" one of his men whispered from behind.

"Draw swords, gentlemen," Hank said, drawing his own. "We don't know what we're facing here."

Hendrick stepped closer to Hank's side. "You think it's her, sir? You think it's the ranger master's sister?"

"What do you think?" Hank scoffed openly, not bothering to even try to hide his disdain.

"I think so. I saw her work her blade at the manor. Terrifying stuff," Hendrick said solemnly.

Hank glared at him. "Was that before or after you got violated by a vampire? Learn when a question is rhetorical, Hendrick."

They explored the village together. Hank had brought thirty of his finest men with him for the task in the hopes that they could bring the whole ordeal to a swift conclusion. Hey, maybe even catch the vampire as she slept and drag her back to the town. He didn't know for sure, but based on what Tyrell had told him—and how weak and ill the vampire had looked back at the manor—he considered it a definite possibility.

The houses were all empty, except for two. In one house—that he could only really assume was Big Bill's' since he'd found the fucker dead as a doornail beneath the bed—he found Petri and Ewan, two of his men, bound and gagged on the floor.

They were fast asleep at first, their lips cracked and dry. He charged one of his men with the task of bringing them round by splashing water on their faces and cutting their bonds. They each sat on the bed, rubbing their wrists and neck.

"Soldier, report," Hank commanded with little compassion. He had been ready for a good killing today, and it looked like he wasn't going to get it.

"She's the devil," Petri said, clutching the skin of water he had been chugging. "She's the devil."

"Who is she?" Hank asked, already certain he knew but needing that final confirmation.

Ewan answered. Hank turned his head. "There was three of them. Two human girls and a...and a—"

"Vampire?" Hank interrupted.

The soldier nodded. "She fed on us."

"Shit," Hank said, scanning over his men who all looked to be instantly afraid of what they were hearing.

"Where did they go?" He moved down to his comrades' level, inches from their faces. "C'mon, soldier. I need to know. Tell me where they went, and I'll make it worth your while. I can get you the governor's favor in a heartbeat. I can make your life a dream when we get back to town. Just tell me which way they went."

Ewan and Petri looked at each other. "I don't know. They left us here and took half the village with them."

Shit, Hank thought. Well, what the fuck was he supposed to do now with no leads? All he had were two beaten-down soldiers, a flock of men, and a field full of blood.

He looked at the floor and spotted something which took his interest. A spare rope, frayed and cut, lay askew on the floor.

"Whose is that?" Hank said, threatening to explode once more.

The guards were silent.

"Whose. Is. That?" Hank bellowed.

Ewan answered. "It's Ash's. They set him free, and he left some time ago. We've not seen him come back."

"He's with *her*?"

"We don't know," Petri said, looking at the floor. "They sent him on his way before they left. Told him to go back to Silver Creek. As far as we know, that's where he's heading."

Hank looked out the window, imagining the guard running through the trees, sprinting back to join them in the safety of the Creek. He didn't expect to see the head poking up, staring through the window.

The man ducked out of the way.

"Get him!" Hank shouted.

A second later, several guards returned into the house with the man wriggling between their clutches. They threw him at Hank's feet. He looked around as if for an escape, but clearly knew it was useless.

"Enjoying the view?" Hank asked, using the rusted end of his blade to force the man's chin up. His eyes were slits, red and bloodshot. "Give me one good reason why I shouldn't use your body to give this place a fresh coat of paint."

"Because I know which way they went!" the rat-man said with a hungry look in his eye, nodding as he spoke. "Please. I can take you to them. I promise. Please don't kill me."

"Excellent," Hank said, turning sharply and slicing his sword across the necks of Petri and Ewan. Blood poured from their throats and waterfalled down their bodies. They slid down and flopped onto the floor.

A smile lingered on Hank's face. If he could use the rat-man to find the rest of the crew, what need did he have for the two guards who had managed to get themselves captured?

Silver Creek Forest

Mary-Anne looked back over her shoulder at Kain as they marched through the forest. Truth be told, he was pissing her off. When she had taken refuge at her old manor last night, it had been with the intention of being able to speed back over to Caitlin and the ship the moment darkness fell.

Now, she had a werewolf trailing behind her, walking so slowly that it felt like her own feet were melting into the ground.

"Will you hurry the fuck up?" she said, trying her best not to go super vamp and simply rip his head off. "The last time I saw a Were move this slowly, it had no head and had painted my bedroom walls in blood." She was exaggerating, of course.

Well, about the painting part.

That fucker was definitely left with no head.

Though she'd had many dealings with Weres in the past —whole packs defending their territories, single Weres sent on a mission, and at one point, a whole army of Weres and vamps battling together and clashing swords—it now felt like so long ago that she wondered if she truly remembered them properly. Surely even a human could walk faster than this shitbag?

"What's the rush? It's a beautiful night. Let's take in the view." He nodded to where the stars shone brightly in the black sky. "I can't remember the last time I merely slowed down and enjoyed the world."

Just like a Were to be difficult.

Mary-Anne stopped. "Okay, look. Here's the deal. You shift your ass into whatever cute, fluffy animal you turn into, and we'll both run on. If you don't, I'll run ahead without you. I'm doing *you* a favor here. You want to tag along with *me*. Not the other way around."

"Don't flatter yourself, sweet-fangs," Kain said. "Besides, Weres can't change as easily as that anymore. Not in today's world. Don't you know anything?"

Kain saw the blank expression on Mary-Anne's face.

"Oh...you don't know, do you?" Kain said.

Though it was only a small detail, Mary-Anne couldn't help but feel a little pissed at the intimation that Kain currently had one up on her. She wanted to ask for more but didn't want him to know she had actually been asleep and in hiding for so long that a lot of the world had slipped by her. All she knew was that vampire-kind were all either being hunted out or turned into zombies. She had no idea what was happening in the wider world with humans, much less with Weres.

"I might know."

"No, you don't. You know nothing." Kain grinned, jogged to catch up with Mary-Anne, and they began walking.

He waited a moment as if thinking about where to start, then said, "The world has changed out there. I don't know if you're one of those ancient-ass vamps who roamed around centuries ago with the Queen Bitch or how much you know of the cities and life before the Madness hit, but since the arrival of the zombies, there have been changes everywhere across the world—or at least, as far as I have traveled and heard."

As if to illustrate his point, through the shadows of the trees, they could see the rusted wreckage of what appeared to be an old vehicle. It could have been a car, or even a boat, at some point. With the wear of time and weather, it was difficult to tell.

"No shit, Springsteen. I've noticed."

"At first the changes were subtle—at least in Weres," Kain continued. "A human contracts the Madness and they go freakin' wild in just a day or two. Zero to zombie, man. Crazy. But with Weres, it's different. There's something in the Were blood that the Madness can't quite get into. Weres don't go Mad. Weres just begin to struggle with their abilities. Something begins to break."

Despite herself, Mary-Anne took an interest. "What do you mean? Like, in the nanocytes? You turn into birds and rabbits instead of ravenous beasties?"

Kain laughed. "I wish. My uncle was a Wererabbit, and let me tell you, stick him with a group of Werebears and wolves, and you've got yourself a tasty fucking meal. I was picking parts of Uncle Hethbert out of my teeth for weeks."

Mary-Anne turned in shock. "You didn't!"

Kain slapped his leg and doubled over laughing. "Of course not!" He struggled to talk between fits of laughter. "Could you imagine...a tiny little...rabbit... That would be...hysterical—"

"Are you going to finish your story?" Mary-Anne restrained the urge to yell or better yet, slap him silly. She felt herself grow red. She couldn't decide if she was enjoying this asshole's company. One minute, she was fascinated by his story, the next minute, he was setting her up as the butt of another joke. If she didn't have so much patience, he'd be somewhere behind her, buried so far into the ground that it would take him a week to climb out.

"Okay...okay..." Kain said, wiping the tears from his eyes. "But seriously, no. It doesn't so much affect *what* we change into, more just...*how* we change. It's almost as if the transformations now are a gun with a limited number of bullets. Those who didn't cotton on early enough got caught out in the trap, but myself and, sadly, a fair number of the assholes from my old pack learned quickly enough to keep our transformation in our reserve tank. Last thing we want is to have to make the choice."

"What do you mean, 'the choice?'"

"Put simply...with every transformation into and out of our animal forms, it gets harder and harder to go back." Kain pulled the sleeve of his cloak up to reveal an arm covered in hair so thick and wiry that it didn't look human. He showed the other arm and revealed the same.

Mary-Anne's eyes widened. She grabbed his arm and pulled it towards her. "This is wolf hair?"

"You know it. Hair from my wolf form." He pulled away suddenly and covered his arms back up. "At some point, all us Weres have got to make the choice. Do we stay as a human, or do we choose to stay as our animal counterparts?"

"And what will you choose?" Mary-Anne asked, trying to imagine which side of the coin she would prefer if she were given a choice: human or Were?

Ah, who was she kidding? Human every time. Who'd want to spend their life as a filthy animal?

"I don't know yet. All I do know is that I need to buy more time. No more changes for me unless I can't help it—or at least until I've made a decision." Kain exhaled into the air with the weight of his burden.

"You best be goddamn handy with a blade, then, because you're going to be a whole lot of useless compared to the Weres I'm used to dealing with." Mary-Anne glanced up and down at the skinny guy walking next to her. His clothes hung so loose they looked like folds of old skin.

"Oh, don't worry, sweet-fangs. You don't get this far in a world turned Mad without learning a few tricks along the way," he said with a cocky wink her way.

Mary-Anne turned her nose up and put her attention back on the forest in front of them. "Yeah. That's exactly the response I'd expect for a guy who got captured by humans."

Kain opened his mouth to retort, then obviously thought better of it and closed it.

Yeah, damn right, pooch. We'll call that one-one.

They walked a little longer, exchanging idle chatter about their kinds. After a short distance, Mary-Anne found herself growing impatient, realizing they still had another mile or so to go before they arrived back at the airship. By that point, who knew what she'd return to. Things were changing so thick and fast these days that it was almost impossible to keep up.

But, fuck it. Caitlin was driving this rollercoaster, and she was strapped in for the ride.

Mary-Anne stopped. "Hop on."

"What?" Kain said, taken aback. He looked at Mary-Anne doubled over and wondered what the hell was going on. "You might think twice about offering a stranger some booty in the forest. Trust me. Things crawl in holes that they shouldn't, birds fly down and target your dangly things...truly, it's a whole big mess—"

"Onto my back, *wolf.*" She couldn't contain the annoyance in her voice. The idea that *she*, a vampire, would want to be mounted by a Were. She shuddered at the thought. "I'm tired of holding back at your pace because of your identity crisis. Either climb on or be left behind. You have three seconds. I won't ask again."

"You're not serious—"

"One," Mary-Anne began.

"Seriously? Why don't we jog together? I don't want to be piggybacked like a—"

"Two," she continued.

"Ah, fuck!" Kain said, submitting at last and throwing his hands in the air. "I swear to cow that if you don't put me down *before* we get to the camp, I'm going to...*woooooah!*"

Mary-Anne turned the throttle to eleven, her grin stretching from ear to ear at hearing the wind knock the air out of that smug bastard's body.

It didn't matter what day she woke up, it always paid to be a vamp.

CHAPTER EIGHTEEN

Abandoned Airship, Silver Creek Forest, Ontario

Caitlin stood at the front of the ship and stared at the night sky. Thanks to the angle that the ship had landed in, the tip extended high enough that she could see above the canopy of trees. Constellations sparkled above her, and for the first time in as long as she could remember, she felt at peace.

Her crew slept below deck. A little way off on the grass was a small fire where Alice could be seen talking with two Revolutionaries. One or two volunteers had agreed to share their time, keeping watch alongside someone who had fast become one of her closest companions.

In all the days she had lived in Silver Creek, tucked tightly behind its walls and dreaming of what lay beyond, she had never really had any true friends.

Well, besides her dog and brother. And you couldn't exactly count those, right?

Jaxon sat by her side. She reached down idly and

stroked the dog's head. He nuzzled into her leg, making sweet noises of affection.

She wondered how it could be that her reality had been so altered so fast. Not only had she learned that vampires were more than legends or myth, but also that Trisk ruled more than only Silver Creek from his golden throne in the town's parapets. They had journeyed a short distance outside of what many rangers had called the "safe zone," and there they had found a village. A village as oppressed as Silver Creek.

Well, maybe even more so.

How many more towns and villages lay out beyond the trees? Were any cities still standing now? It was nearly three hundred years since the fabled World's Worst Day ever—a bedtime story of when the world exploded in a rain of fire and the population was decimated. How many more bedtime stories would turn out to be true?

Caitlin knelt beside Jaxon and looked up at the stars. "You know, boy, we're on to something amazing here. If we play this right, we just might be able to make it so that no more Kiera's may ever have to die. We might never cure the Madness or find a way to stop it from spreading, but if we can unite enough people to rebuild a society like the old days tell of, then that might be enough."

Jaxon licked Caitlin's cheek and placed his front paws on her knees. His tail wagged so madly that she wondered if he'd take off into the sky.

"As long as we've got each other—" Caitlin began. Jaxon let out a low bark and turned towards the three figures huddled by the fire. "Oh, of course." She laughed. "Who could forget them? As long as *we* all stick together, we just might make it."

Caitlin made her way down the ship's slant and waited for a moment in the shadows beyond the fire's reach, listening to the low sounds of voices. She made herself known at a natural break in the conversation and sat and spoke to Alice and her companions—a man with jet-black hair and a missing eye named Marvin, and the girl who had been the first to declare her allegiance at New Leaf, Belle. They both wore clothes that were now caked in mud and blood from their encounter with the Mad.

They spoke for an hour or so, exchanging stories and laughing.

It was as Ash emerged from the ship with his two companions for the watch, rubbing his eyes and yawning, that they heard the sound of a twig snapping somewhere in the forest. As one, the seven Revolutionaries drew their weapons and waited. They formed a near-perfect line of warriors with swords and daggers—one of Ash's companions had even found a mace from somewhere in Mary-Anne's pile of weapons—and watched the trees.

"What do we do?" Belle asked, her voice shaking but her hand steady.

"Let's not be hasty, now. Let them come to us." She looked from side-to-side with a smug grin, wondering at what moment they'd see the glow of red eyes.

Silver Creek Forest

"How much further?" Hank asked, feeling his tired feet beginning to drag. They had followed the rat-man for what seemed like hours now, and day had turned to night. In his head, Hank had envisioned traveling to New Leaf, killing Caitlin and any who stood in his way as an example to the rest of the town, then heading back to the safety of Silver Creek.

That did not happen.

Now, he looked around nervously, feeling like every shadow and rustle was someone out to get them. This was the whole goddamn reason he never became a ranger. How the hell did they put up with feeling like an attack could come every second?

But he wouldn't show his fear to his men, not now.

No way, no how.

They paused rather abruptly when they saw firelight in the distance. The rat-man turned to Hank and waved an arm as if to present what he had found.

"Just ahead through the trees. Draw your weapons. Remain quiet until the last possible moment," he said.

Hank looked down at the rat-man with contempt. "*I* give the orders here." He turned to his men. "Draw your weapons. Remain quiet until the last possible moment. If you find the rebel bitch, leave her to me. My sword is more than ready to acquaint itself with her throat."

The guards nodded, drawing their steel.

They ran ahead, emerging into the small clearing where a tiny campfire burned. Insects swarmed around its light, but there were no people to be seen.

Hank whirled around, looking in every direction. "What the—" He looked for the rat-man but found that he was nowhere to be seen.

Realization dawned, and he felt himself grow crimson.

Rage burned hotter than the fire inside him and he clenched his fists, roaring to the stars. *"Fuuuuuck! Shit, damn, balls, frick, shitty-twat-smack, fuuuuuuuuck!"*

Somewhere far off in the trees, he heard the rat-man laughing.

"We've been tricked, haven't we, sir?" an innocent-looking guard asked as he scratched his head.

Hank could almost see the rage etched onto every line of his own face. Without a word, he swung his sword and removed the guard's head in one clean blow.

The head flew through the air, landing with a *thump* next to the fire. Some embers escaped and caught its hair on fire. Soon, the whole thing was alight, and the smell of cooked meat began to waft around them.

Hank stood with his shoulders rising and falling, his back hunched with anger. He spoke to the remainder of his men who stood patiently, awaiting their next orders.

"Anyone else here think we were tricked?" he asked through gritted teeth. Every guard shook their heads as one. "Good. And that's how the story stays. If I hear anyone tell anybody about this, they'll wake up with their head next to their body. Understood?"

They all nodded.

"What do we do now, sir?" another guard asked, looking nervously at the trees around them.

"We make our way back. We re-group, rest up. Tomorrow morning, we double the Silver Creek defenses."

"Double? But, sir, we're already low on men as it is." He looked at the melting face in the fire. "You really think the girl is that much of a threat—"

The guard stopped talking when *his* head was also removed.

"Any more questions?" Hank asked.

A round of heads shaking was the only response.

"That's what I thought."

Abandoned Airship, Silver Creek Forest, Ontario

"I was starting to get worried about you, Ma," Caitlin said when they saw Mary-Anne appear through the trees. She wasn't alone. Along the way, she had found another man, though this person was strange to look at.

Skinny as fuck with a cloak that swallowed him, when he lowered his hood and introduced himself, she saw that his skin was covered in scars. Whatever this guy's story was, he had definitely been through some shit.

"Never worry about a vampire, Cat. We can hold our own," Mary-Anne replied, glancing along the line up of men and women standing beside Caitlin. "Seems you've kept yourself busy today."

"I'll sleep when I'm dead," Caitlin replied.

"That can be arranged." Mary-Anne winked.

"And who is this?" Caitlin eyed the new guy up and down. "You look like a scrotum had sex with a tree trunk."

"I guess that could be taken as a compliment." The man's voice was low and croaky. His eyes fixed on hers in a kind of mild amusement. "The name's Kain. I'm an... acquaintance...of Mary-Anne's. We encountered each other out in the forest, and when she spoke of a woman looking to overthrow the governor and exact revenge, I found it hard not to say that I wanted in."

Caitlin cocked an eyebrow as they sat by the fire and offered around chunks of cooked deer that they had hunted earlier that night. "You know him?"

"I was a prisoner. It was only recently I made my escape," Kain said between mouthfuls of meat. He didn't worry about manners, tearing at the flesh and sucking every bit of juice off the bone he could manage.

Not that Caitlin could blame him. If she looked as skinny as Kain did, she'd be tempted to grab a knife and fork and tuck into every one of the Revolutionaries.

"A prisoner? My brother is a prisoner in there. Did you see him? Did you see Dylan?" Caitlin leaned forward, the fire lighting the desperation in her face. "Tell me you did."

Kain nodded. "Yep. Hell of a guy. Can't sing for shit."

He then proceeded to tell them all about his experience in the dungeon, and how he had come face-to-face with their governor and managed to escape. He left out the parts about how or even the reasons why Trisk had him imprisoned but focused more on the setup of the guards and his time speaking with Dylan.

The whole time, Mary-Anne watched him without blinking, seeming to try to judge his words and read his mind.

Could vampires do that?

She couldn't remember.

As the night wore on and the next watch came out to take their turn, nobody left the fireside. Talk turned to plans and tactics. Under Caitlin's instructions, they were to divide into smaller sub-groups of Revolutionaries, each led by those whom she had formed a bond with and trusted. There were twenty-three of them in total, which meant that Alice was assigned six people to lead, Ash was given six, and Mary-Anne was given seven.

She figured Mary-Anne would appreciate Kain's company.

Well, from the disdainful look Kain gave Mary-Anne as she dished out instructions, she thought it wouldn't be long before *they* visited the land of bumping uglies.

Hate leads to love, right?

They sketched out the lay of the land on an old piece of parchment someone had found on board the ship. It was dry and cracked, and they needed to be careful not to tear the paper as Mary-Anne sketched a rough outline of the forest and the way back to Silver Creek.

"So, if we were to walk a straight line, we'd reach the Creek within two hours. But we're not walking a straight line, so it will take a little longer. If you're planning on going tonight, Cat, I'd advise against it." Mary-Anne looked up at the sky which was already beginning to turn the light purples of dawn. "The sun will be out before long, and as much as I'd love to join you in its light, I've left my sunscreen at home."

There was a chorus of laughter at that.

Caitlin looked fondly around at those gathered by the fire. All but a few had awoken now and sat around its dying embers.

Alice said, "I think you'd look great with a tan, Ma."

"Don't tell me that name is catching," Mary-Anne said, glaring at Caitlin.

She shrugged in response and smiled. "What can I say, the people want what the people want. If you're set on giving nicknames, be ready to get your own back."

"Yeah, sweet-fangs. Lighten up," Kain said as another rumble of laughter rippled around the circle.

Mary-Anne furrowed her brow.

"Besides, we're still not ready yet," Caitlin said. She addressed the whole group. "Though everyone here has shown a capability with a weapon beyond what I could have already imagined, there is still work to be done. Techniques to be refined. In three days' time, we will be marching on Silver Creek, ready to overthrow the governor and begin to build the old ways of the world. Hundreds of years ago, there were cities, great colonies of people who lived together in harmony. Technology we can only dream of now. But even they had to have started somewhere, right? Some small group of Revolutionaries who paved the way and removed any dictators who stood in their way. That is who we must become. That is what we will now share with the world, and work together to liberate those oppressed by others, so that we can have a brighter tomorrow."

"Yeah!" Ash and Alice said, standing up.

"Together, we can take our heads out of the sand, and we can build the world we want to see. Together, we can claim back the cities and tear those down who don't share our vision of a world where folks can walk free and live their lives without fear of punishment, without fear of the Mad."

One-by-one, eyes widened and gleamed as all attention turned to Caitlin.

"Do you swear this oath, my Revolutionaries, to stand beside me and join me on this mission? Never faltering. Forever loyal. For a future of hope, love, and life?"

To their surprise, Caitlin drew her sword and sliced it across her palm. She walked to the center of the fire, aware that Mary-Anne's eyes were now fixed on her hand, her nostrils flaring as she smelled the blood, and squeezed her palm. Several globs of red dripped into the fire, landing with an audible hiss as they did.

Mary-Anne gulped.

"Maybe you should make yourself scarce for this next bit," Caitlin said quietly for Mary-Anne. "Unfortunately, I'm not making a mini buffet for you."

"Such a waste," Mary-Anne said, her hands gripping so tightly to the floor beneath her that they dug deep into the soil.

"So...who's with me?" Caitlin cried.

One by one, the Revolutionaries joined Caitlin in the middle of the circle. They each took a blade to their palm, wincing as the metal parted the skin, and dripped their contribution onto the fire. The old man who Caitlin had rescued earlier that day ran back onto the ship and emerged with linen which he handed out to the others to stem the bleeding and keep the wounds clean.

Caitlin kept an eye on Mary-Anne, aware that this would be difficult for her. The vampire's eyes pulsed with a dull red glow the entire time, though she did well to stay put. It was only when Alice stepped up that she let a moan escape her lips.

Linen was passed to Alice, but she refused, instead choosing to sit next to Mary-Anne.

"I'll trade. You have a sip, you heal me."

Mary-Anne bit her lip. "No...I can't."

"Honestly, it's fine. We wouldn't be here if you hadn't have helped in New Leaf. It's fine. Go."

A gentle wash of relief fell across Mary-Anne. She nodded, drew out her fangs, and sucked gently on Alice's palm—much to the disgust of Ash and several others sitting nearby. When she was done, she popped a hole into her wrist with one fang and offered it to Alice.

"What are you doing?" Alice said.

"Drink. Yours will heal faster."

Alice hesitated, then drank a mouthful of the warm vamp's blood. She closed her eyes, then opened them wide as, within seconds, the gash on her hand healed.

A few Revolutionaries now looked at their own hands, bandaged in blood-soaked linen, then back at Alice and Mary-Anne with a hint of jealousy.

They looked away when Mary-Anne's red eyes caught them.

"I'm not a reservoir for you to drink from," she muttered.

They remained by the fire until the embers died. As sunlight hit the horizon, Mary-Anne made herself scarce, finding refuge in her dark cabin beneath the deck of the ship. It occurred to her that just over a hundred years ago, a group of vampires, Weres, and humans might have done exactly the same.

Caitlin left Ash and Alice to train their groups, finding that Kain was also a fair hand with a sword. While Mary-Anne's group waited for the vampire to rise when the moon did, Kain took position as her number two without question, teaching techniques which Caitlin watched and learned for her own practice in her cabin.

Caitlin retired to her bedroom at some point before midday. What with Mary-Anne working on a nocturnal schedule, she had begun to feel her body begging to do the same.

Not for the first time, she imagined what life must be like as a vampire. How fun it would be to be so damn kickass that no other creature could stop you in a fight.

Speed, strength, heightened senses, prolonged life—was there even a downside?

Then why the hell was Mary-Anne following Caitlin's orders? She wasn't quite sure, but even the mere fact that she was gave her confidence a boost. If she had to get used to a vampire's sleeping schedule, then so be it. She would do whatever it took to get the best results.

And, as far as she knew, no one in Silver Creek had a vampire fighting beside them.

When Caitlin's head hit the pillows, she dreamed of pirates. The abandoned ship she slept on was soaring high in the sky. She captained the helm in clothes so lavish that they seemed impossible to create. A purple leather jacket fell to her knees, and a large-brimmed tricorn hat shone black in the sunlight.

And on the deck in front of her, an ensemble of twenty-two of the best damn pirates the world had ever seen had gathered. They weren't fighting for gold, nor coin.

They were fighting for fucking justice.

CHAPTER NINETEEN

Prison District, Silver Creek

Sullivan adjusted the collar of his shirt and poked his head around the corner of the building he stood beside. He could see the stairway up to the parapets which would lead onwards to the jailhouse. Stationed at the bottom of the stairs was a set of guards standing to attention, looking like nothing more than statues as people milled on by.

"What's the situation?" Sykes, a short ranger with a ginger beard asked. He stood behind Sullivan, trying eagerly to catch a glimpse ahead. "Have they gone yet? Have they moved?"

Behind Sykes, a man with a grim face and a wide brow remained silent, his arms folded. Sullivan already knew that Carl wasn't happy to be there with them. But after three days of watching over guard patterns and trying to figure out how the fuck he could free Dylan, they were in far too deep now to pull back.

"Not yet." Sullivan spoke in a hushed tone, elbowing behind him.

Sykes hopped around impatiently. "Why not? It's time, right?"

Sullivan glanced at the sun. "Not quite. Almost, though. Take your positions."

Sykes made a funny little *squee* and stepped out from the shadows. Carl rolled his eyes and followed. Sullivan watched and waited as Sykes moved to the center of the thoroughfare and waited, seemingly at ease and adjusting his boots. Carl held back slightly, busying himself with a fruit cart that had stopped at the side of the path.

They had all dressed in casual clothes. While most people knew everyone and would instantly recognize a couple of rangers after seeing their faces, it was worth the attempt to try and blend in. At least then, they wouldn't be so conspicuous.

The time came. Two men in armor approached the guards, waved a greeting, and changed places with them. Carl and Sykes watched as the two guards who had been relieved began marching away. Sullivan followed them both, trying to pick his target.

When one of the guards split off and headed down a side street, Sullivan pursued. After another turn, the guard was alone and out of sight.

Sucks to be him!

Sullivan pounced from behind and smacked him on the back of the head with a rock, and the guard fell unconscious. Not two minutes later, he emerged into the square, clad in the guard's armor. It was a clumsy fit. He felt sick wearing it. The smell inside was cloying and nauseating.

What would the rangers think of me if they saw me now?

He nodded to Carl and Sykes who understood their cue and rolled into position.

When Sykes was a few feet away from the guards, Carl sprinted at him, lowering his shoulder and knocking him to the floor. The two began to scrap, throwing blows left and right as rehearsed. Neither made any real effort to hurt the other as they knew what was coming.

They rolled around on the floor, moving closer to the guards. One of Carl's legs kicked out and booted the guard in the shin.

"Hey! Watch it," the guard said.

Carl rose. "Or what? What's an itty-bitty guard man going to do about it? Go suck on the governor's titty or whatever it is you guys do when you want some action."

That was all it took.

The guard moved towards Carl who turned and moved off. The guard gave chase.

The second guard was so distracted by it all that he wasn't aware that Sykes had moved behind him. He reached towards the guard's hip and removed the sword out of its sheath.

"I always did like a long prick," Sykes said, holding it high where the guard could see it.

"Oi, give that back!" the man said, suddenly torn between remaining at his station or giving chase to the weed who had stolen his sword.

He decided on the latter. What good was he without his weapon? He was like a porcupine without its quills.

Sullivan grinned from the sidelines. The whole thing had gone *so* much better than planned. He'd have to buy

Sykes and Carl a drink or something to say thank you after this was over.

If none of them ended up in jail before then.

With a final look over his shoulder, Sullivan headed up the stairs, navigating the parapets as best he could in the leather armor he now wore. No one batted an eyelid.

This is crazy, he thought, feeling his hands shaking from the adrenaline. He had never dreamed it would be so easy to distract and take down a guard. Now, though, came the real challenge. He could only study so much of the route before realizing he would have to do the rest of it blind. No one, neither ranger nor citizen, ever saw the dark corridors that led to the jails unless they were stupid enough to get caught.

Two more guards were stationed further along the wall, a set of stairs leading down just beyond them.

Sullivan's heart thudded as he approached. They could have been statues, but for the gentle rise and fall of their chest.

"Halt, who goes there?" one of the guards said, stepping forward.

A sudden stroke of inspiration hit Sullivan. "Step down, maggot. I've got direct orders from Captain Hank Newman to deliver a message to the prisoners." The guards looked at each other nervously.

"We can pass on your message," the guards said.

"Afraid not. The Captain has instructed that I deliver the message directly."

The men seemed to contemplate this, eyeing Sullivan with suspicion until he added, "Do I need to report to the captain that I have been delayed in my task?"

To his delight, they stepped back into position and shook their heads. "Of course not. Go ahead now. Give our regards to the captain."

Sullivan passed them by, not daring to look them in the eye.

God, this was so easy. How did I not think of this before? Even the guards are so scared of the governor that they won't question his orders.

He took a left and found his way down a set of stairs. Immediately, darkness closed in, and he could guess from the smell that he was in the right place. A mixture of urine, hay, and desperation greeted him with a vengeance. Instinctively, he clapped a hand over his nose and mouth until he adjusted to the stench.

His footsteps echoed as he descended. At the bottom of the stairs, he found a corridor lit by torches. At the end of the corridor were two more guards.

Wow, the animals really did come in two by two, *hurrah...* Sullivan thought back to the children's stories he had read as a child, tatty tomes with crusted yellow pages.

This time, he had an inkling that the guards wouldn't let him pass so easily. He was in the right place. Lining the walls were iron bars, and beyond the guards was total darkness.

The smaller of the guards called a challenge, putting his hand on the hilt of his sword.

Sullivan tried repeating what he had said to the guards above. Twice was the charm, right?

"And *I've* got direct orders not to allow anyone through without the governor present. Do you have a signed order, or maybe you've got the governor there behind you?" the smaller guard replied.

"I doubt the fat lard-ass could hide behind anyone," the other guard mumbled.

"Hey, now, that's the kind of talk that could land you on the other side of the bars." The smaller guard paused, then said under his breath, "If the bubble butt ever finds out."

Interesting...

"You best watch your tone, soldier. I'll hightail it up those stairs right now and tell Trisk what you said, word-for-word, without even looking back. That what you want?" Sullivan tried his best to put on an intimidating voice but wasn't sure it was really effective. He actually had quite a soft voice for a grown man.

The smaller guard immediately stood at attention at that, a look of curiosity dancing across his eyes. "And what is it that *you* want?"

Sullivan stepped forward. The two guards stepped towards him.

"Ah, what the hell," Sullivan said, removing his helmet and throwing it on the ground. "I want to knock your asses to Kingdom come and rescue my captain."

He moved before the guards had a chance to think. Dashing ahead, he reached forward, grasped a handful of each guard's hair in his hands, and smashed them together like two coconuts. There was a hollow noise, followed by their grunts, then they both folded to the floor.

"I guess Mama was right. Actions do speak louder than words," he said, running into the dark.

. . .

Silver Creek, Silver Creek Forest

Hank looked down at his new recruits with a look of disgust he found hard to conceal. A room full of nearly forty men all lined up and looking at him.

It was a sad display. Since the establishment of Silver Creek as a settlement, there had been strict guidelines and regimes in place to identify the best of the best from the boys who grew into men. Under Hank's careful scrutiny, only the strongest and most fearsome men had ever made it onto his guard force.

But this…

This was utterly humiliating.

Nearly half of the new recruits were still a summer or two out of reaching manhood. Several of the men were overweight, with a beer gut protruding so far out that he wondered what kind of armor would ever fit. And then there were those on the opposite side of the scale, who were so skinny that their arms looked like he could break them with a flick.

Still, desperate times called for desperate measures.

Hank addressed the room and gave everyone their orders. He wasn't the master wordsmith that the governor was known to be, but he could strike fear into those whom he wished to do his bidding.

He didn't mention the vampire.

He didn't even mention Caitlin.

What he did talk about was increasing security and ensuring that Silver Creek remained the safe haven that it had always been in a world gone Mad. This was their chance to bring honor to their families and future children.

As they filed out of the room, Hank dished out their

orders and gave them their weapons. These were as sad as the folks themselves. Though their smithy had worked his ass off to produce a horde of weapons on short notice, half the swords weren't even straight, and those that he did make were too short to stab anyone from a distance. Half of them looked like they might snap at any moment, much less cut through a person.

"You really think they're going to help our cause?" Hendrick asked, looking down his nose as the last new recruit filed out the room. "I've seen dead folks who look more useful."

"We need more numbers, Hendrick," Hank replied. He looked more tired than he had in months. Dark patches shadowed his eyes, and his stubble had grown into a thick carpet of gray and white hairs. "And, in case you've forgotten, there's a bitch, a vampire, and half a village heading our way that we need to be prepared for."

"Why don't we get some more women involved? Leon's wife is just as fearsome as any guard I've ever met. Only last week, he got into a scrap with her and ended up with a black eye."

"No," Hank snapped back. "No more women. We're still cleaning up the last mess we made when we got the ladies involved. They don't think like men. They're far too sensitive. Won't obey orders the same."

Hendrick opened his mouth to reply, then closed it when he saw the dark expression on Hank's face.

Hank sat a moment, listening to the voices in the streets as the excited new guards discussed their responsibilities with each other. He often forgot how much of an honor it was to serve the governor. Many men offered their lives each year, only to be turned down when they didn't quite meet the credentials required to join. Now, an entire new cohort had been given an opportunity to serve.

And likely die.

After taking the girl down and capturing the vamp.

Hopefully.

"What did Leon do to make his wife so pissed?" Hank asked.

"Something to do with sticking it to Mother Wendy."

Hank raised an eyebrow. "You're kidding?"

Hendrick shrugged.

"Well, let's go kick these deadbeats into gear," Hank said, rubbing his tired eyes. "We've got to make vampire hunters out of children."

Prison District, Silver Creek

At first, Sullivan could see nothing when he walked through the archway and into the gloom. He darted back and pulled a torch off the wall and waved it in front of him, squinting and covering his nose as he looked into the empty jail cells.

Hygiene didn't seem to be a factor here. Damp straw littered the floors, questionable stains clumping in patches and something dark and red that looked like blood.

"Dylan?" Sullivan whispered? "Captain?"

A gentle cough sounded to his left. He turned, shone the light in front of him, and saw Dylan tucked into the corner, wrapped up in his traveling cloak.

"About fucking time you showed up," Dylan croaked.

"What the hell are you doing here? The guards...they'll slaughter you if they catch you."

Sullivan smiled and held the bars. "They'll have to catch me first."

He nodded over to the entranceway where the two guards were unconscious on the floor.

"Nice," Dylan said, his grin growing wide. "But what are you supposed to do now? I heard the guards talking before, after I last saw the governor. Another prisoner escaped and ran off with the key. They say it was their only one, so unless you've got something strong enough to break through metal, I'm kind of trapped—"

Sullivan fished in his pocket and pulled out the key Kain had given to him. "You mean, like this?"

Dylan's eyes grew wide. "But...how? Does that mean you—" He checked to see that the guards were still unconscious. "You met him?"

"Who?" Sullivan asked, already fiddling with the key in the lock. "Oh, the Were?"

He said it so casually that Dylan was taken aback. "Kain? Yeah. Did you see it? Did you see him transform?"

The gate creaked open. Dylan stepped outside for the first time in several weeks. He stretched.

"No, he didn't transform. I did ask, though. He just made his eyes glow a bit. Was super creepy, to be honest."

Sullivan proceeded to tell Dylan about how he had helped Kain find his way outside the walls. He related how they had snuck him out as a ranger, then parted ways in the forest.

"And what of my sister? Is she alive? Is she home?"

Sullivan smiled, reeling off the information he had

overheard at Mother Wendy's tavern. Caitlin was very much alive and, it seemed, forming her own army to bring back to Silver Creek and storm the gates. Sullivan even filled Dylan in on Hank's recruitment efforts. Every man in town was jumping at the chance to join the ranks of the guards and serve the town to prove themselves to the governor.

"Shit. It's really starting to heat up right now," Dylan said, stroking his chin.

"Yeah. There's a storm coming," Sullivan replied.

"No, you idiot," Dylan said. "Watch that torch! It's catching on my cloak!"

Sullivan muttered an apology before they hurried out of the prison. Daylight filtered down the far end of the tunnel, illuminating the stairs.

Four guards now stood there with shit-eating grins on their faces.

"Well…fuckety fuck fuck *fuck*," Sullivan said.

"Hey, that's my line."

The guards drew their swords and pointed back to the cells, giving Dylan and Sullivan no choice but to obey.

Their captors closed the gate and muttered something about negligence as they kicked their comrades on the floor in turn as they passed.

They were gone not long after.

The idiots, fortunately, never thought of taking the key.

CHAPTER TWENTY

Abandoned Airship, Silver Creek Forest

Caitlin rose from bed with a smile on her face. Despite the years of wear on the ship, the bed was the most comfortable thing she had ever slept in. She was surrounded by some of the most amazing people she'd ever met, and training had gone better than planned across all teams. Ash, Mary-Anne, and even Alice were doing her proud.

She stood up, rubbed her eyes, and thought of her brother. It wasn't hard to imagine how his face would shine with joy when she rescued him. No matter what would happen over the next few days, she would try her hardest to ensure that hers was the first face Dylan would see when he was given his freedom.

And she couldn't wait.

She crossed the bedroom, running her hands along the furniture and trinkets that decorated the room. Oil lamps with no oil. Old posters and maps from journeys long gone. Scratches and holes in the wood from Lord only knew what.

On the floor, next to a dresser that had toppled to its side lay, a photo frame with an image inside. A man and woman stood side-by-side. They were beautiful together. Her hair was as light as his was dark, and they were clearly in love. She wondered what had happened to them. Perhaps they were the residents who had flown the ship, or maybe relatives or friends of the old captain.

Outside, the air was crisp and breezy. Caitlin stretched and strode down to the grass where Kain sat with two others around the dying embers of the fire.

"I was going to go out and fetch some wood, Caitlin," a man whom Caitlin had come to know as Vex said as she approached. "But Kain mentioned that today was the day we'd be moving out and not to bother. Is that true? Has it already been three days?"

Caitlin nodded. "That's right, beefcake." She said the words ironically, but they seemed to boost Vex's ego despite his skinny frame. "Best prepare to saddle up and take down the bad guys, because I need you all to bring your A-game today. Okay?"

Vex nodded, an eager look on his face.

"Go rouse the others," Caitlin said, nodding her head at the ship. "We leave in ten. Anyone left behind stays behind."

Did Caitlin want to leave anyone behind? Not really. But, dammit, she knew that if she wanted to lead the Revolutionaries, she would have to do so with a stern rule. They needed all the bodies she could get. But she needed them to work *for* her, too.

"What about Ma?" Vex asked, turning around as he ran halfway to the ship. "She can't travel in daylight."

Caitlin and Kain exchanged glances before he nodded. "We've got it covered."

Silver Creek Forest

They traveled through the woods in something close to silence. Caitlin led from the front atop Shitallion with Alice and Ash on one side and Kain and Jaxon on the other.

Following a little way behind, in three rows of two, six Revolutionaries carried a large handmade casket which housed the sleeping Mary-Anne. Over the last few days, Caitlin, Kain, and a few volunteers had worked their asses off to meet Mary-Anne's sleeping requirements. The casket was the exact height, depth, and width fit for a female vampire and, most importantly, was impervious to sunlight.

They hoped.

A goddamn genius contraption, if Caitlin did say so herself. A way to remain portable while living by the clock of a vampire.

At first, Mary-Anne had been impressed by the entire construction, climbing into the casket without hesitation. But now, it seemed that the ride was maybe not as smooth as she had wished. A couple of times along the way, one of the volunteers carrying her stumbled, causing the casket to dip and shake. They heard her muffled shouts from inside and, while the volunteers looked terrified at the prospect of facing Mary-Anne's wrath, Kain and Caitlin laughed into their hands.

"If you sons-of-bitches don't learn to drive steady, I'll find somewhere nice, cozy, and tight to stick those carrying poles right up into your—"

"They get it, Ma!" Caitlin called back, shutting Mary-Anne up in an instant.

Around midday, they started to slow their approach. Aware that they would soon reach Silver Creek's borders, they listened carefully for any sign of Mad or others lurking in the woods. While the sun made them feel much more at ease in the trees, they all knew the dangers that lurked out in the wild.

Many still had the zombie blood on their clothes from their last scrap.

Caitlin made a mental note to make them all scrub up when this was done. The last thing she wanted was to be the leader of a mucky group of tramps. Her group would be pristine, a proud band of heroes.

Caitlin looked down and smiled as Jaxon followed in step with Kain. It was strange, really. Jaxon had always been a fairly obedient dog—hell, that was the whole point of spending hours training him herself. But she had never seen him so at ease with a complete stranger, something that he certainly hadn't shown with Mary-Anne.

Before they set off, Jaxon had sniffed and sniffed at Kain, who had simply smiled and let him do it, proclaiming that he had always been a master of animals. They just loved him, or so he said.

But in the several hours they had now been walking, Jaxon hadn't taken his eyes off Kain once.

What the hell was that about?

Kain caught her eyes. "I told you, pooches just love me."

"Well, they do spend most of their time sniffing assholes," Caitlin replied. She looked for Ash and Alice, expecting to find them laughing, but they were deep in their own conversation.

Instead, the laugh came from behind.

Belle was carrying the front of the casket. Her laughter caused the pole to slip from her hand. The other five volunteers responded by re-balancing and countering the drop.

"Oh, for *fuck* sake," Mary-Anne grumbled.

No one said anything.

"You don't need to say anything for me to know who you are. I can smell you, you know. Once darkness hits and I'm out of here, I'm coming for every one of you."

They all looked at Caitlin with eyes that asked for help.

"Ignore her," Caitlin said, then raised her voice loud enough for Mary-Anne to hear. "Ma's just cranky when she hasn't had a full day's rest."

Kain chipped in. "Ain't that the truth, sweet-fangs?"

"You two are my first targets," Mary-Anne called back.

Suddenly, Ash ran a few steps ahead. He raised the back of his fist to the rest of the group, and they stopped altogether.

"What is it?" Caitlin whispered, kicking Shitallion to move up to stand next to Ash.

Kain answered, taking a deep breath as his head cocked to the side. "It seems as though we're here."

Silver Creek, Silver Creek Forest

Caitlin tied Shitallion to a tree as she instructed

everyone to hold back, lie low, and wait for the cue. There was enough foliage and greenery to hide everyone, but that didn't mean someone wandering past wouldn't be able to spot the group from a fair way off.

Which is why it worked in their favor that hardly anyone strolled through the forest anymore. It made a sad sign of the times when you couldn't simply go for a walk out in the fresh air without being chomped on by zombs or hunted by bandits.

Not for the first time, Caitlin wondered what the world had really been like before it all fell to shit. She hoped she'd soon be able to find out when she rebuilt the damn thing.

She took Ash, Kain, and Jaxon with her. Ash because he knew the lay of the land better than Caitlin ever did, and Kain because his hearing and sight seemed to be leaps and bounds ahead of everyone else. He proclaimed he could see a few guards lining the walls of the town. Caitlin couldn't even see the walls.

But she trusted him for some unknown reason.

Her trust had stood her in good stead so far.

Alice stayed behind, keeping watch over Mary-Anne and the Revolutionaries.

They snuck closer, remaining as far away as possible while always keeping the walls within their sights. The common knowledge of the townspeople was that Silver Creek was a fortress. One way in, one way out. No entry or exit except through the main gate.

"Bullshit," Ash had said to her the night they made their plans around the campfire. "What kind of governor would trap himself in a fortress without a secret way in or out."

"There's a hidden way?" Caitlin had asked.

"That might have been useful to know a little earlier," Kain said, rolling his eyes.

"Several," Ash continued as if no one had spoken. "Four at intervals around the walls. They're guarded, of course. But barely. Only the most trusted of guards are told. Imagine if a stray zombie managed to crawl its way through the holes and into the town. We'd be pretty fucked. So there's always one person, and that's all that's needed."

Caitlin couldn't believe it at the time. But skirting along the walls, it all made sense. Of course, Trisk had put in secret passageways. What else could she expect from a slimeball she wouldn't trust to feed her dog?

An image of the governor trying to squeeze through a gap small enough for an average adult to crawl through flashed into her mind. In her head, he was stuck halfway, his face growing red and his greasy folds bunching against the walls as three guards tried to pull him through. His legs kicked and flailed like mad.

No. Not like *Mad*. More like *fat*.

"Just a little further," Ash said as they ducked low and hid behind some tree trunks. A little further on, Kain spotted something in the wall that was so easy to miss that it wasn't a surprise it was a secret.

Kain looked up at the parapets, took a big sniff of the air, and nodded to them. "Clear," he said with a conviction Caitlin couldn't deny.

But why the fuck did he sniff the air? Could he *smell* the guards or something?

Caitlin's intuition started to work as she thought of Mary-Anne and the secret she had uncovered.

So, vampires exist. But what the hell are you?

Dashing out of the cover of trees and into the open, they ran as fast as they could, practically slamming their backs against the wall. Ash found a small nodule in the wood with his hand and pulled, revealing a tiny doorway that creaked open into blackness.

"This is where we part ways," Ash said extending his hand for Caitlin to shake.

She batted it aside and hugged him tightly. When she pulled away, she said, "Thanks. You know what you're doing, right?"

Ash nodded, then turned his attention to Kain. "You keep her close. The last thing we need is to—"

He cut off short when a light appeared at the end of the tunnel. Footsteps sprinted quickly towards them.

"So much for the guards hardly paying attention, eh?" Caitlin said.

The man was fast, his sword already out. He advanced quickly, a crazed look in his eye as he swung at Caitlin with death in his eyes. She parried adroitly, pushing him back.

"You're dead, bitch," he growled. "The governor wants any intruders to be brought to him—dead or alive."

"I'll have to choose death," Caitlin said, running her blade across the guard's throat. The light faded in his eyes, and he fell to the floor. "For you."

"Impressive," Kain said, his eyebrows raised.

Jaxon trotted ahead and sniffed the body on the floor. At first, for some reason she couldn't explain, Caitlin imagined Jaxon licking up the man's blood. Instead, he cocked a leg and began peeing over the dead body.

"Well...talk about your metaphors for success," Ash said, closing the door behind them and returning to the Revolutionaries to wait for their cue.

"Metaphors?" Kain asked when the door closed and darkness resumed.

"Y'know, like when you say that something represents something, even if it's not directly related."

"I know what a metaphor is, I just don't get how it applies here," Kain said, his eyes glinting in the dark.

Caitlin chuckled. Though she had spent the last few days with her needle moving between the hate-him-like-him meter, it was definitely starting to settle more on the like him side more often. There was something about Kain she found intriguing and that reminded her of Mary-Anne —an animalistic *something* she couldn't quite put her finger on.

"Well, my dear Sudeikis, let's put it this way." Caitlin pulled her hood up over her face, stepped over the guard, and began walking. "Much like Jaxon here, we're about to piss all over the governor's parade."

CHAPTER TWENTY-ONE

Silver Creek, Silver Creek Forest

It was a strange feeling, being back home. Though Silver Creek had been the place where she had spent all her life, it somehow felt different, as though she were stepping into a part of her that didn't seem to fit right anymore.

With their hoods up, Kain and Caitlin snuck through town, clinging to the quiet suburbs and avoiding the routes where Caitlin knew guards were most likely to walk. That didn't make it any easier, though. Not by any standard.

Caitlin noted that the captain's numbers had increased, and there were men clad in the leather armor of the guards nearly every way they went.

Many of them didn't seem to fit the requirements of the captain's usual high standards.

At one point, a young lad of no more than seventeen marched over to Kain and raised his hand. There was a smug grin on his face, as though the kid's birthdays had all come at once.

He tried to stop them and ask them where they were

going. Kain stepped forward, head-butted him in the face, and told him to get lost.

"Way to not draw attention to yourself," Caitlin said, rolling her eyes.

"Sometimes words just won't cut it," Kain replied.

"You could still try."

Caitlin looked at the poor kid, now snoring gently on the floor. She recognized his face but couldn't think of his name.

So young. Too young to be playing grown-up games.

What the hell was the governor thinking?

They continued through the town, doing their best to remain inconspicuous. A couple of times, Caitlin caught people looking their way with interest, but no one else stopped them.

After a short while and a lot of turns, they found what they were after.

"You're sure about this? You're sure this is safe?" Kain asked.

Caitlin nodded. "It's strange, but out of everyone who lives here, she's the only one I trust now." She raised her fist and knocked on a small red door.

They waited a moment and heard footsteps approaching cautiously on the other side. The door swung open to reveal a woman who looked as though the years had not been kind to her. Her hair was greasy and clung to her head, her clothes tattered and torn. Huge bags hung beneath her eyes as she looked them up and down.

"Miss Harrison?" Her voice was barely a croak. "I'd heard a rumor that you were dead."

"Not yet," Caitlin said. "Can we come in?"

The woman looked Kain up and down. "Both of you?"

"Please. We need your help. It's about the governor."

The woman winced at that word, a shadow crossing her face. She leaned forward and scanned the street, looking for anyone who might be watching. She waved them both in. "In you come, in you come."

Kain looked around the room, and his face clearly said he couldn't believe what a mess it was. His nose wrinkled, and Caitlin surmised that the smell had caught his attention. He had the look of a man who had been reminded of something he hadn't smelled in years but recognized all the same. Dust, grime, and... Caitlin waited for the moment of truth.

Gunpowder? The silent inquiry showed in his eyes.

She raised an eyebrow in response, sure now that he knew exactly what so many others missed. His gaze swept the room and over what clearly left him speechless. Strewn across the floor amidst clothes, foodstuffs, and dirt were pieces and parts of weapons that had not been seen in years.

Silver Creek Forest

"This is boring," Alice said as she sat with Ash in the forest and waited for dusk to fall.

Ash smiled and took Alice's hand in his own. "There isn't a boring second when I'm with you."

Alice put a finger to her mouth and pretended to throw up.

"Hey!" Ash got to his knees and pushed her playfully.

"I'm kidding! I'm kidding," Alice said. They both smiled

and stared into each other's eyes. "Y'know, I never thought I'd feel the way I feel so soon after...well..." She trailed off, remembering the brute of a man whom they had left to rot beneath a bed in New Leaf.

"I'm sorry," Ash said. "How long were you married?"

"Married?" Alice looked confused. "Marriage doesn't count for shit anymore these days. It was much more of a 'you're mine' situation. After I was old enough to... y'know...we were paired up, and I didn't really have a choice in the matter. My parents weren't thrilled that Bill had claimed me, but they got caught by Mad out in the wilds not long afterward and the rest was history."

"I'm sorry," Ash repeated.

"Quit apologizing, you big turd," Alice said, pushing him back and straddling him.

They were far enough away from the other Revolutionaries that they would not be heard but close enough that they could jump into action should anything happen before their time was up.

"I'm not a pity case to be had by a Silver Creek guard. Now, are you man enough to take me, or do I have to take you myself?" Alice leaned forward, and they kissed.

They rolled and frolicked, doing their best to keep their moans of pleasure as quiet as they could. That was always a tough sell, though, especially in the heat of the moment. They never expressed it outright, but there was a little fear in both of them. What if they were to charge Silver Creek and never make it out alive? What if only one of them did? Caitlin was an easy leader to fall in behind, but there was always that 'what if.'

Make every second count, Alice thought as she felt Ash in

places she'd only dreamed of, unaware that merely a hundred meters away, two Revolutionaries, Belle and Vex, sat with their eyebrows raised.

"And they told us not to draw attention to ourselves," Vex said, eyeing Belle up and down with a wink.

"You touch me, and I'll cut your cock off," Belle replied, only half joking as she giggled at the gentle moans which floated on the wind.

Silver Creek

Monica Chapman bustled around her house, never really taking a second to sit down. There was a frenzied air to her, as though if she ever stopped, she might die.

"As long as you keep that dog in check, we'll be just fine," she said, her voice croaky and dry.

Jaxon looked at Caitlin, then Monica, then lowered his head onto his paws.

Caitlin smiled and watched Monica with fascination and pity. She had come to know the woman over the years. As a child, she'd been sent on errands by her mom and dad to get small trinkets and tiny pieces of technology from Monica and her husband. That had been back when she was fair and young and carefree, before that moment in the market square where Trisk had given his speech and ordered Hank to shoot her husband right up there on the platform.

Since those days, there had been a visible decline in her health. Despite the governor's orders, Monica continued tinkering and inventing, and Caitlin guessed that no one had ever really bothered too much on checking in with her. They had much bigger fish to fry than to waste their time with a deranged lunatic.

"Here you go," Monica said, the tray in her hands shaking so furiously that the contents of the three cups spilled in every direction. By the time she laid the tray down, there was hardly anything left in the cups. "I'm sorry. It's been a while since I've had visitors. How have you been, dear? It's not often I hear of a person's death and live to see them darken my doorstep another day."

Monica sat for all of thirty seconds, her leg tapping non-stop. She stood up and began to pace around the room.

"We need your help," Caitlin said without any preamble.

"Oh? Straight to it, eh?" Monica stood dangerously close to the fire in the corner.

"The governor has my brother," Caitlin said. Monica cocked her head to listen.

Caitlin told her everything from her inauguration as a ranger, to her kidnapping at the manor, to her travels at New Leaf, and now, her return. The only thing she excluded was the vampire part as, given the current state Monica was in right now, she hardly wanted to chance an overload of information.

She told Monica of the Revolutionaries, and the woman's eyes lit up at that. She continued to circle around the room, her feet kicking odd parts of metal on the floor —coils, springs, and cogs, pieces of the old world.

By the time she had finished talking, Monica had reversed her age five years. Her eyes were vibrant and alive with hope and possibility.

"You're really taking on the governor?" It emerged

more rhetorical than as a real question. "After all these years, the time has come?"

"Yes. That's why we came to you. I know it's beyond the realms of possibility that you have had time through the years to test and try any more weapons, but as much as swords, bows, and daggers are great, we really need to one-the-fuck-up the guards. We've counted nearly double on the streets than there were before, which means they know we're coming for them." Caitlin took a sip of her drink, instantly regretting her decision and doing her best to fight back her own gagging.

Kain chuckled quietly. She threw him a quick look, his subtle gesture revealing that his own drink now fed the dead plant in the flower pot next to him.

"Oh, dears," Monica said, a wry smile playing on her face. "You think I'd let Trisk slaughter my husband and not spend every day since dreaming of ways to blow his tits into the stars? I thought you knew me, Caitlin."

"She goes by Kitty Cat now," Kain chimed in.

"No, I don't," Caitlin snapped. She turned to the older woman. "Ignore him."

Monica picked up a long piece of metal from the floor. Black powder painted its tip, and when she prodded it into the fire, it roared into life. Caitlin and Kain gasped as the flames burned red, then blue, then green.

Jaxon growled.

Monica laughed, something she hadn't done in years. It had been so long that it sounded more like a crow coughing than the tinkling of bells.

"I'd be careful what you say around that one," Monica said to Kain. "There's always been something about her.

Something fierce. The last place you want to end up is on her bad side."

Caitlin slapped Kain hard on the arm. "See! Told you," she said, poking out her tongue. "What kind of magic is that?"

"Flavors of the old magic. The burning of chemicals the folks of Silver Creek have long forgotten." She opened a door at the back of the room and motioned for them to follow her. The corners of her mouth wrinkled into a smile. "You want to see?"

Kain gulped, looking suddenly fearful of what magic the woman had referred to. Caitlin instructed Jaxon to stay put, then followed without looking back, a steely determination on her face.

They walked down a narrow hallway with doors off to either side, then took a right and found themselves in a small cupboard-sized room. Monica lit a torch, dropped to her knees—Caitlin heard them clicking—and lifted a small square of carpet.

"I'm warning you," Kain said, his face a strange cocktail of emotions. "The last bastard who tried to lead me into his sex dungeon found himself without his genitals and coughing up blood."

"Relax," Caitlin said, a hint of amusement in her voice. She had never seen Kain afraid before. The last few days, he'd been nothing but cocky and arrogant. She didn't doubt he could hold his own in a fight—judging by the way he swung his sword—but it was fun, all the same, to see him worried. "If anyone's on the good guy's side, it's Monica."

Monica lifted a trapdoor and revealed a set of stairs.

They filed in one after the other into a cavern of blackness. It was cold down there, and the air smelled stale.

Monica lit a final torch on the wall, and the room came alive with light. Where her upstairs looked like several pigs had had an orgy amidst a pile of scrap metal, this room was incredibly tidy, organized, and clean.

Lining the walls was a vast array of weapons. Pistols, shotguns, and submachine guns—at least, those were the names that came to mind, though where she'd heard them or what they really meant didn't seem all that important. A hundred relics of the old world hung within reach, contraptions that blew Caitlin's mind into Kingdom come and made her breathless. She had no idea how any of them worked. How anybody had ever had the knowledge to be able to assemble the damn things in the first place was beyond her.

"Okay, *now* I'm turned on," Kain said, crossing the room to where a table of handguns, pristinely ordered and displayed, lay temptingly on top. He reached to pick one up. "I haven't seen one of these in years—"

"Nah-uh." Monica reprimanded him, moving instantly to his side and slapping his hands. "No touching. Not yet, anyway. These ones are just works in progress."

Caitlin's mouth wouldn't close. "Where in the name of holy hell did you find all of these? I'm not being funny, but there are so many guns here, and it's not like these things are just lying around, ready to be pillaged, collected, and restored."

Monica crossed the room and removed a small black gun from the wall. Its barrel was immaculate, gleaming in the torchlight. She rolled it over in her hands, then aimed it at Kain, closing one eye and staring straight down the barrel.

"Woah. *Hey*, woah!" Kain said, immediately backing up against the wall and lifting his hands in surrender. "Are you fucking crazy?"

"You like snakes?" Monica asked, but didn't wait for an answer. "This is a Colt Python .357 Magnum revolver. Near mint condition. Now, that's rare. After the leaders of the world cracked themselves up on imbecile juice and tried to blow the fucking world to pieces, there wasn't a whole lot of stuff that wasn't damaged by the bombs. By the explosions. But every now and then, just occasionally, you can stumble across hidden gems and treasures. Buried in basements. Taken from the hands of dead men. A lot of bandits and hoodlums out in the wild have no idea just how precious the things are that they're aiming at strangers on the road."

"You found that gun in working condition?" Caitlin asked.

Kain jittered uncomfortably against the wall.

"Don't be stupid, my dear. My dear Zach found this beauty while out on the road, years ago." Monica's eyes glanced at a large sketch of a younger version of herself with her late-husband, Zach, on the wall. "He was an adventurer. A wanderer. No matter what I told him, he'd sneak through the hidden ways he'd found and explore the world beyond the walls. Sometimes for weeks at a time. Every time, I'd worry myself sick, but it was all for naught as he'd return with a sack full of treasures he'd found soon enough. Obsessed with it, he was. The old world. Which is where my interest came from."

A tear pooled at the corner of Monica's eyes. "One day, he returned covered in bruises and cuts. He'd been ambushed on the road by bandits. Four men, each holding pistols or guns, asking that he turn over the goods he'd foraged that day. He'd taken them all on one-by-one, stealing their weapons. It was never often you had to fear them, really. Guns hardly ever worked in those days, and when he squared up to them and saw that flicker of fear, he just took them down."

Monica lowered the gun. "This is just one of the guns he brought back from that trip. Left in the finest condition I've ever seen."

She lifted it back up at Kain who instantly straightened.

"No!" he screamed.

"No point shouting. This room is so soundproof you couldn't even hear gunfire from the surface. Believe me. I've tested it."

Monica's finger tensed on the trigger. She pulled. There was a click. Both Kain and Caitlin gasped and took a deep breath in.

Kain opened his eyes when he heard the laughter. Monica was in stitches, doubled over and wiping tears from her eyes as she clapped her knee and pointed at Kain.

She opened the cylinder and displayed it to them.

There were no bullets inside.

Kain's eyes flashed amber. He shouted with rage as he dashed across the room at unbelievable speed and picked up Monica by the throat. Coarse hairs began to sprout across his face, and his teeth began to turn razor sharp.

"Kain!" Caitlin shouted, springing after him. "She didn't mean it. She didn't *mean* it."

Kain felt the sharp tip of Caitlin's sword against the back of his neck. He looked into the fearful eyes of the human in his grasp, the lunatic lady who pined after her husband day in and day out. He set her on her feet, stepped away, and looked at his hands in shame. Dark hair had sprouted on their backs which, years ago, would have already receded to where they'd come from. Not now, though.

Kain looked at Monica who, to his surprise, didn't look frightened. She looked excited. He turned to Caitlin who had an eyebrow raised and a knowing smile on her face.

"Vampires, guns, and werewolves, oh my," she said. "So that's what you are."

CHAPTER TWENTY-TWO

Silver Creek, Silver Creek Forest

At first, he wasn't sure what the shape was in the dark. Then, Clint saw the woman with dark skin emerge from the trees and walk along the dusty road to the gates.

"Here you go, Balski," he said, patting a guard with snow-white hair to his left. "Another bimbo for your late-night romps."

Clint turned back to his view of the road from the top of Silver Creek's gates. The woman now stood directly below them, waiting patiently.

He blinked and rubbed his eyes.

How had she moved that fast?

"Halt. In the name of Governor Trisk, who goes there?"

The woman looked up at him, and his heart froze.

Mary-Anne looked up at the guards above. At least two dozen of them stood up on the parapets, half of them with bows. The one who called down had nothing more than a sword.

What a stupid choice of weapon for a gate-guard.

The air was still, the calm before the storm.

Mary-Anne cracked her neck left, then right. She closed her eyes. When she opened them again, they glowed red. Her fangs extended, and she had to stop herself from laughing as the shouts of panic came from above.

Just like old times.

With an order shouted, arrows rained at the spot where Mary-Anne had been, but she was already at the gates now. They were nothing more than wood fashioned into a doorway, strong enough to hold back the Mad, but a freshly fed vampire? No. She charged, punched through the wood, reached through the hole she had made with her fist, and unlocked it from the inside.

A swift kick with the bottom of her foot, and she was in.

"Get her!" the gate-guard shouted from somewhere above as guards appeared from all angles. "Get her!"

She saw a guard sprinting for the walls where a large bell hung. Immediately, she saw his intention—to alert the entire town to her whereabouts. That wasn't about to happen.

She picked up a rock, tossed it with deadly speed and aim, and the guard fell instantly to the floor.

"School's out for summer," Mary-Anne muttered as the first guard leapt at her and she side-stepped elegantly, giving him a helpful shove away from her while she knocked another guard's sword aside and socked him with a right hook.

She tugged his own sword from his hand, then drove it down into his leg and through the floor.

An arrow whistled through the air and landed an inch or so from her feet. She looked up at the guard on the parapets who had fired, his hands now shaking and eyes wide. Clearly, he couldn't quite believe that he had just shot at a freakin' vampire.

Mary-Anne darted up the stairs at vampire speed, leaving a guy behind her to swing and strike at nothing but air. His sword swung through where she had been, and instead of his intended target, found a new home in the flesh of his own comrade's bicep.

There was already a wet patch around the archer's lower half. Mary-Anne could smell it a mile off. She stopped in front of him, took his bow, and set an arrow. "It's more like this," she said, drawing the string and firing at a guard below. The arrow sang and found its target in the guard's eye socket. There was an audible *pop,* and blood splurged into the air.

"See? It's all in the breathing. Steady breaths equal steady fire," Mary-Anne instructed in soothing tones and handed the bow back to the guard. He was young with freckles on his cheeks. One day he might grow up to actually be a useful tool in war.

Not today, though.

She left him standing there, frozen, with tears streaming down his face.

Mary-Anne ran, dodging several more arrows with ease, then turned to look out at the darkness of the trees below. It was a hell of a view from up there, but it was about to get prettier.

She put her fingers to her lips and whistled.

A whistle echoed back from the trees. A second later and Ash emerged, a Silver Creek guard atop Shitallion. The rest of the Revolutionaries sprinted behind, their weapons raised. Cries and shouts. A line of rebels at the back dropped to one knee with their own bows and dispatched the rest of the guards on top of the walls.

"Took your sweet fucking time," Mary-Anne called down as Ash and Shitallion made it through the gate.

"Barely heard you. You whistle like a girl," Ash said, looking up and winking before jumping in and clashing swords with one of Hank's new recruits. He was a large man who by no means had traditional sword skills, but he did have a hell of a weight behind him and flaunted it to his advantage.

"Shut up and focus on tub-tubs," Mary-Anne shouted, then dashed down the stairs and re-joined the battle.

The Revolutionaries filed in, and before long, the area around the gateway was a mash of steel and cries.

Alice sprinted into the fray and found herself locked in a scrap with a guard who, in other circumstances, she might have considered handsome. Though with the blood on his face, his gritted teeth, and his sword trained on destroying her, that kind of took the edge off.

He swung down, and she crossed her two daggers to catch the blade. She grunted at the impact, then looked through and pursed her lips. "C'mon sweetie, it doesn't have to be like this," she said, watching him instantly grow red.

In that distracted second, she threw her left arm right

to bat the sword away, then brought her right arm round to drive the dagger into his neck.

"Bitch," the guard said as he fell—or something like that. It was hard to hear with all the bubbling in his throat.

"Some men just can't take the heat," Belle said from behind her. "The blood rushes to the wrong place and...—"

"Shut the fuck up!" the man Belle was fighting shouted. Where Belle was a little under five foot, this man was a mammoth. He stood tall at well over six feet, and Alice couldn't help but be reminded of Big Bill.

Her brow furrowed and the two of them paired up against the asshole.

On the other side of the battle, Ash and Mary-Anne became a well-oiled machine, keeping their backs to each other. Mary-Anne stuck guards with their own swords, drew her claws out to scratch those who came near, and chomped into necks like a homeless guy at an all-you-can-eat buffet.

Ash, on the other hand, fought like a pro. Knowing all the guard's usual tricks of the trade when it came to battle, he was able to predict their moves ahead of time, taking those who approached him down with ease. At one point, it had crossed Mary-Anne's mind that maybe Ash wouldn't actually be able to take down his former comrades, that maybe he'd grow sentimental and switch sides, but he was certainly proving his worth.

He was a goddamn Revolutionary now, and it was kill or be killed.

"You know this is going to hurt in the morning, right?" Mary-Anne said between stabbing a guy in the chest and fending off a blow to her right.

"What the fuck do you care? You'll be fast asleep in your bed. We'll be the ones cleaning up your mess."

"Always nice to have the roles reversed. For years, it's been vamps cleaning up your goddamn mess." Mary-Anne smiled.

It was dark by the time they emerged from Monica's hidden chamber.

Caitlin looked out the window and at the sky. "*Shit,* how long were we down there?"

"I don't know, but I want to go back," Kain said. "Plug in an Xbox, a TV, and a mini-bar, and you've got yourself a proper little man cave, Chapman. Be just like the good ol' days."

Caitlin didn't even entertain that comment, though wondered what the hell he was talking about. Why would he want egg-boxes down there? Was that an old-world target practice thing?

She couldn't imagine what TV stood for.

They gathered their stuff while Monica quickly knocked up a drink and some food. Caitlin had been open with her intentions for the town and her plan with the Revolutionaries, and in true 'oh, mother' fashion, Monica had demanded they eat and get their strength up.

Caitlin had rushed her bread and water down. Kain swallowed all in practically one go.

"You can breathe between mouthfuls, you know," Monica said.

"I thought people loved folks who swallow," Kain replied with a cheeky grin on his face.

When Kain, Caitlin, and Jaxon left Monica's house, it was so dark outside that hiding was easy. Their cloaks were dark, and the shadows were dense. Even when several guards sprinted past them with their swords drawn and disappeared around the corner, they weren't noticed in the slightest.

"I wonder where they're going?" Caitlin said with a knowing look. The plan would be in full throw by now, the cover of darkness Mary-Anne's ally.

"Sarcasm?" Kain replied.

Caitlin rolled her eyes. "You're getting better at that, eh?"

Navigating the streets was easy for Caitlin, even more so now, knowing that she had a Were on her side. They rounded a corner and slipped down through the network of side streets between houses, ducking low as they passed windows where they could hear citizens going about their nightly business—preparing for bed, shouting, or fucking.

She had to drag Kain away from those windows.

Little known to them both, though, they soon came to the exact same spot where just that morning, Sullivan had hidden with Carl and Sykes, plotting their takedown of the frontrunners of the prison's guards.

Only this time, there were three guards.

Caitlin smiled. She liked those odds.

She motioned for Jaxon to stay low.

"Excuse me, gentlemen," she said, approaching with a sultry swagger that caught their attention. The closer she got, the funnier she found it that they all looked so alike, as if they could've been triplets from the same womb. "I don't suppose you'd mind helping a little lady like myself out at all? I've dropped the contents of my purse back there, and I can't find the stuff that fell on the ground."

She bundled her cloak in her hands to give an impression of nervousness while actually showing the guards the lower part of her calves.

Their eyes practically dropped out, and they elbowed each other as they argued over who would help her.

"We can't," the one on the left said, clearly wanting to be the one to go. "We've got orders."

"Oh, Sam. Can't you see this lady needs help?" The guard on the right winked and nudged him in her direction.

"I'll help, miss!" the guard in the center said, running to Caitlin's side.

She gave him a swift kick to the groin and brought him to his knees. The other two charged in an instant, their weapons still in their sheaths as they reached for Caitlin with their hands.

"You little slut," the first guard shouted, grabbing Caitlin's arm. "Wait until you see what we're going to do with you."

Caitlin didn't bother to look scared. She merely smiled. It was enough to distract them away from the sight of a cloaked figure with dull orange eyes dashing out of the alleyway. He launched through the air like a puma pouncing its prey and knocked one of the guards off his feet.

Kain kept his own weapon sheathed, obviously

enjoying the thrill of old-fashioned fisticuffs as he dished out blow, after blow, after blow.

Caitlin drew her sword and swung at the guard. The blade knocked against the armor, sending a shockwave up her arm. He threw back her hood and grabbed her hair.

He gasped. "*You?*"

"Sorry, no autographs today," she said, spitting in his eyes. He wiped his face but kept her hair in his fist. "Er, a little help?"

Kain sent a mean sucker punch to the guy's cheek, then pivoted and ran for Caitlin. "Dear Lord, and I thought guys were impatient. Just a second, sweet-cheeks," he said, leaping into the air again and round-housing the guy in the face.

Caitlin couldn't believe how agile he was. A skinny guy with little mass, he darted around and between them all like he was made of lightning. She'd seen his practice drills in training, but to see him perform his magic in the heat of a real battle…she was in awe.

The guard released Caitlin's hair as he fell to the ground. She marched up to the beaming Kain and held the sword an inch from his face. "Thanks for the save, but call me sweet-cheeks one more time and I'll put your collar back on and leave your corpse in the doghouse."

"You hear that, Jax?" Kain asked, teasing the sword down cautiously with his fingers. "Looks like it's you and me tonight. Fair warning—I hog the covers."

Jaxon sprinted into the open, accompanying the two. He turned and began growling as a voice came from behind.

"You sons-of-bitches," guard number three growled. In

their little parley, they'd completely forgotten about him. "I'm going to teach you the meaning of...*argh!*"

Jaxon barked and launched himself at the guard. The man fell onto his back and the dog immediately tucked into his throat, ripping his head back and forth as his teeth caught on tendons and cartilage.

"Pain?" Caitlin asked nonchalantly. She turned to Kain, whose eyebrows were raised. "How does it feel to know a common mongrel has more bite than you?"

Kain whistled, clearly impressed. "You've trained him well."

"He just knows who his boss is," Caitlin said, making her way up the stairs. "And soon, the governor will know, too."

Kain whistled again, though when Caitlin turned, she saw it was because he was staring at her ass. She turned away and spoke without looking. "Yes, I know it's nice. But let's not waste time on something you can't have, okay?"

CHAPTER TWENTY-THREE

Hank's Quarters, Silver Creek

Hank couldn't believe what he was hearing.

"I'm sorry, repeat that again," he said, no longer caring that his face reflected a thunderous concoction of color.

The guard standing at his bedside looked around sheepishly. His eyes went everywhere but to Hank's, clearly not happy about being the one to give the captain the news.

He told Hank that the gates had been stormed and that a group of rebels were making their way inside Silver Creek, led by a vampire. He thought his leader would pass out when he told him that one of the rebels was Ash Collins, the same guard who had been missing since being set free by Caitlin in New Leaf.

Hank rose out of bed. He had only been asleep for an hour and it clearly wasn't enough. His rage erupted. He crossed the room to the guard, raised his fist, and took a swing at the wall beside where the man stood.

He turned, breathing hard through clenched teeth.

"How, in the name of Sam Bastard's fucking child, did a group of nobodies smash through the front gates?"

He knew the answer before the guard gave it to him. "They have the vampire woman. Her strength is like nothing I've ever seen. Men ran from her at the sight of the hell within her red eyes."

"Men like you?" Hank snapped, and the guard instantly shut up and blushed. "What of the girl? Is she with them?"

The guard shook his head. "No sign of the ranger master's sister."

"You're sure?"

The guard shook his head again. "No, sir."

A cold shiver ran down Hank's spine. If Caitlin wasn't with the rest of the rebels, then where the hell was she? She didn't seem the type to send others to fight on her behalf—not like the governor did, anyway. In many ways, she was the complete opposite.

"Captain? What are your orders? They're small in number, but they're well trained. We're no match as we are."

When Hank raised his head, his face was deliberately shadowed to hide the clear menace he knew was in his eyes. He calmed his breathing by sheer force of will.

The Governor's Quarters, Silver Creek

Hank had seen Trisk pissed off before on several occasions.

The first had been several years ago, when a duo of town brewers managed to refine the process of making wine. In the collapse of the world, many secrets of alcohol and food had been lost, gone missing or destroyed. So when the day came that a vat of Silver Creek's finest vino was distributed to the governor, they had celebrated in true style.

Food was laid out for all of his closest men. Drink flowed endlessly. Spirits were high, and bellies were full.

Until the morning came, and the governor had been ready for another round of the hair of the dog that bit him, only to discover that all the wine was gone. It had been drunk and devoured by a group of lowly new guard recruits.

Hank had been by his side as Trisk hauled their bodies up with surprising strength, screamed in their faces until his throat was raw, then sentenced them each to one hundred lashes of the whip.

The governor didn't distribute the punishment himself, of course. But he watched every snap and coil of the whip with a disturbingly eager eye. Blood had sprayed in streaks. The men stopped moaning after the count of the first thirty.

The second time had been for nothing more than a disturbance. Trisk had been beyond the realms of the common drunk—years of overindulgence often did that to a person—and Hank, alongside two other men, had had to deliver the news that there'd been another case of the Madness in the town.

Their leader had been in the middle of one of his panty parties at the time and had stumbled to the door with his boxers teepeed around his excitement. He pulled Hank's former right-hand man, Claude, into the room and beat him senseless. Hank had the sense to disappear out the door before the governor could realize what had happened.

He barely remembered in the morning.

The worst part, Hank remembered thinking, was that it was under the man's own orders that he had been disturbed in the first place. He had given express orders to be informed should any case of the Madness break out. Sometimes, even Hank wondered if his master might have had a little bit of the Madness inside him.

But this...this was something Hank hadn't come across before.

When he had finished his sentence, explaining that a group of rebels had breached the town, he'd said nothing at first. He merely looked at the floor, his expression blank.

The governor wandered around the room with his hands behind his back, obviously considering his response. Once again, Hank found him hardly decent for company. He wore striped shorts of the finest cotton weave, with stains and tears that left little to the imagination. The folds of his stomach made his skin look like a bulbous candle had melted, and the actual candlelight caught and shimmered off the grease of his skin.

"Sir?" Hank said, feeling himself get irritated at the lack of response.

Trisk paused at the side of the room where there was a small hole in the wall that Hank had never noticed before. A length of string disappeared through the hole. Trisk hovered his hand over it, seemed to debate his move, then pinched it between his thumb and forefinger, gripping it on the fourth try. He pulled it tight. The string went taught.

A moment later, a bell began ringing loudly, one Hank had never heard rung before.

"Sir?" Hank repeated.

Trisk was on him in a second, moving in a way that Hank couldn't believe possible. He clutched Hank by the scruff of his neck and pulled their faces together. His breath was rank, his teeth all but falling to pieces in his mouth.

Yet, even now, he did not shout. His voice was dark and controlled. There was a fear in his face that his wrath failed to mask.

"You lied to me, Newman," Trisk growled.

The next thing Hank knew, he was across the room. His back smacked into the walls, and he slid down.

He scrambled back to his feet. "Sir... I—"

The governor flushed red and stomped toward Hank like a great bear. "You think my town doesn't have spies, you shit-eating bird-piss pie. You think that *you* are exempt from the truth? How long did you think it'd be before I found out that you've been keeping secrets from me? How long did you think it'd be before I found out that the girl who helped the vampire escape is now leading a rebellion against my fucking town?"

Hank found himself once again lifted off his feet and pulled back to Trisk's face.

"Well?"

He saw his life flash before his eyes.

"I thought I had the situation handled, sir." Hank's legs flailed in vain, seeking purchase on the floor which remained out of reach. "I thought I'd deal with it myself. I didn't want to worry you."

"Well, look how well that worked out, fuck-sack. Now the bastards have burst through my door, and they have a fucking vampire with them. *My* vampire. Do you know how hard it is to kill a vampire?"

Hank shook his head.

"Me fucking neither! Especially when they're not on your side." Trisk let Hank fall to his knees and looked down at him.

He groveled on the floor. "I'm sorry, sir. I'm so sorry. If there's anything I can do, please tell me. I'm forever yours."

The governor knelt with some effort. He placed a sausage-like finger under Hank's chin and lifted his head so that their gazes met.

"I want that girl's head on a spike and that goddamn vampire ready to suck my dick come sunrise," he said, his voice dark and low now with not a hint of amusement. "Because if I don't have them, I'll use your head for both."

Hank nodded, bowed low, and ran out of the room before his leader could say another word. He took a deep breath of the midnight air, feeling its cold energize his body, then ran to gather his troops.

The bell rang loudly about the town. It had been installed when the town was fresh and new to warn of impending attack.

The townspeople had learned the bell meant danger and that every available citizen should flood to the source of the attack.

Whatever kind of supernatural army that bitch had, Hank had to believe it wouldn't be able to beat sheer numbers.

. . .

Prison District, Silver Creek

Caitlin, Kain, and Jaxon made their way along the parapets of Silver Creek as quickly as they could. From afar, they looked like nothing more than three shadows.

Not that anyone looked their way at all.

When the bell began to ring, Kain had clapped a hand to his ears, his hypersensitive hearing overwhelmed by the sound. Down below, they could hear people rousing and making their way through the streets. A few minutes later the people flooded towards the front gates, bleary-eyed and nervous.

"They're not soldiers," Kain grumbled. "They're sheep."

"Right," Caitlin replied. "*Those* are soldiers." She pointed ahead to where a pair of guards ran straight at them.

They both moved their hands to their weapons but needn't have bothered as the guards sprinted straight past them and down the stairs, disappearing into the throng below.

"Huh," Caitlin said.

"Guess the bigger threat is at the gates." Kain sounded amused.

"We need to hurry. The Revolutionaries will need all the help they can get. Come."

They sprinted along the walkway. Caitlin had never been to the jail cells before, but the road was easy. One way in, one way out, with stone walls and iron bars. When they descended the same set of stairs that Kain had used to escape and run, Caitlin ran down two at a time.

"Halt, who goes there?" A voice spoke in the dark, and Caitlin watched as two guards stepped forward into the torchlight. One was considerably shorter than the other.

"I am Caitlin Harrison, founder of the Revolutionaries," Caitlin said, standing straight and putting on her most authoritative voice. There was no more time for mucking around with care and politics. "I've come to release my brother."

The guards looked at each other, then laughed.

"*You?*" the taller one said.

"You hear that? A *woman* has come to release her brother from the governor's prison." The shorter one wiped a tear from his eye. "Look, I'm sorry, miss. We haven't got time to deal with you. Rumor has it there's a raid happening outside, and we're all that stands between the people and chaos. Now, trot your little tush back round to the stairs and..."

His words trailed off as Kain stepped out from behind Caitlin and lowered his cloak. "Hello, my old friends." His eyes pulsed a low amber.

"You?" They gasped, reaching for their swords.

"Uh-uh," Kain said, reaching for his own. "Don't even think about it, scrubbers. Now, we can either play this the easy way or the *hard* way."

His eyes glowed again, and he sniffed dramatically. Caitlin smiled, recognizing that the guards interpreted the small gesture to mean that he could smell their fear.

To her surprise, the shorter one looked at his comrade, then fell to his knees and began begging. "Please...okay, fine. I give up. Please don't kill me."

Jaxon walked over and begin licking the guard's face.

"What are you doing?" the taller one barked. "Get your ass up."

"No, no, no. You remember this is a *Were*, right? A

fucking *Were.*" The shorter one beat his fists on the floor like a baby.

The taller one rolled his eyes. "Yes," he said, approaching Kain. "You're here to overthrow the governor, right?"

"Actually, that's my agenda," Caitlin said, raising a finger. "I just brought him along for the ride."

"You need me," Kain said.

"Like a hooker needs syphilis," Caitlin replied.

The guard bent to his knees. "I pledge my service to you, cloaked princess and canine warrior."

The shorter guard raised an eyebrow. "Why are you talking like that?"

The taller guard smacked him.

"Oh…okay. Me too," Shorty added.

Caitlin looked down at them with pity, hoping that their words were true. "Why?"

"Trisk treats us like shit, ain't that right, Ace?"

Ace replied, "We're here from dusk until dawn with barely a drop to drink and hardly a morsel to eat." He waved his arms around the cells. "This isn't what we signed up for. We wanted to fight for glory. We wanted to serve Silver Creek. Now, we're glorified babysitters, with little more thanks than a visit once a month from a governor who'd rip our heads off as soon as look at us."

Kain raised his eyebrows at Caitlin.

"You want some pets, you keep them," Caitlin said.

"Caitlin?" The voice called out of the darkness ahead. It sounded weak, hoarse and dry.

It made her heart leap.

She ran past the guard folded over on the floor, grabbed

a torch, and headed into the darkness ahead. Her footsteps echoed in the silence until she stopped and whirled, listening into the darkness for some sign of movement.

"Dylan?"

"Is that you?" Dylan's voice came from her left. She turned to see her brother at the bars wearing the biggest smile she had ever seen. "What took you so long?"

Caitlin reached through the bars and hugged him. "I... er...had to take care of a few things. I'll fill you in later. First, we need to get you out of here."

"And me, please," another voice called from behind her.

Caitlin twisted around to see Sullivan standing at his bars, his face pressing through the metal.

Caitlin giggled.

"Wait right here."

Dylan opened his mouth to speak, but Caitlin had already made her way back to the guards.

"Where is it?" she commanded, holding out her hand.

"Where is what?" Ace replied.

"The key." Caitlin's face darkened, and she advanced on him. "No fucking around. Give me the key *now*."

Ace shifted uncomfortably on his feet. He looked at the taller guard. "We don't have it."

"What do you mean, you don't have it?" Caitlin asked, panic rising to almost choke her. "If you don't have the key to your prisoners, then who fucking does?"

"I do," Dylan called.

Caitlin turned to see him and Sullivan standing in the doorway.

Ace slapped his forehead. "Do you guys just shit keys out now?"

Sullivan caught Kain's eye, mouthed the words, "Thank you," and winked.

They all headed up the stairs and out into the night. At the top, they stopped and looked out over the town below. The final dregs of the crowds were filtering through the streets, late-wakers who even the bell had failed to rouse quickly.

"What the hell is going on out here?" Dylan asked. "Is there something that you want to tell me?"

Kain chipped in, counting story points on each of his fingers. "Rescued a vampire, liberated a small town, trained a small army, met a Werewolf, now overthrowing the governor. That about cover it?"

Dylan's eyes widened. Clearly, he was more than a little impressed.

"What are your orders, captain?" Sullivan asked, apparently eager to get stuck into the action.

Dylan threw an arm around his sister and pulled her close. "I'm not your captain today, Sullivan. Today, we follow Caitlin. Ain't that right, sis?"

She blushed before a determined expression settled on her face.

CHAPTER TWENTY-FOUR

The Gates, Silver Creek, Toronto

The battlefield was a little crowded now.

Not solely with fighters, though the guards kept coming, and Mary-Anne, Alice, Ash, and the Revolutionaries did their best to fight them off. But the more people who came, the more they were drawn into a tight circle, their backs to each other.

Around the edges of the fight, a flock of people had gathered—citizens of Silver Creek whose curiosity was greater than their will to fight.

Either that or they were terrified that a fucking vampire would rip their throats out.

A lot of them had heard stories, heard rumors of a time when vampires were as common as their brothers and sisters. Legend had it they had flown the skies around Toronto and even set up small groups on Prince Edward Island. But that had all fallen to rumor and myth.

Or so it had seemed…

It certainly seemed incredibly real now that they

watched a woman with glowing red eyes and dagger-like fangs tear a man's head off and then toss it at another one of his comrades like a baseball.

"Home run!" Mary-Anne yelled with a wicked grin on her face.

"That way," Vex's voice cried back.

"No, not home...*run*... Never mind," Mary-Anne replied, rolling to her left to avoid another arrow as it flew towards her. It grazed her just enough to leave a small scratch down the back of her leg.

She looked up into the terrified eyes of the archer, put two fingers to her own eyes in a V, then pointed back at him.

The man jumped off the parapets of his own accord and splatted on the ground below.

"She doesn't even need to touch people to kill them," Ash said between clangs of his sword on his enemy's. "How is that even fair?"

Mary-Anne tossed her hair back, reminding herself of a commercial she had once seen years ago. "Because I'm worth it."

She was elated, energized by the heat of battle. As she twirled around and took people down, their blood drove her forward as if it surged through her veins. She felt as though she had been made of rusted metal, and every kill made in the name of justice shined it just that little bit more until she gleamed like silver in the starlight.

How had she waited this long to taste human blood again?

It became easier for her, too. The guards and citizens—those who were brave enough to get involved, at least—

began to avoid the vampire and focus on the Revolutionaries. Through sheer numbers, their odds weren't great. Mary-Anne did her best to make her way around the field, and on several occasions, saved the lives of those about to be stabbed or cut. But it was getting messy now, and while a few more guards entered the scene, she realized that their people were growing tired.

"Formation!" Mary-Anne shouted, an idea coming to her head. "Fall in! Fall in!"

The Revolutionaries turned to their surrogate leader and whacked, bashed, and walloped their way together. They stood tight in their circle now, their eyes narrowed.

For a moment, they had some breathing room, the guards surprised at their formation. Beyond the circular wall of brown leather armor, they could see onlookers craning their necks to get a better look at the action.

"Stay together," Mary-Anne said as an arrow whistled towards her, falling short and landing directly on the floor at her feet. She plucked it from the ground and tossed it back up the wall like a dart. An archer to fell back to the ground.

"Woah," Belle said in awe.

Mary-Anne ignored the comment. "Stand steady," she grumbled, feeling the others behind her. "As long as we band together, we'll be fine."

Alice leaned around and spoke softly. "Where is Caitlin? Shouldn't she be here by now?"

Mary-Anne scanned the line of guards—pissed off and terrified. She knew it would only be a matter of time before they charged again, and she wondered how long they could hold them off.

. . .

Somewhere, Silver Creek, Toronto

"This way," Sid, the taller guard, said as they ran along the parapets and down the stairs. Though Caitlin already knew the way, she didn't have the heart to tell him that his services weren't required.

I mean, hey, if he wants to join us and work against Trisk, who am I to tell him he can't make himself useful?

There was no need to hide anymore. All attention was on the bells and the front gates. Guards overtook them without a second glance. The six of them raced past residents who didn't seem to notice them at all. They made great time, and with every step, Caitlin's heart pulsed in her chest.

This is it. This is the moment it's all been leading to. Let's see if I've got what it takes.

She pictured herself standing on the platform that the governor used every week to deliver his messages—only this time, it was her dishing out the news. She would be respected amongst the people, seen as a savior and liberator. Silver Creek would reign as *the* place to flock to for safety in the world gone Mad.

And the Revolutionaries would stand by her side, spreading hope and joy amongst the masses.

All these thoughts flashed through her mind in an instant. There was only one thing blocking her way: Trisk.

Or so she thought.

Where just a moment ago they could hear the sounds of battle at the gates, a quiet now fell. They rounded a corner and found a street emptied except for a perfect V of men clad in the armor of the guards. At the center of the V was a face that made Caitlin's blood boil.

She looked at Hank Newman, hardly recognizing the man standing there. Where he had been fresh-faced and energetic when they raided Mary-Anne's manor, his hair was now unkempt. His beard looked scraggy, one of his eyes twitched, and the bags that hung beneath them looked more like bruises.

"Caitlin Harrison," he croaked. "I thought I'd catch you here." He turned to Dylan. "Seems we've got both the Harrisons, too. Both of the biggest pains in my ass I've ever had—and I've suffered from hemorrhoids."

One of the guards to his right gagged a little.

Hank turned and was on him in an instant, his rage exploding. He socked the guard in the face, then turned his attention back to Caitlin.

"Play time's over, *girl*," Hank continued.

Caitlin hated the way he said that word. It grated on her like the sound of metal scraping against metal.

"When we're through with you, you'll be nothing more than a flesh sack dummy for the training ground." Hank spat on the ground.

Flesh sack, Caitlin thought, remembering the last time she had been called that. That seemed like years ago now. Mary-Anne had said it, standing at the top of the stairs of her manor just moments after saving Caitlin's life.

Back where it all began.

They had come full circle, back to when Kiera was used as nothing more than a dispensable tool in a larger game.

A game led by the governor and fueled by Hank and his men.

Caitlin's brow furrowed as the injustice raced through her. Now was her chance to correct it all, her chance to claim her place and make a difference. "Fuck you, you demonizing ass-maggot packer."

Hank lunged, drawing his sword and going for a stabbing thrust.

Caitlin parried on instinct, stepping to her right as he fell left. He was strong, she'd give him that, but she drove the advantage and swung at Hank's middle, then his neck.

He was prepared, though, his anger sharpening his own senses. He roared, deflected, and went for her legs.

Caitlin jumped.

"She's an agile little thing, no doubt about it," Kain marveled, his knees bent and poised, ready to jump in if needed.

"You look at my legs again, and you'll have a foot in your face," Caitlin shouted back, narrowly missing another attack from Hank. He turned, he swung, and he arced, but nothing he could do could come close to breaking her. She was fitter than he was and wore clothes which weighed considerably less. No matter what he tried, nothing seemed to work.

After another attempt at aiming straight for the heart—in which Caitlin batted the sword away and mouthed a yawn—Hank roared, "Okay, you dickless monkeys, get involved, please."

Kain, Dylan, Jaxon, Sullivan, Sid, and Ace poised, ready to jump in. But to their surprise, there was a moment of hesitation from the troops.

"What are you waiting for?" Hank shouted, his voice

hoarse. He was dangerously red now, moments away from a coronary, or so it seemed.

"They're not going to help you," Caitlin said, holding up the Colt Python in her hand and aiming it at the captain's face.

A flash of fear flooded his features, then dissolved as a realization dawned over him. "Oh, I see. Can't play with the big boys, so you need to get old gunny on your side?"

He took a step towards Caitlin and her arm tensed, her finger poised over the trigger.

"You think that shitty butt-plug scares me? They don't work anymore, hasn't anyone told you? There's only one gun left in the whole of the known world that still manages to spit a bullet, and that little toy is locked away safe and sound. Even ol' Monica is too batshit crazy to put those things back together anymore."

"I'm going to warn you once…" Caitlin closed one eye and stared down the barrel.

Hank took another step. "Oooh, I'm terrified. Little gunny go boom and it's all over for Newman? Bring it on, sister. Show me what you got."

"Final warning." Caitlin cocked the pistol.

"Sis…" Dylan whispered from the sidelines, but Caitlin didn't hear. She was in her zone now, locked on the image of Hank's brains splattering all over the floor in front of her.

That's if Monica was right and the fucking thing worked.

The next thing she knew, Hank reared up and launched himself at her. His sword fell to the floor as he reached with his hands. She managed to duck her shoulders and move to the side, forcing him to dive over her and land on the floor.

A clap of thunder sounded.

The gunshot rang louder than anything she had ever experienced. The gun sprang back in her hand with the force of the bullet. Everyone nearby ducked and held their hands over their ears.

Caitlin stood over Hank, her arm straight, the gun still aimed high in the air.

He looked at Caitlin with surprise and fear. A dark stain spilled down his trousers and onto the ground as his bladder released its contents.

"Surrender, Captain Newman," Caitlin said, bringing the gun down to point at the captain once more. "Surrender or die."

The Gates, Silver Creek, Toronto

Another wave of guards came at them. As a unit, they defended.

Despite having not known many of these guys for long, even Mary-Anne was proud of their efforts. Another guard fell at her feet as she looked around and observed the others.

Belle and Vex had paired up, and their swords were a blur of movement. Ash took down a man with a beard that reached to his knees who charged with what looked to be some kind of dagger-like kitchen utensil. Alice stood not too far away, both hands whirling with her own daggers.

The Revolutionaries shouted, screamed, and roared. It was nearly impossible to think that, just a short while ago, they had been bumbling around in their oppressive regime, merely living their day-to-day lives. Submissive, monotonous, living for the will of the governor.

Now, they were fighting for freedom.

Mary-Anne felt her pride swelling inside her. She brought down another guard effortlessly, then turned to address another when—

Everyone at the gate stopped the moment they heard the gunshot.

"What the hell was that?" someone cried from the crowd.

There was no answer at first. The only sound was the bell continuing its ringing.

Murmurs slowly began to spread as the crowd shifted uneasily. Even the guards had paused and looked around in fear. When was the last time anyone had heard a shot like that ringing through the night? Where had it come from?

What could it mean?

Mary-Anne couldn't see them directly, but she saw the crowds of townsfolk parting. From somewhere just beyond the crowd, near where the houses and buildings began, they came.

Revolutionaries, guards, and residents lowered their weapons when Caitlin emerged with Jaxon at her side. She was trailed by Kain and Dylan, who dragged a bedraggled Hank by the crooks of his arms. Just behind them were two guards and a ranger who was the size of a house.

Everyone turned to look at them as they passed. The pistol hung in Caitlin's hand, still smoking from the tip.

When Caitlin and company reached the Revolutionaries, they threw Hank on the ground. Many faces turned to her, some whispering behind the back of their hand to their neighbor. Many of them knew her, but there were some who took a while to recognize her face, remembering Caitlin as the happy little good girl from the district.

"Perfect timing," Mary-Anne whispered, leaning in close.

"Oh, she's the queen of it," Kain replied.

Mary-Anne smirked. "We vamps already have a Queen."

Caitlin turned to address the crowd. "Citizens of Silver Creek, I am Caitlin Harrison, sister of your ranger captain, and now, your liberator." She held a hand out to Hank on the floor. "This man and his guards have you blindsided under an oppressive regime of fear and terror. Under the governor's orders, you hide in your houses and cower behind these walls, but I'm here to tell you that the world outside, as much as it has changed, is still ours to thrive in if we choose to be free."

"Hear, hear," Kain murmured.

A portly woman with thick eyebrows stepped forward, curiosity clearly getting the best of her. "And that *is* a vampire, right?"

Mary-Anne extended her fangs again, and her eyes burned red.

Caitlin laughed. "Yes, Mary-Anne is a vampire. A vampire who saved my life as I have saved hers. We have fought alongside our Revolutionaries for freedom." She paused, wondering whether now was the time to reveal more. "And this man is also a Werewolf. Kain had been taken by Trisk and forced to transform. Tortured and beaten until the governor took what he wanted, as he does with all of us."

"Vampires and Weres? Like the stories tell?" A small child spoke, held back at the shoulders by his father.

Kain replied. "Yes, kid. Just like the stories."

"There was a time"—Mary-Anne spoke now—"when humans, vampires, and Weres existed in harmony. Great cities and towns were founded from the rubble of the old wars, technology thrived, communities were created. With the Madness has come great destruction, and now is a time for change."

Caitlin held the gun at Hank's head. He shook and blubbered.

"But it is not from the flowerbed of death that hope can grow," she said, holstering the gun and stepping back from Hank. "Hank Newman is an asshole who has convinced guards that rape and bullying is an okay way to live. His lies have fed the governor and influenced his ways for as long as we have lived. Yet, now, Hank Newman, as an example of the new order, I offer you the choice of life or death."

Hank looked confused.

"Either stand with us as a changed captain in the new world. Or be set free into the wilds to seek a new destiny," she finished, motioning to the hole in the gates.

Hank got to his feet, his eyes wide. All eyes were fixed on him, the man who many of the townspeople had come to think of as their savior and protector. Now revealed as nothing more than a twisted liar, he'd been offered a chance at redemption by one of their own folk.

He drew his sword, and there was an audible gasp. Caitlin saw the father of the child covering his eyes.

Hank bent to one knee and held his sword in his hands. "By my honor, my life, my freedom, I swear—"

"*Watch out!*" someone called from the crowd as Hank's other hand moved to a dagger by his waist. He struck out with a violent oath.

But the person in the crowd needn't have shouted. Caitlin was already one step ahead, and with a movement that seemed too fast for a human to make, she drew her own sword and thrust it down with all her might. The metal drove into the flesh, stopping at the bone. She cried out, pulled the sword back, and with a final effort, lopped off Hank's head. It made a sound that sent a shiver running down the spines of many, and his body collapsed in a spray of dark blood.

Mary-Anne licked her lips.

"Not now," Kain reminded her quietly.

"I guess he chose death," Caitlin said, her voice loud enough for all to hear.

There was a rumble of whispering, then a gaggle of laughs. At the front of the crowd, a handsome man with clothes that were ripped and tatty stepped forward, his eyes fixed on Hank. He stopped a couple of feet away, took a deep sniff, coughed up some phlegm, and spat on Hank's body.

"That prick has been harassing my missus for years."

Another man stepped forward and spat on Hank. "He's been stealing my linens."

One-by-one, more people came. Caitlin was surprised to see the joy on their faces as each person revealed a snippet of their lives and how Hank had abused, tortured, or harassed many of the folks of Silver Creek. One old man told the story of how Hank had once beaten both him and his late wife, all because they accidentally made him spill his beer.

The old man hugged Caitlin, turned, and pumped his fist in the air.

"Freedom!" he shouted, his voice raspy and worn.

"Freedom!" came the echoes the crowd. Even the guards seemed relieved, pumping their fists and approaching the group who, just moments ago, they had been set on fighting. They clapped Vex and Ash on the backs, hugged Belle and Alice—hell, even Mary-Anne got some sugar from those who were brave enough to approach.

Jaxon barked loudly and hopped around Caitlin in all the excitement. Faces that she had known for years now *saw* her for the first time. Dylan wrapped his arm around her and kissed her cheek.

"You've done a great thing, sis. Ma and Da would be proud."

Caitlin blushed and hugged her brother tight. "There's just one more thing I need to do," she said, looking out at the town.

Her gazed focused on the governor's quarters.

CHAPTER TWENTY-FIVE

The Governor's Quarters, Silver Creek

Caitlin sat in the middle of Trisk's quarters, steaming in her anger.

The governor had gone. Of course, he had. He'd run away when the shit hit the fan and disappeared to Lord only knew where.

Stupid son of a freakin' whore damn bag-ass bandit bitch!

Though she held a huge sense of satisfaction at liberating her hometown that night, the fact that Trisk had fled certainly tarnished that victory.

There came a knock at the door. For a heartbeat of a second, she thought it might be him returning to the scene of the crime.

Instead, Dylan poked his head around the corner. "He's gone, hasn't he?"

Caitlin nodded. "Lard-ass chicken breath smelled the first sign of danger and fled."

"Pussy," Dylan said.

"Pussy," Caitlin agreed.

"Sounds like my kind of party!" Kain said, entering without knocking. Mary-Anne followed behind.

"Let me guess," Mary-Anne said in the calculated way she always had. "The big kahuna took to his feet the minute that shit got hard?"

Caitlin nodded.

"If only you knew where he was going to go next," Kain mused, tapping his fingers against a table where a faded yellow piece of parchment crackled beneath his fingers.

Caitlin stood up and paced the room. "If the governor had New Leaf *and* Silver Creek, who's to say he doesn't have more towns out there? More settlements where he can run to and hide? Who's to say that there aren't more lives out there that we can save?"

"Hear, hear," Mary-Anne said.

Kain continued tapping the paper, resting his head on his hand. "If only there were a map or something written down that would tell us exactly where Trisk could have gone."

"Yes, Kain," Mary-Anne said, annoyance growing in her voice. "That would be abso-fucking-lutely perfect. Now can you stop with the tapping for a second?"

Kain raised his eyebrows and shrugged. "Sure thing. *Whoops!*"

He batted the parchment off the table, and the four of them watched it float like a leaf to the floor.

Caitlin's eyes widened.

There, sketched in faded ink on the paper, was a map. In the center was Silver Creek, with dotted lines spidering out, one leading to New Leaf, another with 'Toronto' in large letters, and others leading to towns Caitlin had never heard of.

"The governor's reign…" Caitlin whispered.

"What are those?" Dylan said, pointing to small symbols that dotted the paper. They were written in fresher ink than the rest, suggesting they'd been added much more recently.

Kain pointed to a symbol of a full moon with a man silhouetted in its light. "Weres…"

Mary-Anne spotted a symbol of a skull with fangs and red eyes. "Vampires."

Dylan held the map up for them all to see. "Holy shit. Trisk has been tracking Weres and vamps?"

"We have to find them. We have to save them all from his clutches."

The others nodded, steel determination on their faces. Though Caitlin knew little of Weres and vamps beyond what she had learned from Mary-Anne and Kain, she suspected that there was a large chance that these would be hiding too. Scared and in the clutches of a world fallen to the Madness. The last thing they needed was an obese madman to round them up and gather them for his own purposes.

What they needed was a savior, a protector.

What they needed was Caitlin and her Revolutionaries.

FINIS

THEY FIGHT. THEY LIVE. THEY ROT.

Eight years ago, an infection hit London, before spreading outwards. 90% of the population was either contained by the military, trampled during the riots, or infected by the disease.

A disease that came to be known as **The Rot.**

Colin Bolton survived the incident but not without losing everything he held dear to him – his life, his love, and his humanity.

Now, he's living at a farmhouse, acting as a bodyguard for a new surrogate family. Life is stable. He's making do. He's *surviving*. That is... until a vagrant scavenger comes knocking at the door, desperate for food and water.

An encounter that will spin Colin's life into chaos once more, bringing him face to face with a murderous family, the dead and the dying, and the failures of his past.

THEY ROT is the first book in a brutal new series of post-apocalyptia set in Great Britain. It's brought to you by Willcocks and Kondor, two of the groundbreaking authors behind the iTunes chart-busting podcast, The Other Stories, and the story studio, Hawk & Cleaver - A digital story studio bringing you the best new stories to watch, read, sniff, and absorb.

Available at Amazon

AUTHOR'S NOTES - DAN WILLCOCKS
AUGUST 3, 2018

What a friggin' blast this has been!

Wait... I can swear in these notes, too? Fucking sweet...

I've been aware of Mr Anderle's work with the Kurtherian Gambit Universe for quite some time now. After discovering the cheeky video in which Michael leaks all of his dirty writing secrets to the world (you know, the one you said you'd never intended to release, Michael), I was quick to shoot a message over to my regular co-author and co-host of my podcast for writers (links at the end of these notes) to invite Michael on to the show.

We had a great time chatting for nearly an hour about all things Kurtherian and, in my cheeky, no messing around, British way, after the show I shot Michael a message and asked if there'd be a spot available to get some gritty horror written into the Kurtherian Gambit Universe.

"What's your favourite genre to write in?" Michael asks.

"Horror, first and foremost," I reply. "Then apocalyptic."

"Hmm," Michael says, metaphorically stroking his chin.

"Perhaps we may have something in the future. But that part isn't quite ready yet."

To say that I was intrigued was a lie. I knew Michael was busy kicking Kurtherian ass and dominating the charts, so I thought nothing more of it. It wasn't until September of 2017 when Michael, Chris, and Lee slid into my DMs (giggedy) and asked me to get involved in the Age of Madness.

"So, we're basically, like, thinking of, like, making zombies and, like, stuff, but with, like, kickass characters and, like, it's going to be, like awesome," I remember Chris saying in a voice which reminded me of a high school girl...

Maybe I'm remembering this wrong... sorry Chris!

Anyway, I was hooked in from the word 'zombies'.

I've always loved a bit of the old gore and blood, though I'm not really sure why. One theory used to be that I was a psychopath (don't worry, I've since been tested and it's only *partly* true). But now I'm beginning to think that maybe I'm just in love with the darker side of life. There's something strange that draws me to zombies—check out my book 'They Rot' for a glimpse at spore-like zombies which breed in cocoons—and getting the chance to thread them further into the KGU is exciting, to say the least.

The Age of Madness will fill in a lot of gaps in the timeline, and I'm having a blast adding my spin into the tale. Hopefully you will have enjoyed the beginning of Caitlin's story, and will want to read more (because, whether you like it or not, more is coming... *mwahahaha!*). There's a lot yet to cover, and there's every chance that you may see the return of some of your favourite characters from fellow authors' series (or descendants/relatives thereof). I won't reveal much more yet as I slave away to the end of book 3, but let me say in my cheeky, British tone: you're in for a right treat, Guv'nor.

Oh, and one last thing before I bid thee farewell. A huge thank you to everyone who has been involved so far in making these books what they have become. Though mine and Michael's names are on the cover, the support and guidance from Michael, Chris & Lee in the creation of this age, as well as the incredible artwork from the amazing Mihaela, the editing prowess of Lynn and Nat, the camaraderie of HJ, the attention to detail of Steve and, overall, the overwhelming support of you. The readers and the fans.

Man, this age is going to be fucking insane. Be sure to hit me up on social and let me know what your favourite bits were, what you'd like to see in the future, and even just what spread you have on your toast.

I'm weird like that.

Peace out.

Social media: @willcocksauthor
www.danielwillcocks.com
www.hawkandcleaver.com
https://www.acast.com/thestorystudio/tss028-20booksto50k-morew-michaelanderle

P.s. If you like my stuff, you might be interested in my fellow writer brothers over at Hawk & Cleaver—the story studio I run outside of this KGU business. We've got fiction podcasts, comics, and novels galore!

AUGUST 6, 2018

First, THANK YOU for not only reading these stories, but also reading through to our *Author Notes*, as well!

I'm going to continue what Dan said at the end. These books, these collaborations, are more of a production of a lot of people than just the author. While we come up with Universes / characters / stories / beats / arcs etc. etc. we have a number of people both inside the company and outside who help us get these stories done.

From fans who help us when we ask for ideas, or supply ideas when the mood strikes, to artists helping bring our vision to life (or creating a vision that we get to riff off.) There are editors and Beta Readers and JIT (Just In Time) support – to the fans that catch mistakes AFTER we have published and email them to readershelp@kurtherian-books.com.

We have collaborators, other authors, industry friends and those at Amazon who support these efforts.

And maybe that is a good place to make an additional

comment. NONE of my efforts to date would be where they are without the people behind the scenes who created KDP (Kindle Direct Publishing) in the first place. Now, we have (Dozens? Hundreds?) of Amazon members who support the infrastructure of the KDP system (servers, software, billing, payables, receivables, Kindle software on Apple IOS or Google Play, PC or Mac, and of course the Kindle tablets themselves.

I get to be an unsung hero of something that wouldn't be around if not for those who had a vision, one that I ruthlessly took advantage of when I got half a clue later in life.

Finally, we come back to you. If you didn't love to read (both our books and others) and are willing to exchange your time and money? Well, we wouldn't have the blessings we do for producing these stories.

I am well aware of the amount of effort we put into what we have done. I know it wouldn't be there without (at least for me and a few others I know) working seven days a week, often ten to fourteen hours a day for the last (going on) three years.

But, without readers? There would be no reason to do any of it. So, thank you.

This week, we are releasing four (4) books. Dan's FIRST book right here, Judith Berens' fourth School of Necessary Magic book, the fifth book in the Shay Series, and we finish the week with the Twenty-third Bethany Anne book (2nd in the Kurtherian Endgame series.)

--- INCOME ---

Someone asked in the Fan group (on Facebook) how we get paid. This question comes up a lot, so I thought I'd drop the answer in here.

If you read on Kindle Unlimited, we get paid for the number of pages you read. We don't know exactly how much each page is worth until the 15th of the month AFTER we get the reads. Historically, we receive about $0.045 per page (ranges from $0.040 to $0.052).

We get paid the first time you read the book. If later, you download it again and read it (similar to having purchased a book) we do not get paid again. However, if you read half a book, then close it before opening it up again six months later are re-read the first half and finish the book, then we will get paid the second half of the pages.

For purchases, we get thirty-five percent (35%) of the cover price for books that sell between $0.99 and $2.99 (US) and any books OVER $9.99 we also get thirty-five percent (35%).

For books between $2.99 and $9.99, we earn seventy percent (70%) of the cover price. As you can tell, Amazon wants us to sell between $2.99 and $9.99.

We get paid sixty (60) days after the month ending. So, purchases / reads here in August of 2018 will get deposited into our accounts at the end of October, 2018.

If you have a few moments, scroll back to the links Dan provided, and check him and his *Hawk and Cleaver* links out. They have an amazing podcast selection for stories here:

http://www.hawkandcleaver.com/podcasts/

Ad Aeternitatem,

Michael Anderle

CONNECT WITH THE AUTHORS

Dan Willcocks Social

Social media: @willcocksauthor
www.danielwillcocks.com
www.hawkandcleaver.com
https://www.acast.com/thestorystudio/tss028-
20booksto50k-morew-michaelanderle

Michael Anderle Social

Website:
http://kurtherianbooks.com/

Email List:
http://kurtherianbooks.com/email-list/

Facebook Here:
https://www.facebook.com/TheKurtherianGambitBooks/